Love Waits

The Davenport Series – by Judah Knight

Judah Knight

GreenTree Publishers
Newnan, Georgia

Love Waits

Copyright © 2018 by Greentree Publishers

Printed in the United States of America
ISBN-13: 978-1-944483-18-0

Follow Judah Knight through the following media links:
    Website/blog: www.judahknight.com
    Twitter: @judahknight
    Facebook: @authorjudahknight

Greentree Publishers: www.greentreepublishers.com

Dedication

This book is dedicated to my six awesome children. You are a joy to your parents and a bright spot in the world. You have helped to make my life the greatest adventure of all.

Thanks

Writing a book is definitely a team project. I'm grateful for the folks at Dorado Buceo in Veracruz, Mexico along with a host of other new friends I now have throughout central and southern Mexico. If you ever have the chance to scuba dive in Veracruz, I suggest you contact Manuel and his team at Dorado Buceo for a wonderful experience. Thanks Chucho and Iris for making me feel at home from the first time I walked into the dive shop. I enjoyed meeting Andrea and her team from Espora Producciones. I wish you guys the best.

GreenTree Publishers wouldn't exist without the sacrifice and willingness of a lot of people to make these projects work. I have the greatest editorial team in the world. I'm also grateful for my early readers and everyone who sacrificed to bring this project to reality.

Special Offer

Thank you for choosing *Love Waits*, the fifth book in the Davenport Series. While you can enjoy this novel as a stand-alone book, you'll see that it is connected to the previous books in the series. You can find the first four books at your local retailer: *The Long Way Home; Hope for Tomorrow; Finding My Way; Ready to Love Again.*

Special Request:

We would like to ask for a special favor. When you've completed *Love Waits*, would you be willing to go to the retailer's website where you purchased the book and leave a brief review? Your review will be such a help for someone looking for a clean and wholesome romance/adventure book. Thank you.

Offer:

As a way of saying thanks for your interest in Judah Knight's *Davenport Series*, we are offering you a free copy of his novella entitled *A Girl Can Always Hope* by visiting the following website: www.Judahknight.com/free-gift.html. In *The Long Way Home* (Book 1), you learned that the two main characters knew one another as teenagers, and Margaret Robertson (Meg Freeman in *The Long Way Home*) had a crush on her brother's best friend, Jon Davenport. Read the fun, short-story of one awkward middle schooler's attempt to capture the impossible catch. We will send you a free copy in a pdf format.

Now, we hope you enjoy the *Love Waits*.

Contents

Conclusion

Ready to Love Again

The final night arrived, and Jon had Chef Marceau come to the house in Rock Sound to prepare a celebration dinner. Jon asked each of the boys to share one thing that meant the most to them about the summer, and every boy agreed that the one thing was not a thing but a person: Lacy. Lacy wept as the boys took turns hugging her. She couldn't bear to see them leave.

"You boys mean the world to me," Lacy said between sniffs. "You've taught me some important lessons about life and love."

"Kerrick's the one who's taught you about love," Tae teased.

"If Kerrick doesn't treat you right," Barry added, "you call me. I'll get the boys together, and we'll come down to Miami and give him a lesson or two."

"And then you can marry me," Randal beamed.

Lacy blew her nose into a tissue. "I'll keep that in mind." She hopped over to Randal and kissed his cheek.

The boys howled with laughter and demanded to be next. The evening continued with a lot of stories and laughter. Jon ended the evening with a challenge to the boys to make sure that the summer was not spent in vain.

"Boys, you're not leaving the same as you were two months ago. It's important that you realize this time was not about doing something cool during your summer break. It's about life. I've seen enough in you these weeks we've had together to believe the best in you. I expect to hear great things from each of you. Just remember that your future has everything to do with the choices you make. You can choose to define your future."

Lacy was sad that she and Kerrick would not be able to make the trip back to Miami with Marcy and the boys. She and Kerrick had an appointment on Nassau with Dr. Williams and lunch with Debra. She hugged each boy and gave them a kiss on the cheek as they left for the night. Marcy's flight back home was to leave from Miami, so Lacy agreed to stay in touch her friend.

Because he was still restricted to a wheel chair, Randal would have to wait until the following morning to get aboard *The Discoverer*. Lacy and Kerrick had to leave for Nassau early the next morning, so they told Randal goodbye before they went to bed.

"You know my family's going to be moving," Randal told Lacy. "Thanks to Mr. Jon."

"I heard that," Lacy admitted. "I'm so excited. Meg told me your mom planned to buy a house from Uncle Jon."

"Yeah. It's out in the suburbs. He's the best."

"I'm sorry I won't get to see you off in the morning," Lacy said. "I have your e-mail, so I'll stay in touch. Remember to respond to my Facebook friend request."

"I will, Lacy. Good night."

Lacy stopped at Kerrick's bedroom door. "I don't think I can cry any more for a month."

"I'm going to miss those boys," Kerrick agreed. "What about us?"

"Uh, well," Lacy stammered. "What about us?"

"I don't want our relationship to just be a summer thing either. Maybe we should take Jon's advice."

"What advice was that?"

"Instead of letting the future define us, let's define the future."

Lacy placed her hand on Kerrick's cheek. "I'm game." She pulled his face toward hers and kissed him. "See you in the morning."

After their day on Nassau, Jose took Kerrick and Lacy back to the marina where they docked the *New Beginnings*. To her surprise, Jon, Judy, and Ann were sitting in chairs on the back deck of the yacht.

"Carla's asleep in the cabin," Meg whispered as she stepped out of the galley, "so you guys be quiet."

As Lacy hopped aboard the boat on a set of crutches, Jon stood up to offer his chair. "I decided to give the crew a month off, so Captain Buffington dropped us off here. I figured we could all head back to Pirate's Cover together."

When they returned to the Davenport compound, Judy and Meg got right to work on dinner. They grilled hamburgers while Jon dropped some French fries into a deep fryer.

Dinner around the table felt a little funny with such a small group.

"I've been thinking about my medallion," Lacy said.

"Really?" Meg sat forward in her chair. "What have you been thinking?"

"I've been thinking that I never got it back from the jeweler."

Meg got up from the table, grabbed an envelope containing Lacy's medallion, and gave it to her niece. "Here you go. I had Diego pick it up."

"He's such a good man," Ann added. "You were lucky to find someone so dependable to take care of your property."

"We are thankful," Jon admitted.

Lacy pulled the medallion out of the envelope and stared at it. "Thanks so much, Meg. You know that I'll cherish this for the rest of my life."

"I suppose we can assume Miguel has a medallion that contains a clue," Jon said. "The medallion the little girl had didn't seem to say much."

"Don't you have a picture of that one?" Lacy asked.

Meg grabbed the file Queen Ella gave her that contained pictures of the medallion. She laid it down on the table for the group to see.

Ann pointed to the picture of the little Swedish girl's medallion. "A cross in a circle. I guess that's referring to the King's conversion."

"It makes me think of the trelleborg," Meg suggested.

"That's strange," Jon said. "I had that thought when we were swimming through the tunnel beneath Skull Island."

"Why?" Meg asked.

"Jose and I came across intersecting tunnels when we swam from the ocean to the pond. For some reason, it reminded me of the trelleborg."

"I'd love to visit the Trelleborg Museum one of these days," Ann said.

"We better go before the baby comes," Jose suggested.

"I'm so sad that this is our last night together," Meg said. "Lacy, what are your plans? I mean, about the future?"

"I'm thinking about transferring to the University of Miami in January."

"Really?" Meg winked at Kerrick. "I didn't think there was anything special about their exercise science program."

Lacy blushed. "Maybe not, but there's someone special at the University."

Jon flew with Kerrick and Lacy back to Miami the following day on a private charter. Saying goodbye to Kerrick was difficult, but she knew they had plans to be together over the Labor Day weekend. She was grateful they had a lot of private time earlier for the real goodbyes. Before climbing aboard the Delta flight for Atlanta, she hugged Jon and Meg tightly.

"You've changed my life," she offered. "I love you both so much."

"We love you, too, Lacy. You know that you have a home with us anytime."

Lacy waved goodbye one last time and sat down in a wheelchair that a Delta attendant rolled up behind her. Once aboard the plane, she got out of the wheelchair and hopped over to her window seat in first class. She smiled as she thought about the benefits of having a broken leg.

As the plane began to taxi down the runway, she thought back to her summer and touched her medallion. *It's been a crazy summer. Who would have thought that a small medallion with one little word on it could cause so much trouble?* She laid her head back against the seat and closed her eyes. Her mind raced over the events of the summer. She thought about Mr. Phil. She would never forget the sweet, old man who tried to save her life.

She thought about the discussion from the previous night as images of trelleborgs, medallions, crosses, and tunnels filled her mind. She jolted upright in her seat and said out loud: "Beneath! That's it. Beneath! I've got to call Jon."

She pulled out her cell phone, but the flight attendant told her that she would have to put it away until they landed in

Atlanta. *Oh, well. I suppose the secret has been hidden for hundreds of years. It can stand to remain a secret for a little longer.*

Chapter One

Heinrich's Demise - 1871

Blood seeped between Henry's fingers. He could still move his arms and legs, but his heart raced out of control, and his breath came in short gasps. His helplessness drew him slowly to the edge of a bottomless pit as he wondered if it were even possible to keep the life-giving fluid in his body. The bullet hole in his stomach was so large that he began to realize that he would not survive the gunshot wound. Why had he been so stupid to try to get the medallion back?

He knew something was amiss when Ludvig Olsson came to his home some days ago asking for Heinrich. Henry hadn't gone by his given name in over twenty years. The man asked so many questions about the gold medallion that even the slowest fool would have picked up on something suspicious, but Henry had always been too trusting. *How did he even know the medallion existed?*

Ludvig must have had an accomplice, but the Polish priest was the only other person in the world who knew about the mysterious, gold medallions. Surely, a man of the cloth wouldn't send a bandit to kill an old friend and steal the medallion.

Father Vincent was such a kind man. He wasn't a killer. *So, what happened? Where did this guy come from?*

Henry's mind raced back almost thirty years to a small Polish village that was at least a lifetime away. He used to curse being born in Poland in 1830, but 1841 turned everything in a new direction. He and Father Vincent found the treasure that would change their lives forever. They both agreed that it was God's blessing on them for working to build a new church.

He had been so pure at eleven-years-old, and Father Vincent was a saint.

Henry faded in and out of consciousness as his mind returned to a much simpler time several decades earlier. Father Vincent wanted to check the depth of the old foundation, so he asked his young friend to dig in the dirt beside the ancient rock. An old church had once stood on the property, so the priest thought it was a perfect place for the new church to be built. He told Heinrich many times that the little hill was *holy ground*. One minute he had been shoveling dirt out of the growing hole, and the next minute, the dirt fell into blackness. Heinrich nearly toppled into the abyss.

"Oh, my God!" Father Vincent breathed aloud, and Heinrich knew he was not taking God's name in vain.

"What is it, Father?"

"It appears to be an underground cavern. Run back to my room and fetch a lamp and the rope lying on the floor under my bed."

Within thirty minutes, Heinrich dangled at the end of the rope and held a lamp as the priest lowered him toward the cavern floor. The flame flickered in the stale air, and Heinrich prayed it wouldn't go out.

"It looks like boxes," Heinrich's tiny voice echoed around the small room. "I see four, no five." He felt both frightened and exhilarated to be the first person in this room in possibly hundreds of years.

"It must be a crypt. That's fascinating. I had no idea."

Heinrich's feet hit the hard-packed dirt floor. "I also see a smaller box."

"Can you open the smaller box?" The priest called down into the darkened room.

Heinrich reached a trembling hand toward the box. What if the box contained the body of a baby? He fully expected a ghost to appear any minute. The latch on the box had fallen off long ago, so the boy just raised the lid up and one side of the box fell to the earthen floor.

"What is it, boy?"

Heinrich stared in disbelief. He opened his mouth to speak, but words wouldn't come.

"Heinrich. Are you okay?"

"I'm…I'm fine."

"Well, what did you find?"

"Father, it's gold."

"Gold? Oh, my. Tie the rope around the box and let me know when to pull it up."

It took a while, but Heinrich managed to replace the lid on the box and tie a rope around it. He was afraid the box would fall apart. After Heinrich called up to the priest, Father Vincent pulled the rope, but the box wouldn't budge.

"I'm going to my room to get a basket with a handle. You'll have to transfer small amounts of the treasure into the basket. We'll do this gradually."

Over an hour later as darkness began settling on the little Polish village on the banks of the river Dziwna, the two friends gaped at the pile of treasure on the floor of the priest's simple cottage. Most of the treasure was gold coins, but the most intriguing pieces of the lot were three golden medallions with odd

marks written on them. One of them was easily legible and written in Latin. Father Vincent translated it: "Harald Gormsøn king
of Danes, Scania, Jomsborg, town Aldinburg."

"Would you believe that?" the priest exclaimed.

"What is it?"

"It seems that this medallion must have belonged to King
Harald Bluetooth."

"What about these other two?"

"Well, I see marks on them, but I don't know what they
mean. I imagine that would be Runic."

"What's Runic?"

"The language of the Vikings. The letters are made up of
lines and unusual marks. You know, Bluetooth was the Viking
King who brought Christianity to Denmark."

"No. I didn't know that."

"It seems he was a good man. Legend has it that he was
killed by his son, Sven Forkbeard. The whole story is very sad. I
suggest we divide this treasure up. You take a third, I'll take a
third, and the church can have a third."

"Wow! You mean I can have some of this treasure?"

"You found it. Which one of the medallions do you want?"

"I wish I knew what they said."

"We can probably get some help figuring that out. Just
choose one."

"Okay. I'll take the one with the least amount of marks on
it."

"Fine. I'll take the other one. Let's save the one with the
cross on it for the church."

"That doesn't look like the crosses I've seen."

"You're right, my son, but I'm sure it was meant to be a
cross."

After the treasure was divided, Heinrich wrapped up a small portion of his gold in a cloth and pocketed his medallion. He put the rest in a new box and found a perfect hiding place for it in the crypt. He figured he would come back and get the rest eventually. He and the priest shook hands in agreement to keep their discovery a secret.

A few years later, war was brewing in Poland, and Heinrich wanted no part of it. He felt anger boiling in his heart every time he saw a man in uniform. This coming war was all about greed, and he wanted to be as far away from it as possible. He decided to take a small portion of his treasure and leave his homeland. He could find a new life in the United States. He promised to stay in touch with Father Vincent and assured the aging priest that he would one day come back to claim the rest of his gold.

Before leaving, Heinrich copied the scratch marks from both medallions onto a piece of paper. "I'll send you the translation in a letter, Father. Just as soon as I can find someone who can read these marks, I'll forward the message to you."

After arriving in New York, Heinrich attended church and happened to sit across from the most beautiful young woman he had ever seen. He couldn't remember a thing about the priest's comments that day, but he remembered everything about the girl's face. He had even heard someone call her name: Elaina. Elaina! Even her name was intoxicating.

In hopes of meeting Elaina, Heinrich attended church as often as possible, and he soon had his opportunity. He saw her volunteer to help feed the poor in their city, so he volunteered as well. With a little creativity, he managed to serve on Elaina's team, and in time, he began walking her home. She was kind and tenderhearted, and Heinrich could think of nothing else but being with Elaina. He decided to leave Poland behind and pursue a life with Elaina. In an effort to become fully American, he changed his name to Henry. The markings on the medallions soon became the last thing on his mind.

Henry and Elaina eventually married and had four beautiful children over the years, but when their last child was two-years-old, she developed a serious fever. While in the hospital with his daughter, Henry happened to meet the curator of a museum in New York City, and Henry remembered the curious markings on the gold discs. He told the man about the medallions. He was careful, however, not to reveal that he had one of them. The curator offered to review the markings and try to get them translated.

Henry was extremely nervous when he went to the museum with the paper containing the markings. He was also ashamed. He had promised Father Vincent he'd discover the meaning of the markings, but he had neglected his promise for many years.

Once in the curator's office, Henry laid the paper out on the man's desk. "A long time ago, I copied the marks from the two medallions that my friend has in Poland. I've wondered for all of these years what they may have meant."

The man adjusted his spectacles and peered down at the markings on the yellowed piece of paper. "Hummm. Well, are you sure these marks are the same as the original?"

"Yes, sir. I was very careful to make them exactly the same."

After pouring over several books, the curator was confident of the translation. "If you are sure of these marks, then your two medallions say 'beneath' and 'island of the skull.'"

"They're not my medallions," Henry blurted out. "What do those messages mean?"

"I don't know. I'll be happy to do more research."

"Thank you. That would mean so much to my friend. The strange markings have always been such a mystery."

"And you said these medallions were found in Poland? Give me a few days and come back by my office."

Three days later, Henry was stunned to hear of the legend of King Harald Bluetooth's medallions.

The curator removed his glasses and leaned back in his chair. "The legend has it that the king's family was divided, and he wanted to do something to bring them together again. He had worked so hard to unite his country, but his own children wouldn't even stay in the same room together. His daughters were as loving as ever, but his son, Sven, was angry at his father for becoming a Christian."

"So, what do the medallions have to do with their family problems?"

"The story goes that one of the king's men discovered an ancient Mayan city filled with treasure somewhere in the Americas. Most likely in Mexico."

"Mexico?" Henry interrupted. "The Vikings didn't go to Mexico."

"I'm just telling you what the legend says. It is hard to believe they would make it that far south."

"I've heard of El Dorado in stories. Did they find El Dorado? You know, the city of gold?"

"To begin with, the story about Bluetooth's men is a legend and most likely not true. I've also never heard the words *El Dorado* connected to King Bluetooth.

Henry nodded his head. "I didn't think El Dorado had ever been found or was even a real place.

"King Bluetooth envisioned a plan to unite his family," the curator continued. "He took three medallions and created clues his children would have to use to find the treasure."

"So, they would have to work together. I suppose the king thought his children could be reunited if they had a common cause."

"That's my guess."

"Did they ever find it? I mean in the story?"

"As far as I know, they didn't. Most people think Sven killed his father. He became the leader of the Vikings and led them to sack England in 994."

"You're right. It doesn't sound like he searched for treasure in Mexico. If this legend is really true, it means that treasure worth millions of dollars is hidden away somewhere."

"I'm sure that's not the only treasure tucked away. I hope your friend doesn't get the idea of heading south to Mexico to search for treasure. That would be a fool's errand and quite dangerous."

"I doubt he will. He's an old priest. Thanks so much for your help. I'll at least tell him about it."

"I suppose if a third medallion turned up," the curator continued as he walked toward his office door, "it might make you think twice about the legend."

"True," Henry agreed.

Over the next couple of years, Henry began the hunt that took him to port cities where he met with mariners who had sailed all over the world. He was told of a couple of places in the Caribbean that had islands resembling a skull. No one knew of a skull island up north around Denmark or anywhere near Mexico.

He decided to write Father Vincent to tell him the good news. He had received only one letter from the old priest a few years earlier that indicated he was now serving a church in Sweden. He had assured Henry that his portion of Bluetooth's treasure was safe. The old man had hidden it in a casket and placed it in the cellar of an old building on the church property. Now that Henry had news of the meaning of the medallions, he feared telling Father Vincent about it in a letter. It seemed too risky. He decided to send a letter with some information and to make a trip to Sweden so he could give the priest all of the details face-to-face.

"I plan to come visit you to talk with you in person about this exciting discovery of treasure," Henry wrote in the letter. "You have a clue on your medallion, and I have a clue on mine. I'll tell you more when we're together. If we are to follow the clues, it might mean taking a trip to the islands of the Bahamas or somewhere in the Caribbean. I hope to arrange passage sometime this summer."

A jolt of pain riveted Henry's body and brought him back to his present predicament. He winced as he moved a little to try to ease the burning sensation that seemed to be growing throughout his body. He had to somehow get out to the main road before it was too late, but he couldn't move. Though he didn't know the whole story, he was sure that Ludvig had intercepted his letter to Father Vincent. That's how the villain learned about the medallions. *I wonder if he hurt Father Vincent. Did he steal the other medallion too? I should have known this guy was a thief.*

A noise out on the main road got Henry's attention. He weakly called out for help, but his voice sounded like a whisper in a meeting of the Tammany Hall Society. No one heard him.

He knew that he wasn't going to make it. The blood was pooling around his body now, and it would only be a matter of time. He felt so cold and alone.

I was such an idiot. Why did I have to come into the city to chase down Ludvig? He set me up, stole my medallion, and now he's going to steal the treasure. He must have the other medallion.

Henry thought about Elaina and his precious children. He would never see them again. Tears spilled down his cheeks as another painful spasm wracked his body.

I love you, Elaina. I'm so sorry. He closed his eyes and felt a wave of peace flood his mind. He saw Father Vincent standing before him with open arms, as if the old priest were welcoming his young protege home.

Chapter Two

Summer Recovery

Jon closed his laptop when Meg walked into the salon of their forty-four-foot Carver yacht. He smiled up at his beautiful wife as she sat down across from him.

"Did you get your cell phone working?" Meg asked.

"I put it in a bowl of rice. Someone once told me that if you drop your phone in water, rice will help soak up the moisture."

"I'm sorry I got it wet."

"It's not your fault, Meg. I shouldn't have left it by a sink full of water."

"Hopefully, your plan will work." Meg reached across the table for Jon's coffee cup and took a sip. "Ann told me that she and Jose want to go on a short vacation."

Jon knew that Meg and Ann had gone ashore earlier to shop and have coffee together. She had invited him and Jose to come along, but shopping was Jon's least favorite activity. Both men had suddenly thought of pressing responsibilities that kept them on the boat. Ann had been Meg's best friend for most of her life, and Jon was so thankful to have her and her husband as a part of their salvage business. They had been so wonderful with the boys in the program this summer.

"They want to go on a trip?" Jon teased. "Really? And leave us all alone?"

"Well, we're not exactly alone."

As if on cue, Carla toddled into the salon from the cabin holding her stuffed lamb. "Mama. Baba."

"Yes, sweetie. I see Baba. I think Baba needs a little surgery on her ear."

Carla crawled into her mother's lap and held her lamb up for closer inspection. "I'll get a needle after dinner, and she'll be as good as new."

"Now, what were you saying, Meg?"

"I was about to suggest that while Ann and Jose head off to wherever it is that they want to go, we should go on a trip too."

"Like where? We've been on a trip all summer."

"Well, I'd enjoy going back to Conception Island. I'd love to dive the reef again where we found the medallion I gave Lacy."

Jon smiled as he thought back to that dive with Meg. It was Meg's first time back in the water after having Carla. It was a wonder that she even saw the gold disc floating to the bottom because she had already turned to start her ascent. When Meg gave it to her niece as a high school graduation gift, they had no idea that it contained part of a clue that could lead them to great treasure or that ruthless people who would go to any lengths to get the medallion. Lacy had even worn the gift around her neck on a chain without realizing the true value of her medallion.

"Ah. The most beautiful island in the world. When I told you that three years ago on Nassau, I don't think you believed me."

Meg laughed. "I didn't know what to think. All of my stuff had been stolen, and I just wanted to go home. I guess I figured if I was going to get back to Miami, I had to go with you to this island." Carla wiggled and wanted to be put down, so Meg set her on the floor beside the table.

Getting up from the bench, Meg walked over to Jon and sat in his lap. She wrapped her arms around his neck and kissed his cheek. "I'm sure glad I didn't refuse you. I got the trip of a life-time and an amazing husband out of the deal."

"It was indeed the trip of a lifetime," he said as he wrapped his arms around her waist, "and I'm the one who got the deal. I know it's past time for our annual trek to Conception, but I fig-ured you'd want a few days at home first."

"We will need to go home to drop off Judy and Carla, and I am dying to spend a little time at home for a change. I know Judy is tired of being away, and she says that she has a lot to do back at the compound. What would we do without Judy? She's more like a grandmother than a house keeper."

"I agree," Jon said breathing in his wife's scent. "I've always felt like she was part of the family."

"I suggest we do an overnight trip to Conception and then head home for a break from the ocean. I've got quite a list for the both of us."

"I like the idea of Conception Island, but I'm not sure what I think about your lists. What if I don't want to work on a list?" Jon deadpanned.

Meg grinned as she got up from his lap. "Then I will need to use my powers of persuasion."

Jon grabbed Meg's hand as she walked toward the cabin. He pulled her back into his lap and kissed her passionately. "And you can be very persuasive."

"Dada." Carla giggled.

"Jon! Not in front of the baby."

"She already knows I'm deeply in love with her mother," Jon protested as Meg pulled away from his grasp, "and I want to remind her of that fact as often as I can."

Meg turned and winked at Jon as she walked into their cabin. "Maybe later you can remind *me*."

****

"Why doesn't he answer his phone?" Lacy groaned

Liz looked into the rearview mirror before changing lanes. "Who are you trying to call?"

"I need to call Uncle Jon. I figured something out, Mom, but the plane was about to take off when all of the clues made sense to me. The flight attendant made me put my phone away. It's something that will blow your mind."

"I'm sure it's important, dear. Do you mind dropping me off at the gym? I've just got to get my workout in before my pedicure today. Connie is going to pick me up there after my workout. You remember Connie?"

"Sure, Mom. I suppose it's okay for me to drive with a cast on my left leg. So, will you be coming home after that?"

"I have a date with George tonight, so I'll be out late."

My guess is that means you won't even be home at all tonight – my first night back from the most wonderful summer of my life. "Who is George?"

"I'll have to tell you about him, but I don't have time now. I'm glad your flight wasn't later this afternoon. We never would have gotten through the traffic."

Lacy repositioned her casted leg and reached into the backseat to grab the rubber boot the doctor had given her in Nassau. She began working to strap it around her cast.

Her mother glanced down at the cast before nearly rear ending the car in front of them. "Stupid drivers. I swear they must have gotten their license at Dollar General."

"Mom, you don't have to be in such a hurry. There's nothing you can do about traffic accept endure it."

Liz glanced at Lacy again before zooming past another car. "We'll need to get an appointment with Dr. Schenk this week. Meg tells me you should get the cast off next week. You will be as good as new. What a summer – kidnapped, broken leg. You know I meant to come down for your birthday, but I had something really important come up. I didn't know about the whole kidnapping thing and surgery until everything was all over with."

"That's fine, Mom."

Forty-five minutes later, Liz pulled against the curb in front of the gym. "Don't wait up on me."

Lacy drove into her driveway with mixed emotions. *Am I happy to be home? Not really.* Everything looked the same as it had when she left three months earlier, and her mother hadn't changed either. At least, Lacy had Jon, Meg, and Kerrick. She pulled out her phone as she dragged her suitcase toward the house. The rubber boot on her cast sure made getting around a lot easier. She spoke Kerrick's name into the phone and heard Kerrick's phone ringing hundreds of miles away.

"Hey gorgeous," Kerrick's voice sounded as soothing as a stringed symphony.

"Do you always answer your phone that way?" Lacy simpered. "That's quite a pickup line."

"I have this amazing feature on my phone called caller I.D." Kerrick teased. "You ever heard of it?"

Lacy ignored his jab. "It sounds to me like you've been sitting around waiting on me to call."

"I thought I might hear from you after you landed. I had decided to give you a little time with your mother, and then I was going to call you."

"Well, you can nix the time with old mom. She's too concerned about workouts, pedicures, and George."

"Who's George?"

"Her newest fling. What are you doing?"

"I'm packing my things," Kerrick answered. "I can move back into my dorm in a week, so I thought I'd start getting my act together. It's kind of hard to switch gears back to being a mere student after such an amazing summer."

"I'm feeling the same way. I don't want to be in Griffin, and I don't want to go back to Georgia College."

"I have an idea that could solve all of our problems."

"All of them?"

"Well, maybe not all of them, but it's a good idea. Why don't you move down to Miami and stay in Jon and Meg's house this year so you can establish your residency. You can take online classes at Georgia College so you don't get behind on your degree program. Then, next year you can go with me to the University of Miami."

"I love that idea. I'm sure my mom will be happy to get me out of her hair for good. I'll talk with Jon about it. Speaking of Jon, I've been trying to call him, but his phone goes straight to voice mail. Meg doesn't answer her phone either. Any idea what's going on with them?"

Kerrick paused for a second. "Nope. No idea. Maybe they took a break after everyone left for home. You've got to admit that running a program for boys all summer had to be a bit stressful."

"True, not to mention the stress we caused him with the whole Miguel thing. Well, I've got awesome news. I figured out the clue."

"You mean on the medallions? How could you do that? You don't have the third medallion."

"I don't need the third one," Lacy revealed. "Think about it. Those idiots had the third medallion and chose to put their compound on that skull looking island. My guess is that their medallion identified the specific island, and my medallion located the spot on the island."

"That makes sense."

"My medallion says *beneath*. I think that we'll find the treasure 'beneath Coral Cay.' You know how Jon and Jose swam through the caves to get to that pool behind the house? Well, I think we'll find the treasure somewhere in those tunnels."

"I'm game to give it a try," Kerrick agreed. "How does the other medallion with the Latin words fit in? You know, the one that the little girl found in Sweden?"

"I've been thinking about that, too. I was going to ask Jon to send me a picture of it."

"You won't have to. Just Google 'Harold Bluetooth disc,' and you'll find a picture of it."

"Okay, hold on." Lacy opened up Safari on her phone and typed in the search. She scrolled down and found the picture. "I've got it. Do you have the picture pulled up?"

Kerrick hummed a second. "Yep. I got a version of it from Wikipedia."

"Me, too. Do you see that cross? I think that's a map of the tunnels under the island. Do you see that little dot on the left arm of the cross?"

"Got it."

"I'm betting we'll find the treasure where that dot is in the tunnel to the left."

"What are we waiting for?" Kerrick's voice nearly jumped through the phone. "How soon can you get down here?"

Lacy sighed. "It's not quite that easy. I've got to figure out my life first. If I'm going to move to Miami, I've got some work to do on this end."

"Like what? Like buy a plane ticket? If you need some money, I'll help you out."

"No. If I'm moving to Miami, I'll need to drive my car. I hope it can make it."

"What kind of car do you have?"

"It's a 2002 Chevrolet Malibu."

"Does it run okay?"

"Most of the time. A guy who lives down the street is a mechanic. I'll get him to look it over for me. He usually doesn't charge me."

"See. It pays to be beautiful."

Lacy smiled as she felt her cheeks heat up. "I think he's just a nice guy. He's invited me to go with his family to church several times. I almost did once, just because he's been so nice to me. Of course, I haven't driven my car in three months, so hopefully all is well. I'd better go. I'll figure things out and call you back. In the meantime, if you hear from Jon or Meg, tell them to call me. I want to tell them about the clue, so don't mention it."

"Yes ma'am," Kerrick teased. "When's the cast coming off?"

"That's one more thing I'll have to do before coming south. I'm supposed to go to the doctor next week. Hopefully, he'll take it off."

"Let's hope so. We'll talk soon. I love you."

"I love you too, Kerrick."

Lacy stared at the wallpaper picture on her phone of Kerrick hugging her on the deck of *The Discoverer*. The summer had changed her life, and no one in Griffin really cared.

She had to get to Miami as fast as she could. She wished she could pack up, get her car checked out, and head south the next day. Surely, Jon and Meg wouldn't care if she showed up at the house in Miami. They wouldn't be there anyway, so why would they care? The house was huge. Unfortunately, she would have to make a trip to Milledgeville first to work out her school issues.

What about Marie? She was living there this summer to help with the boys' program and to take care of the house. Even if Marie is still living there, Lacy knew that she would have plenty of room. Jon bought the place thinking that he might temporarily house up to ten kids plus Marie. It also has an unbelievably beautiful pool in the backyard.

She smiled as she thought about life in Miami. *Finding sunken treasure sure has its perks.*

Chapter Three

Conception Island

Miguel looked across the room at his new partner, who sat glued to his computer screen with headphones covering his ears. The short, Cuban drug runner had heard a beep that signaled a call had come in on the girl's phone. "Andrew, did you get that phone call?" Andrew didn't move. "Andrew!" Miguel repeated as he reached out and uncovered Andrew's right ear. "Did you get that phone call?"

"No. I wasn't able to make the connection."

"No?" Miguel growled. "I didn't go all the way to D.C. to pick up someone who can't hack a cell phone."

"We're not locked in right, Miguel. That's all. I just need to tweak a few things."

"You'd better get to tweaking fast. They'll steal our gold out from under our noses if we're not careful."

Miguel thought back to the night he had to flee his compound on Coral Cay. He hated leaving his island. He had searched for the island that looked like a skull for many months, and he was confident he had found the right place. His medallion's message was simple: island of the skull. No island in the Bahamas or anywhere in the Caribbean bore the name *Skull Island*, but the northern end of Coral Cay looked just like a skull. It had to be the right island.

It took some creative work on Miguel's part to get hired by the guy who owned Coral Cay. He smiled as he thought about how the rich Floridian trusted him as the grounds keeper and never even came around. Miguel wasn't even sure why the man bought the place.

Miguel boiled with anger as he thought about his former associate, Fernando. The stupid loser blew everything. They had the girl in their hands, and the second medallion was as good as theirs. He would have easily found the treasure by now if he had the message on the second medallion.

He heard that Fernando had been killed, which was a good thing. It kept Miguel from having to do the job himself. *Fernando was a stupid fool. At least now, I've got a partner with some brains.*

"Is this a picture of Jon Davenport?" Andrew asked as he looked up from the Google search on his computer screen. "Who's that woman with him? She's beautiful."

"That's his wife: Meg. She's a looker, but she's got it coming along with her stupid husband. She's caused me and my family a lot of problems over the last few years, and now it's about payday. I want you to stay right here at this computer until you learn of Davenport's plan."

"You know that I can't seem to tap into his number."

"I know. You told me. I think that all you need is that coed's number. You know she's going to run that pretty little mouth of hers and tell us everything we need to know."

"Pretty don't describe that girl, boss. She's in a category all by herself. How did you manage to be chasing two beautiful women?"

Miguel let out a string of curse words. "They may be beautiful, but they have wrecked my life. Their time will come."

****

Meg watched as Jon maneuvered the *New Beginnings* into the bay of Conception Island. His tall, tanned body exuded strength and confidence, yet he was the most tender person she knew. He seemed to understand her every need. His chiseled physique came from a commitment to stay in shape, even when they spent days or weeks at sea, and his heart seemed to be as big as the ocean. She was so blessed to have married a man like him. On top of his love for her, he was the best father to their little girl that she could imagine.

Instead of pulling up to the long, weathered dock protruding from the island, Jon dropped anchor about 100 yards from shore. Meg slipped into the salon to begin preparing lunch. She smiled as she thought about the fact that Judy had really done the preparing. Just a few years ago, Meg was heart-broken over the death of her first husband, lonely, and nearly broke. It was hard to believe how everything in her life had changed so dramatically. Now, she was married to an incredible man and had all the money anyone would need for several lifetimes.

Having so much money made her a little overwhelmed at times. She knew that to those who had been given much, much was required. She had heard that phrase throughout her life and never imagined it applying to her. After spending these few years in the Bahamas, she came to realize that she had been wealthy her entire life, even though her bank account had once been nearly empty. Jon was one of the most generous men she knew. He always helped people and gave money to various causes. Joy and gratitude swelled from within her like a gushing spring as she added up her blessings.

Meg was most excited about the work they had begun with inner-city boys. While she and Jon had experienced only one summer of work with five boys, it had been a huge success. They had already begun dreaming about the next summer. The progress that thrilled her most, however, was the change in her niece, Lacy Henderson. Lacy's frozen heart of bitterness and anger had begun to thaw. *I need to call Lacy and see how she's doing. I'm sure Liz didn't give her much of a homecoming. How can a mother be so cold toward her own daughter?*

Meg jumped as she felt Jon's body press against her back and heard him clear his throat. "Hey, sweetheart." He kissed her tenderly on her cheek and nibbled on her ear. "What's for lunch?"

A shiver ran down Meg's back. "Looks like Judy packed us our normal fried chicken."

Jon opened the refrigerator and pulled out a bottle of water. "I don't think we can make a trip to Conception Island without fried chicken. I can't believe I haven't been to our cave in a year."

"Why weren't you with us at the beginning of the summer when I came here with Lacy and Kerrick? Finding that skeleton was a little spooky."

"I was bringing up a fishing boat. You remember. That guy's boat sank in the storm. What a disaster."

"Oh, yeah. I remember. Was he able to have it repaired?"

"I guess so. We got it up and floating again. All of the electronics were ruined, of course. I don't think the insurance company would have wanted it salvaged if it hadn't been brand new."

"I'm ready to go ashore if you are."

Jon grabbed a small backpack that sat in the chair across the galley, and Meg picked up the picnic basket. When they walked through the door to the main deck, Meg noted that Jon had already lowered the Zodiac into the water.

She loved their rubber inflatable, though it was unlike any little raft she ever had as a kid. She remembered the raft her father had won through his work when she was a little girl. She and her sister, Liz, called it *Rover*. The Zodiac she and Jon kept on *The Discoverer* was twelve feet long, and the twenty horse-power, Yamaha outboard motor was strong enough to get them ashore quickly. She had been concerned the first time they took it into the inlet, thinking it might drag on the shallow bottom, but they had never had a problem.

After lunch in the cave, Meg lay on the blanket beside Jon with her head on his chest. He gently slid his hand through her brown hair. Their annual trip to Conception Island was always a highlight to Meg.

The first trip to the island as a married couple lived up to the island's name. It had first embarrassed her a little when Lacy figured out the importance of this beautiful slice of tropical paradise. Meg tried to convince her that the reason the place was so special was because she and Jon had hidden out in the cave during a hurricane while trying to escape from a band of thugs who had kidnapped them. That reason was true, but it was the second trip to the island that gave the place the most significance to Meg. Lacy was sharp, and once Meg absentmindedly told her the date of the start of their tradition, Lacy did the math.

"Oh, my God," Lacy had nearly shouted. "You two had…"

"Had lunch and started a wonderful tradition," Meg interrupted.

"You did more than lunch, and Carla is proof. That's hilarious."

"I think it's miraculous," Meg insisted.

"It's really sweet. I don't think I'll ever get married, but if I do, I hope to find someone like Jon."

"He's pretty special."

Jon's gentle voice brought Meg back to the present. "What are you thinking about?"

"Oh, I was just thinking back to trying to convince Lacy that we love this island because it saved us from the hurricane."

"You know where you go for lying?"

"Yeah. Washington D.C. You've told me that before."

Jon laughed and tenderly lay Meg on her back. His hand brushed hair from her face, and his lips found hers. Electricity shot through her body as it had the first time he touched her. Passion swelled within her, and the familiar desire for her husband engulfed her.

"I love you, Jon Davenport," Meg whispered in her husband's ear.

Chapter Four

Miami Bound

Lacy took the ramp onto Interstate 75 and pointed her car toward Miami. She couldn't believe she was actually moving to Florida without even saying goodbye to anyone. What would her mother think? She wouldn't care because she hadn't even bothered to come home for the last week, except to take Lacy to the doctor. *My mom doesn't even know I exist, or if she does, she doesn't care. She will be glad that I've moved to Florida. It will probably be at least a week before she notices that I've gone.*

A large eighteen-wheeler blew by Lacy as she wiped a tear from her wet cheek. Moms were supposed to care. *Why does mine have to be such a selfish...?* Several words filled Lacy's mind that would complete her thought, but they were words from her past, from the old Lacy. After escaping from Miguel this summer, she had pledged to be a new person, and one way meant no more profanity. It shouldn't be too hard at this point. Somehow, she had managed to make it through most of the summer with only a few slip ups.

"I pledge to be like Meg and not Mom," Lacy said aloud. "I'm not going to let the pain of the past define my future," *Boy! That sounds just like something Meg would say.*

Lacy thought over the blur of the last week. Getting the cast off her leg had certainly been one highlight. Changing all of her courses to online classes had been a cinch. She had assumed that dealing with her counselor would be the greatest stumbling block to her plan, but it turned out to be a breeze. Talking her way out of her lease had been a greater challenge, but she remembered a girl in her English 101 class who was in need of a place to live. Lauren practically screamed with joy when Lacy offered her the room in the apartment.

When Lacy stopped by the property manager's office to present the idea of a change to him, he just stared at her for what seemed like a year. He slowly shook his head.

Before he could say no, Lacy pleaded with him. "Please Mr. Murphy. It doesn't affect you in the slightest. As a matter of fact, Lauren is a much nicer girl than me. She'll be a far better tenant."

He finally caved to her pleas. The fact was that Lauren could have passed for Lacy's twin. The thought had crossed her mind to just make the switch without telling the landlord. He probably never would have noticed. In the end, everything worked out perfectly. Lauren had a new place to live, and Lacy jumped her final hurdle to becoming a Floridian.

Turning on her right blinker, Lacy took the Forsyth exit and pulled into the McDonald's parking lot. Not only had she pledged to stop cussing, but she had also made a commitment to stay away from fried foods. After sitting in her car for a few minutes, she decided that it was best to break only one vice at a time. French fries would offer some measure of comfort. *I hope McDonalds serves fries this early.*

She looked in her visor mirror, wiped away a black smear of mascara from her right cheek, and walked into the restaurant. She'd barely been driving for thirty minutes and was already stopping. *At this rate, it will take me two weeks to get to Miami. I cannot keep doing this all the way to Florida.*

She got in line behind a cute teenage girl that was hanging all over her boyfriend. It was kind of disgusting. The girl was really pretty and looked to be at least eighteen, but Lacy heard her say something about her first year of high school. *The kid is only fifteen!* Lacy was shocked when the girl dropped a few words that would have made Meg cringe. She even used the worst word in Meg's potty mouth list of banned words, well, maybe it wasn't the worst word because it wasn't taking God's name in vain. Meg especially hated those words.

Does this girl not realize what she's asking for by using a word like that? Lacy jerked as if someone had slapped her when the girl dropped the bomb again. Just a few months earlier, Lacy had been using the same word. What had people thought of her? Meg's rule about language now made a lot of sense. At first, Lacy had thought that her aunt just wanted to protect her daughter from profanity, but now Lacy realized that there was a lot more to cleaning up her language than just Carla.

It occurred to her that she not only had never heard Meg use a bad word, but her aunt had never even lost her cool. *Do she and Jon ever fight? What does Meg do when she's really angry?* It was odd that Lacy couldn't even remember ever seeing Meg get mad. Meg versus Liz. What a contrast! *How did my mom become such a jerk, and Meg is the sweetest person in the world?*

Ten minutes later with a large order of fries placed carefully in the console of her car and a large Diet Coke in the cup holder, Lacy was once again bound for the Sunshine State. *Maybe whatever Meg has will rub off on me.*

As she drove passed Perry, Georgia, she picked up her cell phone to try to call Jon again. Just like the last few days, it went straight to voice mail. This time, however, when she called Meg's phone, it began to ring.

"Hello," Lacy recognized the sweet voice of Judy on the other end of the line.

"Hey, Miss Judy. This is Lacy. How are you?"

"Hello, Lacy. I'm doing so good, but I sure do miss you. I'm putting a puzzle together with Carla."

"That sounds like a lot of fun. I've been trying to call Jon for days, and he doesn't answer his phone. Meg wouldn't answer either. Is everything okay?"

"Yes, dear. Everything is fine. Jon's phone got wet. I think he dropped it in a sink full of water."

"Ohhh. That's bad. I wasn't too surprised when Meg didn't answer her phone. She doesn't carry it with her much."

Judy laughed. "I know. Jon gets a little exasperated with that at times.

So, Jon gets exasperated. I'm at least glad to know that he is human after all. "I really need to talk to Jon. Is he around?"

"No, dear. He and Meg went over to Conception Island for their annual ritual."

Lacy stopped herself just short of a snort. She knew at least some of what their ritual included. "Well, in that case, I'll just call back."

"Jon is supposed to check in with me shortly on his satellite phone. Do you want me to have him call you?"

"Oh, no. I'd hate to interrupt their *ritual*. Just tell him to call me when he gets back."

A long, loud horn blew as a huge truck raced by Lacy. She jerked the steering wheel to the right.

"Lacy? Are you okay? What was that noise?"

"Sorry, Miss Judy. I guess Meg is right again."

"What do you mean?"

"She told me I shouldn't talk on the cell phone while I'm driving. I nearly pulled in front of a truck."

"Oh, my. You be careful. Are you driving back to school?"

"Actually," Lacy said with a bit of a hesitation. "Judy. I've made a huge decision. I should have talked with Jon about it first, but he seemed to think it would be a good idea a couple of weeks ago. At least, he sort of said something about the idea."

"You're not making sense, sweetheart. What decision have you made?"

Lacy told Judy about her plan to move to Miami and complete a couple of semesters online while working toward her Florida residency.

"Let me guess," Judy interrupted. "Then you're going to transfer to the University of Miami."

"You sure are perceptive," Lacy teased.

"I'm also guessing that there's one certain young man that draws your interest more than your educational pursuits."

"Right again."

"You know. You could move into Jon's house in Miami. It's just sitting empty right now."

"What about Marie? I thought she lived there."

"Technically, she does," Judy agreed. "She's taken some time off to go back to Tampa to take care of her mother. You would have that big old beautiful house all to yourself. At least, for a while."

"Can you keep a secret?"

Judy paused on the other end of the phone. "My lips are sealed."

Lacy imagined her sweet, older friend zipping her lips. "I'm headed to Jon's house right now, but I have a long way to go. I know I should have checked with Jon first, but I couldn't stay in Griffin for one more second. Jon wouldn't answer his phone, and…"

"Sweetheart! You know that Jon welcomes you here any time you want to come. He will be so glad to have someone living in the house while Marie's away."

"Do you really think so?"

"Indeed, dear, and you know that pool really needs to be used."

Lacy laughed. "You are so right, Judy. Just tell Jon to call me, and I'll break the news to him slowly. Who knows? I might be in *his* pool when he calls. I'll talk to you soon."

"Okay, dear. You be careful. Call me when you get there so I'll know you arrived safely. Goodbye."

Lacy felt warmth fill her heart as she thought about her sweet, elderly friend. Judy was so sweet. Lacy thought about getting old and wondered if she would be a kind old lady, or would she be a grouchy biddy? She decided that old people must be an exaggeration of what they were when they were younger. *If that's the case, then I'm going to start practicing so I can be a sweet old lady.*

As Lacy crossed into Florida, she picked up her phone and called Kerrick. "You'll never believe where I am," she cooed into the phone once Kerrick picked up.

"Let me guess. Hawaii? No, Nassau?"

"You're cute."

"Thanks."

"You crack me up. Actually, I just crossed into Florida, and I'm dying to see you."

"You've only got about six or seven more hours to go, that is if you can drive without stopping to use the bathroom or get gas. Are you okay on money? I forgot about asking if you had money for gas."

"I may be broke, but I do have a little money, Kerrick." Lacy said defensively.

"Okay, okay. I just care. That's all. I've been thinking about our conversation from earlier."

"Which one?"

"The one about your last thought before your plane took off from Miami a few days ago."

"Oh, you mean about…"

"That's the one," Kerrick interrupted. "Have you talked with anyone else about that topic?"

"No, why? I couldn't if I wanted to because my cell phone battery is about to go, and I forgot my charger."

"If you are where I think you are, you're about to pass an exit that has a truck stop. There's a pay phone on the right side of the parking lot."

"You're not making sense, Kerrick?"

"Just a little game to keep you awake," Kerrick said.

"Okay. A pay-phone? What a relic."

"I know. I can't believe they still have those things around. Stop there and call my sister."

"Call Kelsey? Why?"

"She wants to talk. It shouldn't cost too much, but she REALLY wants to talk to you."

"Kerrick, you're being weird."

"I've got to go. I'll talk soon."

Lacy nearly ran off the road as she looked down at her quiet phone. What was Kerrick's deal? She looked up just in time to see a sign advertising a *Loves Truck Stop* on Highway 129. That had to be it. She took the exit, found the pay phone, and dropped a few quarters into the slot on the phone before dialing Kelsey's number.

"Lacy?"

"Kelsey! How are you doing?"

"I'm great, and I'm already missing you. Listen, I'd love to talk, but Kerrick just gave me specific instructions not to talk too much before telling you to hang up and wait on his phone call."

"What's going on, Kelsey?"

"I'm not sure, but he told me to get your number off of caller ID and text it to a number he gave me. He said he'll call you immediately."

"Okay. Something must be up. I'll call you after a while."

Lacy hung up the phone and stood quietly for a couple of minutes before the pay phone rang loudly. "Hey. What's going on?"

"You better be glad it was me," Kerrick insisted. "Listen. Right when I hung up with you the last time, I heard a little noise. I don't know if it means anything or not, but Miguel once told me that he had ways to listen in on anyone's phone in the world. We know he's still around, and he's not going to give up on your medallion easily. I suggest that we assume he's got our phones hacked."

"You're kidding. Are you calling from your phone now?"

"No. I just got to my dorm room, so I'm using a friend's phone. I think we should give Miguel a little run for his money."

"Like a wild goose chase?"

"Yes. Why don't you call me on your phone and tell me that you changed your mind? Say you decided it was better for your career to stay at GCSU. Our conversation will have to be convincing. Also, we can't talk about what we're doing or our location. I'll get us a couple of temporary phones to use to talk to one another and to Jon and Meg."

"Okay, but we'd better still call one another on our regular phones or he'll know something is up. I like the idea of making Miguel think I'm going back to school in Milledgeville."

"That sounds good. I'll send Jon a text and tell him that you'll call him tonight at 11:00."

"Send the text to Meg's phone. Jon's phone fell in the toilet or the sink."

They talked for a few more minutes before Lacy hurried into the truck stop to buy a phone charger and then continued her trek south. Surely, Miguel was not still after them. As a misty rain began to fall, she tried to imagine what Miguel would be thinking. If she were Miguel, she wouldn't give up searching for the treasure. If that were true, then her phone could certainly be tapped, and she could still be in danger. She felt a shiver of dread run down her back as the light rain turned into an all-out storm.

Chapter Five

Home Again

Jon pulled the Carver up to the dock in Pirate's Cove and let it bump gently into its familiar berth. He looked down on the deck and heard his beautiful wife singing, and then he turned his gaze to his home on top of the bluff. A huge smile covered his face, and he shook his head slightly in disbelief. He loved their home on Great Exuma, and the community of Roker's Point had accepted him and Meg as if they were family. He even considered selling his ranch back in Georgia. They may as well sell it. Ever since buying the property in the Bahamas, they had been back to Georgia only two or three times.

Meg often teased him about calling their little spot of paradise *Pirate's Cove*, but Jon insisted that if he were a pirate, he would find refuge in their cove. Because he thought it was a perfect place for pirates to drop anchor, he was confident that they must have used this cove three centuries earlier.

He looked up again toward his house and saw Judy holding Carla. They both waved enthusiastically, and Jon's heart warmed at the sight of his precious daughter. Meg must have heard Carla's little voice drifting down to the dock because she stopped tying the boat to the dock cleat and waved.

When Meg topped the last step and hurried onto the grassy yard atop the bluff, Carla ran into her open arms. "Oh, sweetheart. I've missed you so much."

"Hey, sweet bug," Jon said as Meg set their little girl down so she could hug her father. "We sure did miss you and Grandma Judy."

"Dada. Boat?"

"Yes, sweetie. We were on the boat, but we're home now. What have you been doing?"

Carla began jabbering away, and Meg nodded and laughed. Jon marveled that his wife seemed to know exactly what their little girl said. He picked up Carla, and everyone walked into the house.

"I just made some lemonade," Judy announced, "and I'm about to pull chocolate chip cookies out of the oven."

Jon breathed in the smell of freshly baked cookies. "Sounds like we got home just in time. Anything happen while we were gone?"

"Bird!" Carla said with a frown on her chubby face.

"What about a bird, sweetheart?" Meg said as she squatted down in front of Carla.

"Bird die."

"Oh?" Meg held Carla in a tight hug.

Judy sat two glasses of lemonade on the kitchen table. "A bird flew into the living room window yesterday while I was reading Carla a book. It died, and Carla cried. She has such a tender little heart."

"That's the second one since we've all been home," Jon said, "and there were three there when we arrived from Nassau on Saturday. What can we do to keep that from happening?"

"I've heard of people rubbing soap on the outside of the glass," Meg offered, "but it seems like that would wash off, not to mention make the window a bit cloudy."

"I researched it last night," Judy replied. "I found a website that suggested putting up fine mosquito screen, so I ordered some from Amazon. It should be a perfect fit for the window and shouldn't hinder our view of the cove. Oh, Jon. Before I forget. You need to call Lacy. She's been trying to call you for days."

"Okay. I meant to call her before we left for Conception Island just to see how she was doing. We sent a text to Liz last Friday afternoon to make sure she was at the airport."

"It's sad that we have to make sure my sister wouldn't forget to pick up her own daughter," Meg sighed. "I don't know how she and I can be so different and come from the same family. At least, Liz called me later to tell me Lacy was at home, but I don't think she was with her at the time. It sounded like she was at a bar."

"Lacy is such a sweet girl," Judy said. "She's fortunate to have you two."

"She certainly has a lot of potential," Jon agreed. "I'll call her in a little while. Carla, would you like to color a picture with Daddy?"

After dinner, Jon picked up Meg's cell phone and saw that a text had come in from a strange phone number that had an odd message: "Judy's sister is trying to get hold of her."

"Judy. You don't have a sister, do you?"

"You know I don't, Jon."

"Do you have a text message?"

Judy went into her bedroom to retrieve her cell phone. "Yes, I do. I don't recognize the number, but it says it's from Kerrick. It says, 'Lacy will call you between 10:30 and 11:00 tonight.'"

Meg walked into the living room. "What in the world is going on?"

"There's no telling, sweetheart. We'll find out at 11:00 tonight."

At exactly 10:55, Judy's phone rang. Jon answered, and immediately recognized Lacy's voice on the other end. He put the phone on speaker so Meg and Judy could hear.

"Hey, Uncle Jon. I've been calling you and Aunt Meg for days."

"Hey, Lacy. Sorry, I dropped my phone in some water."

"Yeah. Miss Judy told me about the phone. That sucks."

"Yep. I just got the thing before our summer trip. Oh well."

"Sounds like we might need to find some more treasure so you can buy you a new one," Lacy said with a laugh.

"So, what's with the secret phone calls? Meg and Judy are listening in as well."

"Hey, Meg and Miss Judy. I miss you guys so much. As far as the weird phone stuff, Kerrick thinks our phones have been tapped by Miguel."

Meg inhaled sharply, and Judy moaned something before Jon could reply. "Why does he think they're tapped?"

"It's only a hunch, but it makes sense. Miguel once told him that he could hack into anyone's phone in the world, and Kerrick thought he heard a popping sound on his phone when we were talking earlier. He doesn't know whether or not that means anything, but he feels pretty sure that Miguel would keep tabs on us. If he is listening, we're trying to lead him on a wild goose chase."

Jon gave a thumbs up to Meg. "That's good thinking Lacy. If Miguel is listening in, you can certainly get him off course."

"The real reason I called is because I need to talk to you about something really important, but I'd rather not talk over the phone."

"Is this bad news, Lacy?" Meg asked hesitantly.

"No, Meg. It's great news."

"Are you getting married?" Judy gasped.

"No. I need to talk face-to-face. I also need to ask a huge favor."

"Sure," Jon said. "Whatever you need."

"Wow!" Lacy laughed. "That was pretty easy, and I haven't even asked yet. Would you allow me to live in the house in Miami? I'll get a job and pay you rent."

Lacy went on to tell Jon, Meg, and Judy about her experience at home and her plans to move to Miami. When Jon was hesitant about her getting behind in school, Lacy reassured him that she would be able to keep up her studies online.

"In that case," Jon replied, "I'd be happy to hire you to watch over my house in Miami. I'll pay you $1000 per month, and your rent will be $500."

"Uncle Jon! You can't pay me to watch over your house."

"I was paying Marie that much, and she's now gone for at least six months, maybe permanently."

Meg started to speak, but Jon stopped her before continuing, "Five hundred dollars is a lot cheaper rent than the house is worth, but I'm sure you could find a room for about that much around the school. I'll help you and you help me."

"Deal," Lacy exclaimed.

Meg leaned toward the cell phone. "When do you want to move in?"

"How about tonight?" Lacy laughed. "I'm actually standing on the front porch."

"Ummm." Jon rubbed his chin. "What if I'd refused?"

"For starters, I knew you wouldn't say no, Uncle Jon. If you did, then I suppose I'd come up with something. Kerrick and I could just shack up."

Judy gasped again. "Judy," Meg said as she patted Judy's hand, "Lacy's just kidding."

"You know I wouldn't do that, Meg. I just had to leave Griffin."

"I understand, Lacy," Jon reassured her, "and your timing is perfect. We'll catch a plane over tomorrow morning so we can talk."

"Sounds good to me. How about I fix us breakfast in the morning? Can you be here by 9:30?"

"I wouldn't miss it."

Before Jon disconnected the call, he gave Lacy the code that would unlock the front door. He laid the phone on the coffee table in front of the couch. "It's amazing how things happen around here." He looked over at Meg and took her hand. "Honey, if I know you as well as I think I know you, you were about to say that Lacy could just live in the house without rent."

"You know me pretty well, but I now definitely see the wisdom in having her earn her keep and pay rent. You are so wise."

"I wonder what Lacy is up to," Jon said. "I know she's crazy in love with Kerrick, but what do you think she wants to talk about?"

"I just knew she was pregnant," Judy said as she fanned herself with the copy of the island newspaper that came out once a week.

"I hate to admit it," Meg said, "but that thought crossed my mind, too. She's smarter than that, though."

Jon squeezed Meg's hand. "Sometimes even really smart girls do stupid things."

Meg nodded. "True. Maybe she just needs advice about her next move. Coming down here alone took a lot of nerve."

"I think it has more to do with heart than nerve," Judy said. "She's so in love with that boy, and I think they make such a sweet couple."

Meg stood to go upstairs to check on Carla, and Judy told them both goodnight. Jon pulled a folder out from the end table that contained the translated copy of King Bluetooth's journal he had received from the queen of Denmark and pictures of the two medallions. He stared at the picture of Lacy's medallion for the hundredth time and studied the picture of the Swedish girl's medallion.

Olivia was such a charming little girl and had so many questions for Jon and Meg about scuba diving. The Swedish girl had appeared poor, and scuba diving in Sweden was probably not very common. Jon thought about how much fun it would be to invite the girl over to spend a week or two in the Bahamas. He made a mental note to talk with Meg about the possibility. In the meantime, he sure wished he could figure out the clues on these medallions.

He picked up the picture of Lacy's medallion again and inspected it carefully. "How did you get to Conception Island?" he said aloud. *If Bluetooth's man really did discover a lost city and the king put clues on these medallions, he wouldn't have left the medallion in the cave. The king's children were supposed to have them.*

Jon felt fingers running through his hair and suddenly realized that Meg was sitting beside him. He had been so engrossed in his thoughts that he didn't realize she had come back from Carla's room.

"So, what are you thinking about so hard, Jon? You've looked at those pictures a hundred times."

Jon put his arm around Meg and pulled her toward him. "I was just wondering how in the world these medallions got to the Bahamas. Them being there doesn't make sense to me."

"It is weird. We've assumed the skeleton in the cave was Bluetooth's man, but the medallions were supposed to be given to the king's children. Why would this guy bring the medallions to Conception Island?"

"None of it seems to fit," Jon sighed. "We assume Miguel's medallion came from the dead guy in the cave, but how did yours end up on the reef a mile out from the island?"

"I sure wish I knew," Meg said.

Jon kissed the top of his wife's head. "I suppose that's one mystery that we'll never be able to solve."

Chapter Six

Ludvig Olsson - 1871

As the train rocked south out of New York City, Ludvig looked back to the mayhem going on at the parade celebrating some Irish battle. Why couldn't the Protestants and the Catholics get along? A smile crossed his face as he considered the violence taking place on the streets. One dead man in an alley would be considered another fatality resulting from the Orange Riots. Perfect timing!

He opened the letter again and read Liam's words. Now that he had the medallion, could he really meet his cousin on Santa Maria de la Conception? He had never heard of the island before, but Liam insisted that was the best place in the Bahamas for them to meet.

Liam was a killer. Ludvig knew of at least three men the brute had killed with only his hands earlier in his life. Now, he had killed a priest. Even if the Swede was family, Ludvig wasn't sure if he could trust a guy who would kill a priest. Ludvig thought of Heinrich lying in the alley and was sure he was dead by now. *I suppose that makes me a killer, too. If he had not come after me, I wouldn't have had to do it.*

Ludvig was confident that Liam would try to kill him as soon as he delivered the second medallion. If he had not been working in New York, his cousin wouldn't have involved him in the first place. *It doesn't really make sense to me. Why didn't Liam just come over*

*here and get the medallion for himself? He must need my help for other
reasons. I know the sea a little. That's got to be it. He needs me because I
can help him sail somewhere in the Bahamas.*

Looking once again at the gold medallion, Ludvig knew he
would at least go along for now. His cousin was the one who
contacted him first about this unbelievable story. He marveled
that it seemed the whole thing was true, though he had not
believed Liam at first. Heinrich's medallion verified this crazy
tale.

The main problem Ludvig now faced was in following
Liam's orders in the letter. Getting a small boat that could sail
around the Bahamian islands wouldn't be too much of a problem, but Liam wanted him to come alone. Ludvig knew that his
cousin knew nothing about sailing, so there was no way he could
navigate the islands by himself. He considered the task of just
finding one trustworthy seaman.

The train ride ended in Philadelphia. Ludvig had been told
that he would discover the train tracks in the south were in dis-
repair because of the war, so he sought passage on a boat that
took him down the Delaware River to the bay. He knew he could
board a larger ship there that would take him all the way to Florida, and maybe to Nassau.

Nearly a month after leaving Cape May aboard *The Admiral,*
Ludvig was standing on the deck when the ship dropped anchor
in Biscayne Bay, near Ft. Dallas. He climbed down the ladder to
the waiting skiff that would take him ashore. His voyage south
had been a bit difficult with numerous storms, and he was ready
to step foot on Florida soil. As he looked across the water to the
community he had heard called Miami, he was surprised that it
was nothing more than a rugged settlement. Someone told him
that the fort was essential for the protection of the settlers from

the Seminole Indians, but he had expected a larger city for this southern post. He studied the other ships at anchor and wondered if any of them would be going east to Nassau.

The thought crossed his mind that he could find a small charter vessel here in Biscayne Bay and avoid having to purchase passage on a larger ship. It would have to be small enough that he and one other person could sail it, but large enough to make passage over the Florida Straits. He spotted several possibilities, but he didn't know if these ships would be available for his use.

Once ashore, Ludvig found the steamy room someone called a tavern, but it was more like a wooden box with a tin roof. He reached for his handkerchief to wipe his forehead as his eyes began to sting with the salty perspiration. He rolled up the sleeves of his shirt and sat down in a chair beside an overturned barrel. It was difficult to get over the swaying motion that had become normal to him over the last weeks, and he found himself unconsciously holding his glass of ale as if it might slide off the barrel. Even though it was just past midday, several people sat around barrels with chipped glasses of dark liquid in front of them.

"You must have come in on *The Admiral*," a young sailor said who sat at the nearby table. He stuck out his hand. "Anthony. My name is Anthony Sellers."

Ludvig took the man's hand. "My name is Oliver. It's a pleasure to meet you." Ludvig had made an instant decision not to reveal his real name.

"With an accent like that, you're obviously not from around here."

"No, sir. My home is Sweden, but I work in New York. Are you from here?"

"No. I'm from Maryland, but I've been here a little while."

"Why did you come to Ft. Dallas?" Ludvig asked while thinking that anyone would be out of their mind to want to live in this rat hole.

"I came down from Baltimore on the *Wesser*. It seems that I got a little carried away in a card game and had to spend a night in the hoosegow. Problem is, the *Wesser* didn't wait on me. I've been trying my hand at wrecking for the last few weeks."

Ludvig leaned toward the young sailor. "Hoosegow?"

"Oh. Sorry. That's what they call the jail around here. I think it's Spanish. Anyway, I'm sort of stuck here for now. Good for me that I got paid when we dropped anchor."

"And what does a wrecker do? I've never heard that word either."

"Well, we try to salvage stuff from ship wrecks. There's some shallow reefs around here that snag boats all the time. As long as the boats don't sink, we can get some nice coin for stuff aboard."

The two men talked on for an hour, and Ludvig decided he could trust Anthony. He first thought that the young man had a boat, but it turned out he worked on another man's rig. Ludvig imagined they could find a boat in Nassau easy enough. "I need a partner who can sail. Would you be willing to work for me?"

"What kind of work is it?"

"I need to meet my friend in the Bahamas, and we're on a bit of an expedition. It should take a week or two, that's all. I'll pay you to be my first mate."

"I suppose that will work just fine. What kind of expedition?"

"Well, my friend and I are ornithologists. We study birds. The Bahamas are famous for unique bird species, and we have been hired to research the...the Yellowthroat."

Ludvig once read an article on tropical birds and thought he remembered reading something about a Yellowthroat. Thankfully, the word *ornithologist* had come quickly to his mind. He hoped that the yellowthroat was either a bird of the Bahamas or that Anthony didn't know the difference.

"So, Mr. Oliver, that makes you a scientist? Or should I call you Dr. Oliver."

"Mister is fine. Will you work for me? I'll pay your expenses as we go along and then give you your pay at the end of two weeks."

Anthony stuck out his hand to shake. "Sounds good to me Mr. Oliver. When do we start?"

"Let's get passage to Nassau, and then we'll need to find a boat we can use. Surely we can come across a fisherman down on his luck who's willing to loan us his boat for a couple of weeks in exchange for a little money."

Finding a boat in the Bahamas turned out to be a little more difficult than Ludvig anticipated. He haggled and bartered. He finally found a fisherman who would loan out his boat for a sizable price, but the fisherman insisted on going along. The Bahamian, named Jalen, was huge from years of work on the sea, and Ludvig didn't think he could be trusted.

"I go or no boat!" he insisted.

"Okay," Ludvig conceded. "You can go. I want us to leave at sunrise tomorrow."

"Good. Where are we going?"

"Our first stop will be Santa Maria de la Conception."

The large fisherman looked as if he had been punched in the gut. "No. We can't go there."

"Why not? That's where we must go."

Jalen shook his head violently. "Cursed. The island is cursed. I will not go to that island."

Ludvig couldn't believe what this guy was saying. Island lore ran deep in the Bahamas, and someone had evidently told him a story about Conception Island. "The island is not cursed. I am to meet my friend there in a week. Is Conception Island inhabited?"

"Not by people, but it is inhabited."

Ludvig closed his eyes in disgust at the superstition. "In that case, we'll need to go to an island nearby to wait for the proper time to meet my friend."

"I'll go to Exuma, but not Conception."

"Let's go to Exuma and then we'll talk about it."

The following morning, the three men set sail for Georgetown on Exuma island. While Ludvig was quite familiar with the seas in the north, he had never seen anything like the emerald waters of the Bahamas. Looking at the bottom that was five fathoms beneath the surface was like looking at drinking water in a clear, glass cup. It was remarkable. The large fisherman had a broken, glass jug that he would set in the water, and Ludvig could make out creatures moving along the sand on the bottom. He imagined what it would be like to swim in the ocean and see with clarity. Unfortunately, Ludvig couldn't swim very well, and there was no way to seal the jug to his face.

"Useful for finding fish," the large man insisted as Ludvig continued staring at the ocean floor.

Ludvig suddenly jerked up from the jug and almost dropped it into the sea. "Oh, my God. What was that?"

The fisherman laughed. "Shark. It was a Hammerhead shark. You've never seen one?"

Ludvig sat down in the boat. "I've seen sharks, but never a Hammerhead. That thing was huge."

"Yes. I saw it. Perhaps twelve feet. Good to eat but will also eat you."

After spending nearly five days in Georgetown, Ludvig was ready to head toward Conception Island. He haggled with the fisherman and offered to pay him double. The man finally agreed to tow a small skiff so Ludvig could go ashore to find his friend.

"You must go the last mile by yourself. I will not go any closer to the island."

"Fine. Just get me within a mile."

Ludvig noticed water in the bottom of the fishing boat that must have come from the rain of the previous night. He removed his shoes so he could step into the boat and bail the water. As he stepped from the dock, he lost his balance and fell into the ocean. He landed near the pylon of the dock and reached for the post as he went under. Though he managed to pull himself up out of the water, he cut both of his hands and a foot on barnacles. The salt water burned as blood gushed from the wounds.

"Mr. Oliver!" Anthony shouted as he helped Ludvig get back onto the dock. "We must get you to a doctor."

"I'm fine," Ludvig gasped. "Just get me a cloth. I'll wrap it up, and the bleeding will stop."

"I think you need to see a doctor," Anthony insisted. "I'll go back into town to get help."

In about thirty minutes, Anthony returned and informed Ludvig that the doctor had gone over to Cat Island. "I managed to get a needle. I'll sew it up for you."

Ludvig looked at the young sailor dubiously. The last thing he wanted was for his new friend to stick a needle in his hands or foot.

"I've done it many times," Anthony insisted. "We'll put a little wine on the wound to clean it out, and you'll need to drink a little. You won't feel a thing."

Four hours later, the small crew was sailing northeast toward Santa Maria de la Conception. Ludvig was still a bit lightheaded, but his wounds had been sewn up. His foot was the worst of his wounds, and he still wore a bandage around it to catch the blood that seeped from the cut.

The wind was in their favor, so the small vessel skimmed across the water. Ludvig sat near the front and pulled the gold medallion from his pocket. He made sure that Anthony and the fisherman were too busy to notice him look at the scratch marks one more time. Heinrich had been slow to tell him the meaning of the marks, but with a little persuasion, he had eventually told him the marks were Runic for *Beneath*. What did that mean? Surely Liam would know.

"Mr. Oliver!" Anthony shouted from the rear of the boat.

Ludvig pocketed the gold disc and looked up at the darkening sky. "Yes. What is it."

"That's your island. We're not going any closer. Jalen says a bad storm is coming. We should go back while we have time."

"No. I'll go to the island. You can come back for me tomorrow."

The ocean pitched as Ludvig stood to his feet. He steadied himself by holding to the side of the boat.

"Do you want me to come along?" Anthony asked for the third time.

"I've already told you, Anthony, that I'll go alone. Just come back tomorrow after the storm passes. I'll watch for you from shore."

Anthony pulled the little ten-foot skiff to the side of the fishing boat. Both vessels were beginning to be tossed about by the waves. Sitting on the edge of the fishing boat, Ludvig reached for the smaller vessel with his feet, but it was jerked away by another wave. He felt the sting of salt water as his bandaged foot plunged beneath the surface of the tossing sea. As he finally stepped aboard the small skiff, he noticed the bloody cloth that had been his bandage floating away from the boats.

"Give me another bandage," Ludvig shouted over the growing wind. "My foot is bleeding again."

Jalen threw a piece of cloth toward the skiff as he pushed away to return to safety. "We'll go to Cat Island," he shouted. "It's not too far from here."

Within minutes, the fishing boat became a small spot on the horizon as Ludvig paddled against the wind. If he could just get inside the bay, the ocean would probably push him toward the beach. He needed to hurry because his boat was filling with every crashing wave.

The front of his small skiff jutted into the air on a menacing wave, and before Ludvig realized what was happening, he was tossed into the sea. His boat flipped upside down and nearly hit him in the head. Just before going underwater, he managed to grab hold of the rope that trailed behind the boat. He pulled his body slowly up the rope toward the safety of the capsized boat. *I must not let go of this boat. It will take me to shore. I'm sure of it.*

The cut in his foot burned as the salt water entered his bleeding wound. He had the sensation of something brushing against his leg. Was his mind playing tricks on him? Suddenly, something bumped hard against his side; and then again. He tried to peer down into the dark, churning water. A shock of pain seared his body as if he had been sliced by a large piece of glass. Something pulled him by the leg, but he held to the side of the boat.

His mind went back to the Hammerhead shark he had seen earlier, and a shiver of dread ran down his spine. Whether the island was cursed or not, he was cursed for taking the medallion. He reached for the gold disc in his pocket and considered throwing it into the sea. His body felt as if he were on fire with pain like he had never experienced. The water around him turned crimson as he saw two dorsal fins break the surface.

Those are sharks. How many more are beneath me. God is judging me for killing Heinrich. I never should have come here.

He tried to pull his mangled body atop the overturned boat, but suddenly pain shot through his body as something very large grabbed him from beneath and began shaking him violently. Terror filled his heart, and his lungs filled with water. The medallion slipped from his grasp and drifted to the coral reef thirty feet beneath the bloody surface.

Chapter Seven

Love Embraced

Lacy felt Kerrick's strong arms wrap around her as she punched in the code to the front door of the house. She felt secure in his embrace and giggled as he nibbled on her ear.

"You need to stop that," Lacy insisted, but not with much conviction. "You're going to get the neighbors talking."

"Who cares."

Kerrick pushed the door open. He picked Lacy up and carried her into the foyer.

"Kerrick! What are you doing?"

"I'm carrying you across the threshold."

"We're not married, silly. Put me down. I can walk. My leg's not broken any more."

He lowered her feet to the floor, and eyes seemed to be taking in every inch of her body. She looked down at her feet and twisted her class ring. When she looked up into his eyes, it seemed that all of the world stopped. Kerrick took her head into his hands and slowly lowered his face toward hers. She felt as if her heart might explode as their lips met. His chiseled body was hard, but she knew his heart was soft. She slid her hands under his tee-shirt, and they tingled at the touch of his bare skin. She couldn't get enough of him. She had never loved anyone like this.

"This could be dangerous," Kerrick finally said as he pulled Lacy's head to his chest.

She was breathless, and hearing the rapid beat of his heart nearly made her go crazy with desire. They had only known one another for a few months, but they had already experienced a lifetime together. She loved him with every ounce of her being.

Kerrick pulled Lacy's chin up until they were once again staring at one another. His eyes were beautiful and pleading. "Here we are. Two almost-grown adults who love each other. Alone in a beautiful house. Everything in me says 'stop,' but nothing in me wants to."

An image of her mother with George flashed through Lacy's mind, though she had actually never seen the jerk. Just hours ago, Lacy pledged to be like Meg and not like her mom. Her mom could wallpaper their house with pictures of men she'd slept with, but Lacy knew that Meg thought sex was special and was meant to be experienced only between two people in a committed relationship. For her aunt, that meant marriage. Lacy used to think her aunt needed to get with it and move into the 21st Century, but maybe she was right. After all, look at Jon and Meg. Lacy didn't know anyone in the world who loved one another any more or who were any happier. Her mom, on the other hand, was a miserable, selfish, wreck. Meg would stop things right here in the foyer. Her mom? Well, her mom didn't know what stop meant.

Lacy took Kerrick's face in her hands and kissed him one more time. "I've missed you, Kerrick Daniels. I can't believe I get to live in the same city with you. True, I want you to spend the night, but that's not a good idea. Meg would kill me, and we would regret it. Having Aunt Meg's trust and your respect means more to me than I once realized."

"You're right. Let's get something to eat and make some ground rules on how we're going to manage maintaining Meg's trust. I will do my best to help us not give in to the most natural thing in the world. For starters, I'll never spend the night with you. Well," he grinned, "not never."

"What are you saying Mr. Daniels?" *Is he talking about marriage?*

"I'm saying that you're the most beautiful woman in the world, and I'm so glad I have the honor of taking you out to eat tonight."

"I don't think that's what you were saying, and it's not that I don't want to have sex. I want to more than you know, but I hate what my mother has become."

"What does your mother have to do with us?"

"Kerrick, I've spent a lot of time comparing my mom to Aunt Meg. There's no comparison. I refuse to be like my mom, but I'd do anything to be like Meg."

"And Meg thinks sex is for married people."

"I know that's old-fashioned, but look at their marriage. You have to admit that they really have something special. Not too long ago, I hated men. You changed my mind, but I refuse to become like my mother."

"I knew you had an attitude when I first met you, but why did you hate men?"

Lacy closed her eyes for a moment reliving some experiences from her past. An involuntary shudder ran down her spine.

Kerrick pulled Lacy into a hug. "If you don't want to talk about it, that's okay."

"I'm all right. For starters, my dad is a jerk, but...well, it goes back further than that."

Kerrick led them to a leather love seat in the living area. "If you want to talk about it, I'm all ears. If you'd rather not, then I understand."

"My cousin raped me when I was a young girl," Lacy blurted out. "It actually happened several times through the years. I hated him. When he was asleep one night at my house, I tried to…well, let's just say I tried to hurt him so he could never do that again. He woke up, and I got in trouble."

"Did you tell your parents what he did to you?"

"I eventually did, like a few years later, but they didn't believe me. They said Greg would never do anything like that and that I was a pathological liar. A couple of years ago, he was arrested for sexually assaulting another girl, and he's now in prison."

"Oh, Lacy. I'm so sorry. How old were you?"

"I was eleven the first time. Meg stepped in and tried to help me. I've been to counseling, but I know I still have some things to work through. You don't know it, but you've helped me a lot. Please just be patient with me if I'm a little, well, a little weird."

"You're not weird, Lacy. I'm so sorry you've been through all of that. You don't have to worry about me. I respect you too much to hurt you. Thank you for sharing your past with me."

Lacy felt spent and ashamed. Her counselor had insisted that what Greg did to her was not her fault, but she still struggled with feelings of shame. She could feel tears building up, but she was not going to let that happen.

She stood to her feet. "Well, that's my ugly past, but it is my past. As far as my present, I'm starving. Where are you taking me for dinner?"

"Do you like Japanese? There's a great restaurant called Matsuri near campus."

"I don't think I've ever had Japanese. I'd love to try it."

Nearly three hours later, Kerrick and Lacy stood at the foot of the stairs in the South Beach home. Dinner had been amazing. Lacy eyed the large master bedroom and gazed at the hallway leading to five additional rooms upstairs. Holding Kerrick's hand, she felt the same tingle of anticipation she had experienced when they first arrived, and she thought of another rule that needed to be added to the list they made over dinner.

"Here's another rule," she announced.

"Another one? I think you're starting to like this rule stuff."

"You can't come into my room."

"I thought that would be covered in the previous rules."

"No. We didn't say anything about you staying out of my room. You know that if Meg and Jon were living here with me, they would not want you in my room."

"Okay. Solid rule. There's only one problem, other than the fact that I want to be in your room."

"What's that?"

"That means you've got to carry all of your own luggage up the stairs to your room. I assume you're not taking the master bedroom."

"I have decided to take an upstairs room, and maybe we can break the rules for only a few minutes.

"If you don't take the master bedroom, does that mean we can enjoy the hot tub in the master bathroom without breaking the rules?"

"I think you being in my bedroom may be safer than us being in a hot tub." Lacy grinned mischievously up at Kerrick. "Maybe we'll try it tomorrow night and see how it goes."

"Deal. How about I come over at about 8:00 in the morning and help you with breakfast?"

"I don't know how to cook, so I think that's a great idea."

Lacy carried a box into her room as Kerrick topped the final step with two suitcases. The large room had a canopy bed in the center with a huge, plate glass window that offered a view of the water just half a block away. She turned to face Kerrick and was immediately wrapped in his arms. The kiss was deep and passionate pulling desire from deep within Lacy that she thought she had under control.

As abruptly as the passion started, Kerrick pulled back. "I'll see you in the morning, beautiful. I'm so glad you're here."

"I love you, Kerrick."

Lacy stood at the front door as Kerrick pulled out of the driveway. She climbed the steps in the quiet house and paused at the top of the stairs. She felt good about the commitments she and Kerrick had made that evening, and she knew Meg would be proud of her. She walked into her bedroom and turned around twice. "I can't believe this is my new room and my new home," she said aloud. "I'm going to love living in Miami."

She slipped into a large tee-shirt that once belonged to Kerrick and dropped her shorts in the doorway to the bathroom. *Okay. Meg is not a slob, so I shouldn't be either.* She folded her shorts and placed them into the chest of drawers where she and Kerrick had already put most of her clothes.

Lying in the soft, queen-sized bed, Lacy thought over the events of the last months and marveled at how her life was working out. She was no longer the same person who came to Florida at the end of May to work in the program her aunt and uncle started. She was definitely different—a good different.

As she was about to drift off to sleep, her door suddenly slammed shut. She instantly sat up in bed as a slang word slipped from her mouth. Her heart pounded, and she was momentarily frozen in fear. She then remembered opening the window in the room across the hall to help air out the upstairs and realized the wind must have pulled her door closed. She thought about the ugly word that just came out of her mouth. *Okay, so I may be a different person, but I still have some rough edges.*

After closing the window, Lacy lay back down in her bed and closed her eyes. She now lived in a beautiful home in the South Beach community, had a job making a little money each month, and had the hottest boyfriend that any girl could imagine. She also knew the secret that would help her lead Kerrick and her aunt and uncle to an amazing stash of treasure. Could life get any better?

Chapter Eight

Secret No More

Jon's dark blue F-150 pulled into the circular drive of the house on South Beach, and Meg saw Lacy's Malibu parked next to Kerrick's truck. Meg had almost called Lacy back last night to talk with her about Kerrick. The last thing she wanted was to come across to Lacy like an old-fashioned, busybody, but she knew all too well what could easily happen when the two were alone in the Miami house. Not only could Lacy get pregnant, but Meg knew that if the two were to marry eventually, they would benefit greatly to wait for that kind of intimacy.

Meg knew that Lacy didn't share her convictions, so it may be a bit difficult dealing with their romantic relationship from the island home at Roker's Point. It frustrated her that Liz was not helping her daughter to make the right choices, but of course, Liz didn't seem to have the ability to choose wisely herself. *How can I have that conversation with Lacy so that she knows that I just love her so much and want the best for her?*

After Jon opened the door of the truck for Meg to slide out, he walked over to Kerrick's vehicle and placed his hand on the hood. A grin spread across his face. "It's hot."

Meg let out air as if she had been holding her breath. She couldn't believe that Lacy and Kerrick made the decision not to spend the night together, but she was grateful. Meg had watched Liz mess up her entire life, and Liz's greatest problems always seemed to involve promiscuity with guys. She was still reaping the consequences of living a life out of control. It seems that Lacy must be more determined to live differently from her mom than Meg first realized.

Lacy met them at the door with flour on her face and an apron tied around her waist. "Aunt Meg!" Lacy wrapped her arms around Meg leaving a white imprint of flour on Meg's dark tee-shirt.

Jon enveloped Lacy in a hug. "Lacy! We're so glad you're here. How's your leg?"

"I'm good as new. I've been dying to talk to you about something really important, but I promised Kerrick we would eat breakfast first."

"What do you want to talk to us about?"

Lacy grinned. "You'll see. In the meantime, I've got omelets on the stove and biscuits in the oven. Or, maybe I should say that Kerrick has omelets on the stove. We should be ready to eat as soon as the biscuits are ready. You got here just in time."

Breakfast was exceptional, and Meg mentally checked another box on Kerrick's list. *He's kind, considerate of Lacy, a hard worker, great character, and he can actually cook.* Lacy seemed to have found a real gem. Meg wondered if wedding bells were in their future.

Jon refilled his coffee cup and sat back down at the table. "So, what's the big secret?"

Lacy beamed. "I've been about to bust. I tried to call you from the plane on Friday, but the flight attendant made me put my phone away. I've tried calling you a million times since then, and you guys obviously didn't want to talk to me."

"You know that's not true," Meg insisted. "Jon's phone fell in the sink. I'm sorry I can't ever seem to keep up with mine. We should have called you to check in, but we decided to take a trip to Conception Island."

"Oh, yes. The annual trip to Conception Island. So, is Carla going to get a little brother?"

Meg felt heat rising to her face. She never should have told Lacy about their first trip back to their cave on the island after their wedding. As far as Lacy was concerned, their trips to Conception Island only meant one thing. "Uh, well. We'd like to have a little boy one of these days. Right now might be a little too soon."

"I don't know," Lacy cooed. "Carla is now what? Seventeen or eighteen months old? She'll be over two-years-old in nine months. That sounds perfect to me."

"Let's let Ann have her baby, and then maybe we'll think about it. One baby at a time at Pirate's Cove is enough to keep us busy."

Jon cleared his throat. "Lacy, you were saying something about the big secret?"

"Oh, yes. I figured it out. The clues. I figured them out. I was thinking about everything from the summer. I know we don't know what's on Miguel's medallion, but think about it. They were on Coral Cay. Why would they be on that island unless they thought the treasure was hidden there?"

"I can think of a lot of reasons why they'd be there," Jon admitted. "For example, Miguel worked for the guy that owned the island."

"True, but didn't the FBI agent tell you that Miguel had only worked for that guy for about three years. If I found a medallion that said Coral Cay, or something like that, I'd do everything I could to plant myself on that island, so I could search for the treasure."

"That makes sense," Meg agreed. "If you're right, then your medallion means that the treasure is beneath the island."

"Yes!" Lacy nearly shouted. "Mine just says beneath, and let's assume that Miguel's says Coral Cay. And the third medallion isn't a cross. It's a map. It shows the tunnels under the island that you and Jose swam through to rescue me. Jon, remember how Kerrick said that he first came up inside the cave when the jeep ran off the cliff into the ocean?"

"I remember well," Jon admitted. "That's how we knew that there might be a tunnel leading to the salt water pond behind the house."

"Do you remember when Kerrick said that he pulled himself out of the water and sat on the floor of the cave, but when you and Jose swam through there, the tunnel was fully submersed? I think we're going to find that the tunnel to the left rises to an opening that is always dry, and the treasure will be in there. I don't suppose you have a picture of that third medallion on you, do you?"

"I have one on my phone," Meg said as she got up to locate her phone. She found her purse and took her phone back to the table. "Here you go."

Lacy looked at the picture and turned the phone around for Jon and Meg to see it. "Notice this little dot here on the left beam of the cross? I think that marks the spot in the tunnel to the left."

"I thought they were supposed to use an X," Kerrick teased.

"There's only one way to test your theory," Jon said. "Do you guys feel like taking a dive?"

"That's all I've thought about for four days," Lacy said as she grinned at Kerrick. "Well, almost all I've thought about."

"We only have one problem," Kerrick said as he leaned back in his chair. "Miguel. I know for a fact that he can tap into any phone, and I think he's probably listening in on our phone calls."

Kerrick related to the group the conversation he had with Miguel about a year ago when the creep threatened to kill his sister. Somehow, the guy knew intimate details about what Kelsey was doing and even quoted something she said to her friend, Rachel. When Kerrick asked how he knew what Rachel said, Miguel had simply answered that he knew anything he wanted to know and could listen in on anyone's phone conversation in the world.

"Lacy and I have started trying to use that to our advantage," Kerrick informed them. "We're assuming that they are hearing everything we say, so Lacy told me earlier yesterday that she decided to go back to Milledgeville. We think that if Miguel wants to put his hands on Lacy, he'll start looking for her at Georgia College. We're going to continue talking on our regular phones as if she's in Georgia."

"I like the idea," Jon admitted, "but I think he may be able to locate the position of your phone. He'll know you're not in Georgia."

"Oh, no. I didn't think about that," Kerrick said. "Lacy was in Florida when she made the last phone call."

Lacy leaned forward on her elbows. "I have an idea. What if I send my phone back to my old roommate? She grew up near my home town, so she could probably be mistaken for me."

Kerrick grinned. "So, you're saying she has South in the mouth too?"

Lacy punched his arm. "I haven't noticed you having any problem with my mouth."

"Well," Meg said between coughs. "I think it's a good idea. What's your friend's name?"

"Megan. I can't really call her a friend, but she'll help me. I'll tell her that I'm being stalked by a creepy guy who can tap phones. She can call Kerrick a few times and talk about stupid school stuff. She'll get a kick out of it."

"You're okay with a cute coed calling Kerrick from Georgia?" Jon teased.

"Who says she's cute?" Lacy challenged.

Meg watched Kerrick's hand slip under the table, and a slight smile spread across Lacy's lips. Meg thought back to the picture she saw last year of Lacy and her roommate. Lacy was right. She wasn't cute. She was drop-dead gorgeous, but Kerrick didn't have to know that little bit of information.

Jon pulled out his iPad and suggested that they write out their plans to make sure they were thinking of everything. Meg felt a sense of dread as she considered the fact that Miguel could be back in their lives. She wanted to pack up her family and run away. Jon slipped the iPad over to Meg and asked her to make a few notes. For starters, they all agreed to talk with one another about important matters on prepaid phones but maintain a ruse on their regular phones in order to try to keep Miguel guessing. Lacy needed to contact Megan and get her to agree to be a part of their shenanigans. Lacy would then need to mail her phone to Milledgeville.

"Next," Jon interjected, "we need to plan a scuba diving trip. Why don't you guys come to the compound on Great Exuma this weekend? We can make a dive, but we'll need to somehow do it so Miguel won't be suspicious, assuming he's watching us."

"Why don't we dive at night?" Kerrick suggested. "We could use a different boat and make the dive after dark."

"That would work," Jon agreed. "I could probably put my hands on a shrimper. If Miguel sees a shrimp boat, he'll just think someone is fishing. He'll never know it's us."

"I'm so excited," Lacy blurted out. "I'm fixin' to explode."

"You're fixin'?" Kerrick teased. "What's broken? What are you fixin'?"

"I'm fixin to slap your face," Lacy said with irritation. "If you're going to date a Southern girl, you're going to have to get over your Yankee arrogance."

"I'm not a Yankee," Kerrick insisted. "I just don't talk like you do."

"Okay," Jon interrupted. "Let's finish our planning, and then Meg and I need to head home. I agreed to play in a soccer game at Roker's Point this afternoon."

"I didn't know you played soccer," Lacy insisted. "I thought you played football."

"I played football all of my life growing up, but I also enjoyed soccer. We just didn't have a soccer team at my high school, so I pursued football."

"Obviously, that didn't hurt," Kerrick interjected. "I mean, who can feel bad about a full scholarship to play ball?"

"I'm not complaining," Jon laughed. "I did come to love soccer, however, and I've played off and on in some community leagues through the years."

"He's actually quite good," Meg said. "You'd be impressed."

"I don't think I'll be going pro any time soon," Jon joked. "We really need to talk about how we're going to make this dive."

They discussed the possibility of diving off Coral Cay Saturday night, and Jon called a friend of his who lived in Hollywood, Florida, to try to borrow his shrimp boat. Once that was confirmed, Kerrick and Lacy agreed to meet Jon's friend at the docks in North Bay on Friday, but Jon told them they would need to stop in Nassau to spend the night. He had a friend who owned the resort where he and Meg had run into one another years earlier.

Jon eyed Kerrick. "I'll have two rooms reserved for you."

"Sure," Kerrick nodded. "Two rooms are good."

Meg marveled that this guy in Hollywood, who rarely saw Jon, would let him use his shrimp boat, but then Jon had told her the story of how he had helped this guy keep his boat when the bank was trying to take it away. Meg realized that if the truth was known, Jon probably owned more of the boat than this friend.

An hour later as Jon held the door of the truck open for Meg to crawl in, Lacy and Kerrick stood next to the truck holding hands. Meg was thrilled to see that Lacy was so happy.

"We'll see you Saturday," Kerrick confirmed. "I have no idea how long it will take us to get over there in the boat."

"Maybe you should stay out of Pirate's Cove. Meg and I can ride out to meet you in the Robalo. Why don't you plan to just be out from the cove at sundown Saturday? I'll have the Robalo loaded with dive gear and get Diego to take us out."

"How is Diego?" Lacy asked. "I never thanked him for picking up my medallion from the jeweler."

"He's good," Jon said. "He has become much more than a maintenance man for us. He'll be happy to take us out Friday. Just call me on your other phone if there are any changes."

Meg slipped back out of the truck and hugged Lacy one more time. "I love you, Lacy. I'm so glad you're here."

"I love you, too," Aunt Meg.

"You be careful and slow, if you know what I mean."

"Slow as in not getting married any time soon?"

"That's one thing on my list," Meg said with a laugh.

"I'm good, Meg. You don't have to worry about me. Kerrick and I made up some rules. We're goin' to be fine."

As the truck pulled out of the drive, Meg saw Kerrick put his arm around Lacy and pull her close to his body. That girl was a beauty, and she had a good head on her shoulders. She was going to be all right.

Chapter Nine

Liam's Journey - 1871

Liam stepped from the carriage and looked wistfully out to sea, past the docks and chaos that was typical in any seaport town. He would be glad to leave Trelleborg behind and never planned to set foot in Sweden again. He adjusted his duffle bag on his shoulder and looked for the *Virginius*. He had been quite fortunate to find passage on a ship that was not only fast but was also heading to Cuba. Once he had reviewed a map of that region of the world, he decided to begin his search for the island of the skull by setting up a base on the Bahamian island of Nassau. He felt confident that he would be able to find a sailor who would know of an island that resembled a skull. Getting to Nassau from Cuba should be easy.

He reached into his pocket, wrapped his hand around the medallion, and thought of the other jewels he had packed away in his bag. He wondered how long it would take someone to find the body of the pathetic priest. Liam almost laughed out loud as he thought about the priest praying for him as he was about to slit the old man's throat. *He should have been praying for himself.*

It was simply good fortune that led Liam to learn about the medallion in the first place. His grandmother used to tell him the story of King Harald Bluetooth and his sad little family. She was crazy about Viking stories and had even taught Liam and his cousins how to write letters in Runic. He and his cousin, Ludvig, got quite good at writing notes to one another in the ancient Viking language. It became a great way to communicate when they didn't want anyone else to know what they were saying. He thought the Viking king must have been weak and that the only one in the family who had any real future was the son, Sven. It took some nerve for the Viking prince to kill his own father, but what a stroke of brilliance.

Liam had always wondered if the story about the medallions was true, and then one day at the pub in Copenhagen, he heard someone talking about the old priest's medallion. Liam still wouldn't have given it another thought until he came across an old man on the road to Trelleborg. He thought back to the weak little man. People who were weak needed to be killed. It had been sickening to hear the man whimper just before Liam twisted his neck to end his life. Liam just needed some money, but he found a lot more. The poor fool had a pocket full of money and a single envelope addressed to Father Vincent.

Once Liam read the letter from Heinrich Boldt in New York, there was no doubt that the legend was true. All he needed to do was steal the priest's medallion and get the other one in New York. He also needed someone who knew the sea well enough to help him find the treasure, which meant he'd have to involve his cousin. He hated Ludvig, but his cousin would at least show himself useful for once.

Killing a priest had been no big deal. He had done worse. He only wished he could have found Bluetooth's journal. The priest probably told him enough about what was in the journal that he could probably get by without it, but he sure hated sailing south without knowing all of the details. He feared there could be something written in it that he might be overlooking. He just had no idea where to find the thing.

The medallion in his pocket was his ticket out of this stupid country. The message on it was clear, at least to him. He was sure that the priest had not discovered it's meaning yet: *Island of the skull.* Finding the island might be a challenge, but how many islands would be known as "the skull"?

He had to leave. If he returned to Stockholm, he'd for sure hang. Most people didn't think highly of men who did what he did to a couple of young women in Solna. *They were so beautiful. It's too bad the blonde tried to get away. I didn't have any choice.*

If he went back to Malmo, there were at least ten men that would shoot him on sight. His best option was to leave Sweden and start over. Why not start fresh in the Bahamas? He had heard stories of stunning women who lived on the islands. He could find the treasure and be rich enough to start his own country.

Hiding out in Ystad while he waited to hear back from his cousin in New York had not been much fun, but now, it seemed as if the plan was in full motion. Unfortunately, he had to return to Trelleborg to catch a ship going west. He wasn't too worried, however, because there was no way anyone had seen him kill the old priest.

Now, as he walked across the wharf, he knew he was as good as home free. Once he located the ship, he bought passage all the way to Cuba. The quartermaster first wanted the Swede to work aboard the ship, but then Liam pulled out a few gold pieces. The man's eyes about bugged out of his head. *It's amazing what a little Viking treasure will do. I'm suddenly a prince. All I need is a woman to share my cabin, but I don't suppose that will happen until I get to Cuba.*

Liam hoped that Ludvig had carried out his part of the plan just as he had been instructed. Timing was everything. The last thing Liam wanted to do was to spend weeks on a God-forsaken island waiting on his stupid cousin. He hoped he would at least find a letter waiting on him at the tavern in Havana. He smiled as he imagined the look on his cousin's face once they found the treasure. Ludvig had always thought he was better than the rest of the family. Liam would show him with the tip of a blade who was superior. *I think I'll tie him up and let him watch himself bleed out.*

The voyage to Cuba was worse than Liam had imagined. He had to kill the little thief who tried to steal his duffle bag. The boy said he had picked up the bag by mistake because he said his was identical. Strangling the kid wasn't a problem, but getting him overboard without being seen was a bit of a challenge. The odd thing was that Liam saw a bag exactly like his in a box that was being removed from the ship in Havana. *The kid must have been telling the truth.*

Cuba was nothing like Liam had imagined. The place was filled with slaves and pitiful looking women. Where were the beauties he had heard about? There were a few, but he thought there was supposed to be enough for every man to have two or three. The sooner he could get to Nassau the better. He just needed to wait to hear from Ludvig. He managed to get his medallion put onto a gold chain. He decided it would be safer if he kept it around his neck at all times.

It was also unfortunate that everyone spoke Spanish. He finally found a Swedish girl named Elsa who had been in Cuba long enough to learn Spanish. She looked young, though he discovered the kid was almost 20. She served him well and translated for him, too.

After being in Cuba for nearly two weeks, it happened. A boy from the tavern ran to Liam's room one night. Fortunately, Elsa was staying with him every night now, so she listened to the boy rattle off something in Spanish and then told Liam that the boy had a letter for him. Liam read the anticipated letter from Ludvig, and suddenly, nothing else mattered. The dumb kid expected a tip, but he got a boot on his backside instead.

The letter told Liam that he could finally leave Havana. Good riddance; however, he would miss Elsa. He'd grown fond of her, and he even thought about taking her along. She had developed a cough, however, that was really getting on his nerves, so leaving her behind wasn't such a bad idea. He'd also be glad to get out of the flea-infested room he'd shared with her. She had become so covered with bites that she looked spotted from head to toe. He even had a few bites himself. He'd find more women in Nassau.

Liam only hoped that what he heard in the tavern about the skull island was true. He smiled as he thought back to the old drunk sailor. He got him to draw the island of the skull on a map. The old man was a fool, but Liam hoped the map was right. He considered getting someone else to confirm the location of Skull Island, but he was afraid of giving away his secret.

Santa Maria de la Conception was supposed to be the closest island to the one shaped like a skull, so Liam figured that he and Ludvig could meet there before going to get the treasure. He considered sending Ludvig straight to Skull Island, but then Ludvig may get the idea of double crossing him. That, for sure, wasn't going to happen.

It only took ten minutes at the docks, and Liam had passage to Nassau. He would be leaving Havana in the morning aboard a little clipper. It might take him a couple of days or so to arrive, but he would have plenty of time to make arrangements to get over to Conception Island before his scheduled appointment with Ludvig.

Three days later, Liam sat down at the only tavern in Nassau. He knew he was in the right place when the most beautiful woman he'd ever laid eyes on served him a drink. She obviously had other plans in mind because she winked at him. He might just have to come back here once he got the treasure. A man could get used to seeing a woman like that all the time.

He found a fisherman who was going to Galliot Cay who agreed to drop Liam off on Conception Island for a little coin. At first, the grizzled old fisherman was hesitant to get near Conception Island because he had been told all of his life that it was home to evil spirits. Liam finally agreed to pay the man double if he would just take him ashore. The only bad news was that Conception was not the closest island to the one with a cliff on one end that looked like a skull. His information had been wrong.

Liam thought back to the old fisherman in Cuba who had told him about the islands. He was confident that the old man didn't suspect anything when he was asked about ghost stories in the Bahamas. Fortunately, the man could speak English, and Liam knew enough English to understand the words *Conception Island* and *skull*. He managed to get the old fisherman to talk about the island with a skull, but it turned out to be farther away from Conception than he had been led to believe back in Havana.

"You'll have to go around Long Island and get south of the Exumas," a young, dark-skinned man from Nassau told him.

"Oh," Liam quickly replied. "I'm not going there. I don't want to go to an island that looks like a skull. Haunted, I'm sure." Liam didn't need the man to suspect his real interest lay in Skull Island.

Sailing out of Nassau on the little fishing boat was intoxicating, though Liam had now developed Elsa's cough and felt sick at his stomach. *I miss that girl so much that I'm starting to sound like her.*

The water looked like a sea of emeralds, and Liam noticed several uninhabited islands while in route to Conception Island. The fisherman was surprised that Liam wanted to be left on the island, but Liam assured the man that he had plenty of supplies to hold him until Ludvig showed up. He noticed the old man staring at him more than once, and the fisherman asked Liam about the rash on his chest.

"It's just flea bites," Liam insisted. "My place in Havana was covered up with the pests. I'm glad to be rid of them."

As he watched the fishing boat sail away, Liam realized that his plan was not the best idea. He had considered meeting Ludvig in Nassau, but he'd rather not be seen by anyone with his cousin. The last thing he needed was for someone to accuse him of Ludvig's murder. All he had to do was wait for a day or two, and his cousin would show up.

He pulled his supplies to some small brush up from the beach and began a brief search of his end of the island. He discovered a cave just above a pool of water and figured this would be a great place to wait. He had a good view of the bay and could even see the water on the north side of the island. *Now, my dear Ludvig. I hope you enjoy your last few days on earth.*

Chapter Ten

Miguel's Mistake

Miguel turned right on North Clarke Street and circled the entire campus of Georgia College and State University. Even though it was getting close to 8:00 in the evening, students in Milledgeville were still everywhere on campus. Every girl he saw was a beauty. He was beginning to understand Fernando's fascination with young women. He scoffed at the thought of his old partner. *He may have had an eye for beautiful girls, but he was an idiot. He nearly got me killed.*

The light from his smart phone illuminated the front seat of the car he had stolen at the Atlanta airport, and he followed his phone's directions to Carriage Hills Townhomes. He remembered seeing a picture of Lacy's apartment in Fernando's files, but he had never been to the place. He pulled in the parking lot and located the correct building. He backed his car into a parking place so he could have a good view of the door leading to apartment B-1. *B for blonde or beautiful.*

Miguel slid down in the seat to where he could just see above the steering wheel to the front door of Lacy's apartment. It seemed that while campus was filled with students, no one was around this place. He thought back to the first time he saw Lacy Henderson. She was a babe, no doubt. He would have had to be blind not to have noticed the girl. She was just a kid, though. He might still have some fun with her, but Meg was his real goal.

Before this was all over, he and Meg were going to get to know one another really well.

The light in Lacy's apartment was the only light he could see in the whole building. *Why isn't anyone home except Lacy? That is actually quite good.*

He knew from his phone call to the office earlier that day that the apartment across from Lacy's was empty, so he wasn't surprised to see those lights out. He also learned from a little detective work on the phone that the door he was looking at opened into a hallway. The door to Lacy's apartment was immediately on the left. He just hoped he could get inside and find the hallway empty. Getting into the apartment would be a breeze.

He saw the figure of a girl with short brown hair through the front window of the apartment and decided that was Lacy's roommate. After a few minutes, the light to her bedroom went out, but there was still a light on somewhere else in the apartment. The outside door eventually opened, and a cute brunette walked toward a red Honda. *So, you're all alone now Lacy, and you're waiting on me.*

As soon as the tail lights of the brunette's car disappeared up the road, Miguel climbed out of the car and hurried toward the apartment. He ran through several scenarios in his mind, but all of his plans required the front area of the apartment to be empty. If Lacy happened to be standing near the front door when he entered, she might scream. Of course, it appeared that no one was around to hear her. Then again, Lacy wasn't really the screaming type. Being that no one else was home, he might just go ahead and have a little fun in Lacy's bedroom. If the roommate returned before he left, she would just have to get in on the fun, too. Miguel didn't mind that thought.

Fortunately, no one was in the hallway, and Miguel pulled out his lock pick and knelt in front of the door. In less than forty-five seconds, the door clicked. He gently turned the knob and had a perfect view of the entire living room. *You should have chained the door Lacy girl.* The front of the apartment was clear. As he walked across the apartment, he heard a noise coming from behind a closed door down the short hallway. *Oh, my. Lacy is in the shower.*

He quietly turned the knob and cracked the door open. Through the steamed-up shower door, Miguel could just make out Lacy's alluring body and long, blonde hair. He considered starting the party right away, but then he decided the bathroom wasn't the best option. He pulled the door closed without a sound and slipped into what he knew had to be Lacy's bedroom. He had already seen the roommate's bathroom down the hall in front of another bedroom.

Lacy's room was dark, but he had enough light coming through the outside window to keep him from tripping over anything. He breathed in the feminine smells of her room and felt the quickening of his heart as he thought about the girl in the shower. He stood by the door and pulled out his knife as he waited for the action to begin.

The water turned off, and he could hear Lacy humming. The bathroom door opened a few minutes later, and Miguel pressed his body against the wall by the door. He got a glimpse of a bare leg just before she turned off the bathroom light. He smelled her enter the room before he saw her silhouette. She smelled of some kind of flower. She was intoxicating. Blood pumped through his body like water bursting through an open dam as the brief thought of her standing in the room with him raced through his mind. She reached toward the light switch. Before she could turn on the light, he grabbed her arm and threw her onto the bed. He was on top of her in just seconds with his hand over her mouth.

"Well, well," Miguel hissed. "We meet again. Have you missed me Lacy?"

He thought it odd that Lacy was whimpering. He could feel her warm body beneath his, but she shook with fear. He didn't remember ever hearing Lacy cry when they had her on Coral Cay.

"Now, you listen to me. We're going to have a little fun first, and then you're going to tell me where I can find your medallion." He held the knife up in the dark toward her face. "You may not be able to see what I have in my hand clearly, but if you scream, you're going to feel it carve up your pretty face. Do you understand?"

He felt Lacy's head shake in agreement. As headlights from a car outside briefly lit the bedroom, Miguel saw the light reflecting from the braces on her teeth. Suddenly, two police cars pulled into the parking lot with sirens blaring. Miguel jumped off the girl and looked at her for just a second. She leapt toward the other end of the bed and pulled the towel tightly around her as she began to scream. He ran back into the living room and was out the back window before he heard the police crash through the door. He raced for the trees just beyond the apartments.

When Miguel came out of the woods on the next block, he saw a kid get out of a car and walk toward a house; the guy had left the car running. Miguel hurried toward the car, jumped in, and sped off toward the edge of town. He pulled into the Walmart parking lot glancing at each of the vehicles near the back of the lot. He sat for a moment watching an older man get out of his Buick. As soon as grandpa was in the store, Miguel was in the Buick heading toward Atlanta. His work in Milledgeville was done.

A little over two hours later, he took the exit to Virginia Avenue as a Delta plane took off from the nearby airport. When his phone rang, he looked at the caller I.D. and saw that it was his new assistant, Andrew. "Where have you been?" he barked into the phone. "I've been calling you for two hours."

"I'm sorry, Miguel. You don't expect me to work all the time. I'm sorry I missed your calls."

"I just need to know one thing," Miguel spewed into the phone. "What is Lacy Henderson's address?"

Miguel could hear Andrew clicking some keys on his keyboard. "She lives in Carriage Hills Townhouse and Apartments. She's in B-1."

"Then tell me why the girl who lives in B-1 has braces. Lacy Henderson has perfect teeth. She doesn't wear braces."

"Uh, I don't follow you, boss. Did you see the girl or not?"

"I didn't see her face very well. She had blonde hair and maybe the body of Lacy, but the girl had braces on her teeth. She was also whimpering like a scared puppy. My girl would never do that."

"Maybe it was Lacy's roommate."

"No, it wasn't. I saw her roommate leave the apartment, and besides that, we know that her roommate is a brunette."

"I don't know, Miguel. I'm not sure what to say."

Miguel thought for a minute. "Okay. Listen to me. I want you to get into the computers at the college and tell me Lacy's address. I'm sure they have it. I'll turn around and go back to the right place if I have to. The girl must have moved. I'm going to

get something to eat. Call me when you've got more information."

Thirty minutes later as the IHOP waitress sat a stack of pan-
cakes in front of Miguel, his cell phone rang. "Yeah?"

"Hey, boss. It's me. I've got bad news and good news."

"What is it," Miguel growled into the phone.

"Lacy is no longer a resident student. I've got her address as
being Griffin, Georgia. She's going to school online."

Miguel cursed into his phone, and several customers looked
toward him. He got up and walked into the bathroom. "Then
tell me why we both heard her say that she was going back to
Milledgeville. She told Kerrick she wasn't coming to Miami."

"I know, Miguel. Evidently, she changed her mind."

"Something's not right, Andrew. I want you to locate this
girl. Do you understand? We've got to find her. I can drive south
to Griffin if she's there or catch the next plane to Miami. I'm
going to find her tonight. Do you hear me?"

"I also said that I have some good news."

"Don't play games with me Andrew."

"I thought you'd like to know that someone used Lacy's
debit card tonight at La Carretta in Miami."

"Is that a fact? I want you to find out where that girl is, and
I'll be in Miami just after midnight. We're going to give some
Miami detectives a little work to do in the morning. That girl
won't see the sunrise."

Miguel slammed his fist into the wall, punching a hole in the
sheetrock. He banged the door to the stall closed and stood over
the toilet cursing and swearing to kill that girl if it was the last
thing he did. He went to the sink, splashed water on his face,
and walked out of the restaurant.

After parking his stolen car in the hourly parking lot, he walked toward the terminal where he saw several police cars lining the curb. *Surely, they're not looking for me. The girl didn't even get a look at my face.* He ducked his head and joined a group of travelers heading toward security. Within an hour, he was flying south toward Miami.

Chapter Eleven

A Night Out

Lacy nearly jumped out of her chair when the alarm on her phone split the silence. She turned off the fog horn sound she had programmed into her cell phone and hurried upstairs to shower and step into some clean clothes. The day had been filled with lining up school stuff, but tonight was going to be all about Kerrick. Before she got to her car, her phone rang. "Hey," Lacy rasped into the phone. "So, did you think I was going to forget about our date?"

"Of course not," Kerrick laughed. "You sound winded."

"You'd be winded too. I just set a new world record on taking a shower and getting dressed."

"You didn't have to do all that. I love you just like you are."

Lacy thought of how her hair looked about fifteen minutes earlier and imagined the forest that was beginning to grow on her legs. Nope, he wouldn't have liked all of that.

"I wish you wouldn't insist on driving. I'm happy to come out to South Beach and pick you up."

"You know me. Hardheaded Lacy." *And it's also a great way to make sure nothing happens tonight we might regret.*

"If you insist," Kerrick continued. "I was just going to tell you that I would meet you in front of the Watsco Center on south campus. I've got a parking pass for you. You should be able to find a parking space in the lot right in front of the field-house."

"How did you get a parking pass for me?"

"Let's just say I've got connections."

"Right. Of course, you have connections. I don't know how to get to the fieldhouse."

"Just type in *Watsco Center* on your phone, and let Siri take you there. We can go to La Carreta in my car."

"Okay. I'm just ready to eat now. I'm starving."

"You'll love this place, that is you'll love it if you like Cuban. I'll see you in about thirty minutes or so."

Three hours later, Lacy checked her watch and saw that it was nearly 9:00. She felt bloated and wanted nothing more than a run on the beach. She eyed her plate and considered sopping up what was left of the juice from her meal.

"I've got a little left," Kerrick joked. "I mean, if you're still hungry, I'll share."

"If I eat anything else, I think I'll puke. What does *Ropa Vieja* mean anyway? I assume it has something to do with beef and vegetables."

Kerrick grinned. "Actually, it means *old clothes*."

Lacy started to throw her napkin across the table, but then looked around and thought better of it. "No it doesn't. No one would name something that amazing *old clothes*."

"Yes, they did. I think it has something to do with the colorful vegetables on the top that made someone in Cuba think of a pile of clothes ready for the wash. It's Cuba's national dish or at least one of them."

"It was really amazing."

"So, I guess you don't have room for *pastel de platano*?"

"I'm telling you, Kerrick, if I put anything else in my mouth, it's going to get ugly."

"Fair enough. Why don't we go for a walk down the beach? We could go over to the Oceans and Human Health Center on South Beach. There's a great place to walk there, and it's not too far from your house?"

"Health Center?"

"It's something the University does with some other groups to research how humans affect the ocean and how the ocean can benefit our health. It's a pretty cool place. I did a brief internship there last year."

A cute waitress came up to the table and eyed Kerrick like he was for dessert. "Can I get you anything else?"

Kerrick started to speak, but Lacy blurted out, "Yes, my fiancé and I were just saying how nice a cup of coffee would be."

"Sure thing," the perky coed spouted. "I'll have it out shortly."

Lacy watched the girl twist away, but she was relieved that Kerrick's eyes were not on the waitress but on her.

"Fiancé? When did we get engaged? Do we have a date for the wedding yet?"

Lacy grinned across the table. "The girl just needed to be put in her place. It's imperative that she know that you're mine and not available as an hor d'oeuvre, main course, or dessert. The poor thing was about to drool all over her caked-up face."

Kerrick laughed. "You are something else, Lacy Henderson. I think I might just have to…to…."

"To what?" Lacy smiled innocently.

"I'll think about it and let you know. I am concerned that you're going to take a sip of the coffee and barf because you have no room left in that beautiful body of yours."

"I'll be fine. My dad used to say I have hollow legs. I wanted to tell you about something I've been thinking about anyway."

"I'm all ears."

"For starters, I'm confident that we're going to find you know who's stash tomorrow night."

"You know who? Oh, King..."

"Don't you think it's a good idea not to say certain words in public?" Lacy chided.

"You're right again. I'm pretty pumped about tomorrow night."

"The question remains as to what exactly we're going to find."

"I'm kind of thinking of a T. C. or two."

Lacy raised an eyebrow. "A T.C.?"

Kerrick leaned forward across the small table and paused until Lacy leaned toward him. As the waitress sat coffee cups on the table, he placed his lips on Lacy's and held her in a kiss until the waitress walked away. He then whispered, "Treasure Chest."

Stunned by the kiss but wanting more, Lacy sat back in her chair. "What was that?"

"That, my dear, was called an impromptu kiss of passion. That was what I just had to do. You asked me a minute ago what I had to do."

Lacy grinned and poured cream into her coffee. She knew that the waitress got the message loud and clear. "Okay. So, you think we're going to find a T.C. or two. I don't think so."

"Why not?"

Kerrick shook his head when Lacy offered him cream and sipped his coffee.

"Well," Lacy began. "For one thing, I don't think our Viking adventurer was going to bring a whole T.C. back as evidence. All he needed was one or two items to prove that the stash came from Mexico and to point the children of you know who to the location of the real city that was filled with…uh, you know…T."

"T? Oh, yeah. T, as in T.C. Interesting thought. I can't imagine just leaving one or two items. What if you're wrong about the whole map thing on the medallion?"

"I'm not, but if I am, then I'll cook dinner for you every night for a month."

"Do you know how to cook?"

"That will be part of the deal. I'll learn how to cook and then cook for you for thirty nights."

"Deal. Let's just hope I don't die in the process."

"I think you'll be fine." Lacy snatched the bill and pulled out her debit card. "I'm paying."

"Oh, no you're not," Kerrick insisted.

"Too late. You snooze, you lose. Paying for dinner is an expression of my love. You wouldn't want to reject my love, would you?" Lacy batted her eye lashes.

"You're something else, Lacy Henderson. This will be the last meal you pay for when you're with me."

"Let's get out of here. You need to take me back to get my car."

The drive to South Beach didn't take long, and Lacy couldn't quit thinking about how easy it had been to refer to herself as Kerrick's fiancé. What was happening to her? Just a few months ago, she was determined to spend her life as a single woman. She

didn't need a man telling her what to do. Now, she couldn't get
Kerrick out of her mind, and she couldn't quit thinking about
the possibilities of being his wife. She'd only known him for
three months. She had to get a grip on her emotions. If she were
not careful, she was going to be in way over her head, if she
weren't already. She saw the blinker on Kerrick's truck in front
of her, so she followed him into a parking lot.

Lacy saw Kerrick's fit body appear beside her car. He stood
holding the handle as he waited for her to unlock the door. *He's
sweet, handsome, and has manners. I don't think they make them this way
anymore.*

"Here we are," Kerrick announced. "The Oceans and
Human Health Center."

"So, this place does research?"

"Yep. It's sponsored by the National Science Foundation
and the University. They study all the stuff we do to hurt the
ocean."

"You mean like pollution and stuff like that?"

"That's part of it. They also study things like how toxins pro-
duced by algae affect people and how we can also benefit from
the resources of the ocean. Mainly medical research."

"Sounds interesting."

"It's pretty cool. I had another idea on the drive over. Why
don't you leave your car parked here, and we can ride to the state
park in my truck?"

"So, we're going to a state park?"

"I thought that would be fun. We call it The Cape. It's officially the Bill Baggs Florida Cape State Park. A lot of families
come here to swim and hang out. It has a really cool lighthouse."

Lacy had never heard of the state park, but she had always
loved lighthouses. While driving the short distance to the tip of

the cape, she had a flash back of climbing to the top of the Cape
Hatteras Lighthouse in North Carolina with her mom and dad.
Life had been so innocent back then, and everything seemed
perfect in her world. She had no idea that her father was seeing
another woman, and her family was just a few years away from
a train wreck. She peered through the windshield to the darkened guard house at the entrance of the park. "It looks like
they're closed."

"They are. I just happen to have connections."

"There you go again. Mr. Connections."

Kerrick rolled his window down as a sixty-something-year-
old guy walked up.

"Hey Bill," Kerrick said as the guy peered across the car to
look at Lacy.

"Good evening, Kerrick," Bill bellowed. "You were wrong."

"Wrong about what?"

"She's prettier than you said."

Lacy felt her cheeks redden at the thought of Kerrick and
this old guy talking about her.

"Come on, Bill. I told you she was beautiful. I want you to
meet Lacy Henderson. Lacy, this is Bill Thorp. He used to work
at the University.

"Hey, Bill. It's good to meet you."

"Good evening, darlin," Bill winked. "You need to watch
who you're hanging around with."

"You know she's safe with me, Bill. I appreciate you letting
us in. We won't tell a soul."

"It's best if you leave your truck here and take the golf cart
on the other side of the gate. We have a night guard who drives

around, and he'll be less suspicious if you're not in a strange vehicle. I left the key to the lighthouse in the cup holder."

"You're awesome, Bill," Kerrick said. "I owe you one."

"You'll owe me more than one. Just don't let anyone see you, and if you ever tell anyone about this, I'll insist you're a liar."

"Our lips are sealed," Kerrick promised.

"Also, don't do anything stupid," Bill insisted.

Kerrick drove the golf cart down the road toward the south end of the park and turned left into the parking area in front of the lighthouse. He paused for a moment and then drove off the pavement behind some bushes. "It's probably best that no one see the golf cart parked here. Let's walk down the beach and then climb to the top of the lighthouse. I think 109 steps will help you work off your dinner."

After strolling hand-in-hand down the beach with Lacy and picking up a few seashells, Kerrick inserted the key into the door of the lighthouse, and the door swung open. Light from the moon illumined the way to the bottom of the winding staircase.

Lacy's legs burned from the climb, but once they emerged on the top landing, she gasped at the beauty of the night. She looked north toward the lights of the city and then out to sea. Heat lightening lit the sky as Kerrick wrapped his arms around her. She could hear his heart's steady thud and imagined every beat saying, "I love you."

"I could stay here forever," Kerrick finally said, "but we better get down. I guess you realize it's way past our bedtime."

Lacy tried to focus on her watch. "What time is it?"

"It will soon be 2:00. Let's head on back. We've got to be at the docks by 9:30 in the morning. We shouldn't have stayed out this late."

When Lacy moved toward the opening leading to the staircase, she heard a loud bang. Staring down the spiraling metal stairs was like looking into the black abyss. "What happened? Did someone close the door?"

Kerrick eased up behind her. "The door probably closed by itself. I left it open to give us a little light. Do you have your phone?"

"No. I left mine in the car."

"Here, use mine. I just don't have much battery left."

Lacy saw the light from his phone come on, and she was amazed at how much of the darkness was dispelled by such a small light. She had a memory of something she heard years ago when she went to youth camp with her friend's youth group. *A little bit of light makes darkness flee. Light always wins.* She thought about the darkness that had consumed her life and how Meg had been that little beacon of light for her. *Maybe light is winning in me after all.*

Half-way down the stairs, the phone battery died. It was no big deal because Lacy could easily follow the stairs down without a light. When she stepped onto the concrete floor, Kerrick bumped into her.

"Oh, sorry about that."

Lacy felt his arms squeeze her, and he spun her around. She could smell his cologne and imagine the shape of his beautiful mouth. They had to be only inches apart. She felt the heat of his breath on her face before his lips were on hers. The kiss was long and deep. Passion filled her and blinded her senses. She pulled his body close and felt secure in his hard, firm embrace.

"We better go," Kerrick finally said. "I just can't remember where the door is."

"It's to the right," Lacy recalled.

They felt their way along the sides of the lighthouse until Lacy's hand grazed the door frame. "Here it is." She felt for the door knob. "There's not a door knob. How do you get out of here?"

Lacy could hear Kerrick's hands rubbing all around the door. She heard a sound as if Kerrick kicked the door.

Out of the darkness, she heard his voice. "I don't think we can get out."

Chapter Twelve

Uninvited Guest

Meg called Lacy's phone for the third time, but still, there was no answer. What could she be doing that would keep her from answering the phone? Several things came to mind, but the simplest explanation was that she and Kerrick were out, and Lacy had left her phone at home.

"Any luck?" Jon asked as he walked into the kitchen.

"No. She still doesn't answer. I just hope she's not in trouble."

"Are you sure that the Milledgeville police said this guy was definitely looking for Lacy?"

"I'm sure, Jon. The girl said that the man called her Lacy."

"Now, who is this girl?"

"Her name is Lauren McBee. She's just a girl that Lacy knows from school. Liz sent me a picture she found on Facebook of her, and from the back, she could be mistaken for Lacy. She has long blond hair, and her body is similar to Lacy's. Liz told me that the police said all of this happened in the dark in the bedroom of Lacy's old apartment, so it would be easy to mistake her for Lacy."

"Why did the police just happen to show up?"

"Someone was leaving the apartment complex and saw a man in Lauren's apartment. Evidently, the shades to the living room were open. The girl didn't recognize the man, and she knew the two girls who lived in that apartment. She just said he looked suspicious. She thought about it as she drove to meet a friend and finally decided to call the police."

Jon sat down on the stool at the kitchen bar. "It's a good thing. The guy didn't hurt the girl, did he?"

"Scared her to death, but the police got there just in time."

"It had to be Miguel. Didn't Lauren say he was dark skinned?"

"She thought he was, and he definitely had an accent."

Jon's fist hit the counter top. "It's got to be Miguel. We must get hold of Lacy. She could be in danger."

****

Lacy stood still next to Kerrick and listened intently. Surely, if someone had come into the lighthouse and closed the door, they'd be able to hear something from them. After several minutes of tomb-like silence, she figured that if someone were inside with them, they had more discipline than her.

"If anyone's in here," Lacy blurted into the darkness, "come on out. You win. You've got us."

She paused for a reply, but the only thing she heard was Kerrick's breathing and her own racing pulse.

"I think we're alone," Kerrick concluded. "If someone closed us up in here, then I suppose they'll be back after a while. There's no way we can get out unless someone opens the door from the outside, and we have the key."

A large, unguarded yawn slipped from Lacy's mouth. "I'm wiped out."

"Come on. Let's just sit over by the steps."

Lacy felt Kerrick's hand slip into hers as he pulled her toward the spiraling staircase. She knelt down and felt the floor, and her hands eventually touched Kerrick's leg. She sat down beside him and lay her head on his shoulder. She yawned again and didn't bother covering her mouth.

"Lacy, go on and get some sleep. I'll stay awake."

"No. I'll stay awake with you."

She felt his strong arms wrap around her body, and the two of them slid further down until they were both lying on the floor. Lacy felt his muscular body pressed against hers as she nestled her head into his neck. He smelled good, strong, and safe. His hand slid into her hair, and he lowered his lips to hers. Their kiss was tender, filled with love and possibilities. Locked in a lighthouse or not, she decided that being in Kerrick's arms was the safest place possible.

Lacy suddenly jerked awake as a bright light shown into her eyes. Kerrick stirred beside her, and she realized that they had both fallen asleep.

"Kerrick! What in the heck are you doing in here?"

Kerrick sat up. "Bill? How did you find us?"

"It wasn't too hard. When you didn't come back, I came looking for you. I figured I'd find you here, and then I saw the golf cart in the bushes. I would have come sooner, but I had to wait until I got off my shift.

"Well, thanks for coming," Lacy said as she stood to her feet and combed her fingers through her hair.

"I meant to tell you to make sure you didn't let the door close," Bill confessed. "We need to get out of here. I convinced the guy that just came on duty to keep his head turned until you left. You need to go before he changes his mind."

Lacy looked at her watch and saw that it was after 6:00. Her back hurt, and she felt like her hip might never recover. She limped a little, and Kerrick wrapped his arm around her as if to help her to the golf cart. Within fifteen minutes, they were in the truck driving back to her car.

Lacy laughed out loud as they pulled into the parking lot of the Oceans and Human Health Center. "I suppose I'll have to confess to Aunt Meg that we slept together."

Kerrick opened the door to his truck and turned back to Lacy. "For some reason, I don't think what we did is what she is worried about. Look, why don't you head home, and I'll follow you to your house. Once you're safe, I'm going to need to go back to my apartment and get some clothes and my scuba gear. Then, I'll come back and get you."

Kerrick jumped out of the truck and hurried around to the other side to open Lacy's door. She decided that she really liked this special treatment.

Lacy started her car and pulled out of the parking lot. They were less than fifteen minutes to her house, and there was no traffic. She was talking to Kerrick on her cell phone as she turned into her driveway. She looked toward the house and slammed on her brakes in shock.

Lacy gasped into her phone. "Do you see that? The front door's open. We didn't leave the door open. I'm sure of it."

"Get in my truck. Now. We've got to go."

"I shouldn't leave my car here. Just go. I'm right behind you. I'm going to call the police and ask them to come check things out."

Kerrick backed out of the drive at lightning speed, and Lacy was right behind him. She followed him back toward his apartment near the campus of the university. *It has to be Miguel. He's come back. Thank God we were stuck in the lighthouse.* She felt a shiver run down her spine as she thought back to being held captive on Skull Island. She would never think of that horrible place by its real name: Coral Cay. It would always be Skull Island, and it would be forever known as the place she could have died.

Lacy began to breathe hard as tears flooded her eyes. Her heavy breathing turned into gasps as she picked up her cell phone. "Kerrick! I...have to...stop."

"Lacy. We'll be at the apartment in about five minutes."

She jerked her car into the parking lot of a department store and pulled up next to the building. Though lights were on, the place wouldn't be open for at least another couple of hours. She put the car in park and lay her head down on the steering wheel. *Get hold of yourself, Lacy. Don't be such a wus.*

Out of the corner of her eye, she saw a figure standing beside her door. She gasped as she jerked away.

"Open the door, Lacy," Kerrick said as he knocked on the window. "It's me. You're okay."

Lacy's trembling hand reached for the door locks, and it took her three attempts before the locking mechanism clicked. Kerrick knelt by the door and pulled Lacy toward him. She felt another spasm of fear shoot through her body.

"I'm...sorry, Kerrick. I just kind of lost it."

"It's okay, Lacy. You went through a lot. You're going to be fine. Did you call the police?"

"No. I should have, but I started thinking back to the island."

Kerrick reached across Lacy and grabbed the phone that was lying in the passenger seat. He dialed 911 and reported the break in at Lacy's house.

Lacy could easily hear the woman on the other end of the line. "Would you like to meet the officer at the residence?"

"No, ma'am," Kerrick insisted. "Could you please call us back and let us know what you find?"

"Did you say this is your home, sir?"

"No. My girlfriend lives there. I'm calling on her phone."

"We'll call her back as soon as the officers report in."

Kerrick disconnected the call and held Lacy in his arms for another five minutes. "Let's park your car out at the end of the lot, and you can ride with me."

Once Lacy's car was locked up, the two of them rode the last few miles to Kerrick's apartment. He held her hand tightly as they climbed the stairs to the second landing. He led her into his bedroom where she lay down on the bed and pulled her knees up to her chest. Kerrick eased into bed behind her and held her in his arms.

Several minutes passed and Lacy could finally hear something other than her own breathing. "I just had a thought," Lacy said. "We didn't say anything about staying out of your bedroom."

Kerrick laughed as Lacy turned to face him. He brushed a few strands of hair from her face and traced the outline of her chin. When his fingers slipped to her neck and brushed across the exposed flesh at the top of her shirt, her body shivered again, but this time it wasn't from fear.

"Miss Henderson,"

"Ummm?

"I think our rules mean we should stay out of my bedroom, too." He lowered his lips to hers and pulled away quickly. "I'm going to shower first, and then you can. I've got a clean shirt you can wear, but other than that, you're fresh out of luck."

Lacy felt the heat of embarrassment slip up to her cheeks as his meaning sunk in. "I just need a shirt," she simpered.

As Kerrick began to get off the bed, Lacy grabbed his hand. "Kerrick? Why did you stop?"

"You mean back at Walmart?" He grinned.

"No, goofy. I mean just now."

"It sure isn't because I wanted to. Lacy, I respect you too much not to stop. You have no idea how much you mean to me, and I don't want to treat you like some college bimbo. I think Meg is starting to rub off on me, too. Saying no may be the best way to say yes."

"Yes?"

"Yeah. Yes to I love you more than words can communicate."

He kissed her gently and walked into the bathroom. She heard the shower come on as she lay her head back on Kerrick's pillow. His smell enveloped her, and she imagined sleeping here in his bed with him. She was somewhere between doze and sleep when his hand rubbed her face.

"Your turn, Sleeping Beauty."

The shower felt invigorating. What a night! How she was going to be able to stay awake all day to make the ride out to the Bahamas was beyond her. As she was drying off with a towel, the door cracked open and Kerrick's hand slipped into the bathroom. "Kerrick! What are you doing?"

"Sorry, sweetheart. I'm not peeking. You have a phone call. It's the police."

Lacy noticed for the first time that Kerrick was holding her phone. "Hello?" Lacy said after grabbing the phone. "Yes. This is Lacy Henderson."

She listened as the police officer on the other end explained that two officers went to the house and searched the entire premises. The woman said that the front door had been open, but there was no sign of anything wrong.

"Miss Henderson, you must have just left the front door open. It happens all the time."

"I'm sure I closed it," Lacy maintained.

"Our officers checked everything thoroughly. It's safe for you to return home."

Lacy looked back toward the door and saw Kerrick's hand again, but this time, he was holding a Divers' Direct tee-shirt. She thanked the police officer, disconnected the call, and snatched the shirt from his hand. When his arm snaked back through the door, Lacy pushed the door closed again. She looked at her phone and was reminded that she had missed a few calls from Meg. *I wonder what's up. They've called three times. I'll have to call them on our way to the docks. There's no need to have to tell her I just got out of Kerrick's shower.*

Once she was dressed, she and Kerrick drove back across town toward her house, but they first stopped to retrieve her car. They walked cautiously up the front steps of the house, and Lacy slipped her key into the lock. They walked through the entire house, but it seemed that the officers were right. Lacy finally walked into her bedroom to pack her clothes and bathing suits, and just as the officers reported, the room was in order. As she gathered the last few items for her trip from the top of her dresser, she looked up at the corner of her mirror. Her face turned as white as a sheet. Her gasp must have been louder than she realized.

"What, Lacy? What is it?" Kerrick hurried into the bedroom.

Lacy continued staring at her mirror. "We didn't just leave the door open by accident." She pointed to the corner of the mirror where a necklace dangled. On the end of the chain was a small charm in the shape of a skull.

Chapter Thirteen

Back to the Bahamas

Meg rolled over and looked at the clock on the bedside table. It was nearly 7:00 a.m., and she felt like she had been run over by a truck. Her mind raced back to Lacy again as it had 100 times during the night. *Why hasn't she called back?* She reached for Jon, but his side of the bed was empty. Grabbing her robe, she headed down the stairs to make coffee. She assumed that Jon would be in the gym, which is exactly where she should be, but coffee had to be first on her agenda.

A smile spread across her face when she saw that Jon had not only made coffee, but he had her special cup out awaiting her arrival. It was the heart-covered cup he had given her for Valentine's Day the previous year, and he had stuffed a small gift in the cup that was appropriate for the holiday. He told her that the cup and its contents were actually her gift to him, along with her, his true Valentine. Her real gift that day showed up at breakfast, which he served her in bed. She touched the emerald ring on her finger and thought back to that wonderful morning.

"Good morning, sleepyhead," Jon said as he walked through the mudroom door. "I figured you'd meet me in the gym."

"I didn't sleep much. I've been so worried about Lacy."

"I'm concerned, too. If we haven't heard from her by 9:00, let's call again."

'Okay. You don't think I should call her now?"

"At least give her another hour. I'm sure she and Kerrick were just out late last night."

"I'm going to work out," Meg said as she took her coffee cup upstairs where she could slip into her gym shorts. "Hey," she called back from the top landing. "I noticed you set out *the cup*. Thanks. Are you hinting at anything?"

Jon laughed. "Sweetheart. I'm always hinting, but I actually just set that one out to remind you that you are the light of my life."

A few minutes later, Meg bounded down the steps, being careful not to spill the coffee that was still in the bottom of the cup. Jon was at the kitchen counter when she sat the cup down beside him and pressed her body against his. Their mouths connected, and Meg felt the familiar surge shoot through her body that always made her feel like they were kissing for the first time.

"I've got to do a short work out, but if you're not busy afterward..."

"I think I just decided to clear my calendar."

They both looked up the stairs as they heard Carla calling for her daddy. Meg pecked him on the cheek and headed for the gym in the guest house.

When Meg's prepaid phone rang at about 9:30, she chided herself for not calling Lacy like she said she would do. She looked at the caller I.D. and saw that it was indeed Lacy calling from her new phone. Meg decided that it was probably better for Lacy to initiate the phone call so the coed wouldn't think her aunt was being a nagging parent.

"I'm glad to know you're alive, Lacy."

"I'm sorry, Meg. You won't believe what happened."

"First of all, where are you?"

"We just met Matt, and we're heading to his shrimp boat. He's really a nice guy. He said that the boat is actually Jon's."

"I think Jon just got him out of a bind," Meg insisted. "It's Matt's boat. He's nice to let us use it. Are you sure Kerrick is comfortable driving it?"

"Matt's going to show him a few things, but he says it's pretty straight forward. According to Matt, it's a lot like the *New Beginnings*, that is unless we actually want to start trying to lower the nets to catch some shrimp. I was a little concerned about your phone calls last night. I left my phone in the car, and I didn't see that you had called until it was quite late. I figured you'd rather me wait till this morning to call back."

"So, you guys were out late last night?"

"You can quit worrying about us, Meg. We're fine. We went out last night to eat dinner, and then Kerrick took me to the lighthouse."

"You mean the one at Florida Cape? I thought the park closed at dark."

"It does, but it seems that Kerrick knows the right people. We walked down the beach and then climbed the lighthouse steps. While we were inside, the door slammed and locked us in. I've got to confess that it scared the crap out of me. I thought it was Miguel. Turns out that the door just closed by itself."

"You're right to be worried about Miguel," Meg interjected. "He attacked the girl who moved into your bedroom in Milledgeville."

"Lauren?" Lacy gasped. "Is she okay?"

"She's fine. Scared her pretty bad, but he didn't hurt her. It seems that the police showed up just in time. The interesting thing is that the man, who had a Hispanic accent by the way, called Lauren by the name of Lacy."

"Oh, my God. It was Miguel! I had no idea that our little game would put Lauren at risk. I just wanted Miguel to think I was still in Georgia."

"I guess he knows now that you're not. Lauren said that he stared at her for a long second before he ran out of the room. She thinks he realized that she wasn't you."

"Lauren kind of looks like me," Lacy admitted. "Her hair is about as long as mine, and she is definitely a blonde, though I think hers came from a bottle."

She went on to tell Meg about coming home to the South Beach house and finding the door open. She related her story about calling the police to report the break in, though she managed to leave out the part about taking a shower at Kerrick's apartment. "The police said that we just left the door open, but I'm sure it was Miguel."

"How can you be sure?"

"He left a skull necklace hanging on my mirror. It had to be him."

"Thank God you got locked in the lighthouse," Meg whispered.

"I thought about that," Lacy agreed. "I'm not sure what God has to do with it, but it is an interesting coincidence."

"You know, Lacy. I once heard someone say that coincidences happen a lot more when we pray than when we don't."

"I wasn't praying," Lacy laughed. "I mean, you guys are kind of getting to me, but I'm not ready to drink the Kool-Aid yet."

"I was praying," Meg confided. "You scared me to death when you didn't answer your phone."

"I checked the time of my missed calls from you. Your first one must have come in while I was driving to the health center where I parked my car. I just didn't hear it vibrate."

"When you didn't answer the second time, I figured that you must have left your phone somewhere, but when I heard about Miguel's attack, you better believe I started praying for you. I'm so glad you're okay."

"Thanks for caring, Meg. I'm going to have to go. Will you and Jon still meet us tomorrow night out from Pirate's Cove?"

"Yep. We'll watch for the boat. We want it to be dark when we pull away from our dock, however. Y'all be careful and be smart about the whole hotel thing on Nassau."

"Careful is my middle name," Lacy laughed.

"So, you've told me before," Meg chuckled. "Just don't forget that you're my only Lacy."

****

Lacy climbed aboard the *Misty Dawn* and saw Matt untying one of the ropes at the front of the boat that held the shrimper to the dock. She went to the back and freed the vessel from the back cleat. Matt waved goodbye as they pulled away from the dock and slowly putted through the deep-water marina. The ocean breeze blew through her hair, and a spray of salt water hit her face. She felt a shiver of excitement run through her body as the bay opened up to the sparkling waters of the Atlantic.

The boat was beautiful and clean. It was nothing like what Lacy had imagined. She figured to be covered with the smell of dead shrimp by the time they got to the Bahamas, but this boat was so clean she could eat off the deck. She smiled with that

thought and decided eating from the deck might be taking things
a bit too far.

Before heading into the wheelhouse with Kerrick, Lacy
walked the full length of the boat. It had to be forty feet long,
maybe more. The sides had been painted fire engine red, and the
deck and the insides of the boat were so white they almost
blinded her to look at them in the sunlight. It was actually quite
pretty…for a fishing boat.

She stopped near the boom holding the nets and stared into
the blue water. Her life had taken some really interesting turns
over the last few years. When she graduated from Griffin High
School, she had been willing to do anything to get out of her
home town and away from her parents. Getting away from her
father turned out to be quite easy. He evidently didn't want to
be around her either. Her mother pretended to care, but the
truth was the only person she cared for was herself. When Lacy
finally got around to calling her to tell her that she had moved
to Miami, she wasn't even fazed. She just told Lacy not to do
anything stupid. That was it. *Don't do anything stupid? Like grow up
to be like you?*

Lacy reflected on her freshman year at Georgia College. It
had been fun, but it proved to her that all guys were jerks. They
all wanted one thing, and they were all arrogant, self-centered
jack…Okay. So, she had sworn off the language of her past.
That was the old Lacy. The fact is that all guys were idiots except
for one. Well, counting Jon and Jose, there were three who came
to mind. Kerrick was one in a million. He was kind and considerate. The one thing he wanted was to serve her and make her
happy. Wow. They just didn't come like that often.

She had worked through his deception over the summer. His
sister's life had been at stake, so Lacy gave him a pass. In a way,

it made him even more admirable that he would risk everything to save his sister. She looked toward the window of the wheelhouse. He was definitely a keeper. On top of everything, he was knock down hot.

Lacy climbed a few steps up to the platform where the wheelhouse was located. The door was open. "Hey. Do you want me to get you something to drink? Matt said he had some cokes in the frig."

"Cokes as in Coca Cola or cokes as in sodas."

"You know what I mean smarty. Everything that fizzes is a coke. Would you like for me to get you a *soda*? Next thing you know, you're going to be complaining about my grits."

"What's a grit?" Kerrick joked and then ducked as Lacy threw a small towel at his head. "I'd love a soda. Maybe a D.P. if you have one."

Lacy returned shortly with a Dr. Pepper. "Doesn't this boat go any faster? It's going to take us forever to get there at this rate."

"We're going as fast as we can go. We only have to make it to Nassau by nightfall, and that should be easy. What's the resort called again?"

"Bayview. I'm just wondering how we're going to get a shrimp boat into the public marina at Paradise Island."

"We're good. Matt told me a place where we can dock. I'm wondering why Jon and Meg asked us to bring this boat over knowing that we had to spend the night together. They've made such a big deal about what we shouldn't do, and now, Jon is sending us to a romantic resort together."

"What they're doing is smart," Lacy concluded. "Jon doesn't want us to sleep together, but we need the shrimp boat for the dive. So, what does he do? He taps into your character and your sorrow over what happened this summer to assure that we will indeed sleep in separate rooms tonight. He knows that after what happened, if you say we're going to sleep separately, we're going to sleep separately."

Kerrick lowered his head. "I can't believe I did that to Jon."

Lacy wrapped her arms around Kerrick and hugged him tightly from behind. "You had no choice, Kerrick. I mean, you could have pulled Jon into it from the beginning, but Kelsey's life *was* being threatened. You did what you thought was right and what you considered to be your only choice."

Kerrick steered the boat in silence for a moment and set the coordinates so the cruise control could kick in. "He's right," he finally said.

"Right?"

"Yeah. I'll never lie to him again. You couldn't pay me enough to sleep with you tonight."

Lacy laughed. "I don't know if I should be hurt or happy."

Kerrick turned around and faced Lacy. He kissed her forehead and then her lips. "You're beautiful, and I'll have to reach deep past a resolve that is teetering. If a man doesn't have character, he doesn't have anything."

Lacy's hand went to Kerrick's cheek, and she stared into his blue eyes. "I love you, Kerrick Daniels. There's not many guys like you in the world."

Chapter Fourteen

The Island of the Skull

Jon scanned the Google map of the Bahamas once again as he tried to get into the mind of Miguel. If he were Miguel, where would he choose to place his base of operations? Coral Cay had to be the island where Miguel thought he'd find the treasure, so it was hard to believe that the pirate would get too far away from his former compound. He knew, however, that the old compound was under constant surveillance by the Coast Guard. *There's no way he's back on Coral Cay.*

He zoomed in on the smaller islands surrounding the area but returned to the view of Coral Cay. He wondered if Google Earth would show the skull on the northern end of the island. He changed the view on his computer and zoomed in as close as possible. He saw the top of the skull. A shiver ran down his spine as he remembered Kerrick pushing himself backward off the cliff. The thought still tied his stomach in knots. That had been one of the bravest things Jon had ever witnessed, but of course, Fernando was about to slit the boy's throat. Kerrick confessed that he had been scared to death but felt like he had no choice but to go over the cliff. He had been fortunate to clear the rocks. Too bad Fernando didn't.

Jon allowed his eyes to follow the dirt path that ran north and south down the island and noticed that an east/west road intersected it at about the midpoint of the island. *That's interesting.*

It seems like everything we look at is similar to the cross on the medallion.
He imagined the dot on the medallion that Lacy said marked the
spot of the treasure. He followed the east/west road with his
eyes. *If that cross is pointing to this road, and the dot marks the spot of the
treasure, then the treasure would be right…here.* He placed the tip of
his pen on his computer screen.

He felt hot breath on his ear before Meg's arms encircled his
neck. "What are you looking at?"

"I'm just trying to figure out where Miguel could be."

"That's Coral Cay, isn't it?"

"Yeah. Look at this dirt road. Do you see where it intersects
this other road? Does it make you think of anything?"

"Wow. That medallion could be an aerial picture of the
island. Then again, what are the odds of Bluetooth's warrior having a hot air balloon?"

"True, but of course, he wouldn't really need an aerial view
to create a map. At the same time, it's not very likely these roads
were around hundreds of years ago."

"If the treasure is there," Meg said as she pointed to the spot
where Jon had considered earlier, "then why would Lacy's
medallion say 'beneath'?"

"Good question. Of course, we don't know what Miguel's
medallion says. What if it says beneath something that's somewhere around this part of the island?"

"There is another option," Meg concluded. "These roads
could just intersect and have nothing to do with the medallion."

"I suppose we'll find out tonight. How do you think our love
birds made out last night?"

"Let's hope they didn't. I mean didn't make out."

"Cute, Meg. You should be a comedian. I've always said you
have hidden talents."

"I have a lot of confidence in those two to use their heads and not their hearts. I also think that neither one of them wants to disappoint us. I suggest we not even bring the issue up."

"You're right," Jon agreed. "I trust them implicitly. I need to go fill up the scuba tanks. What do you think about making something to take with us for dinner? I know by the time we meet up with them, dinner time will be long past, but we're going to be up quite late tonight."

"Good idea. Then, I think we need to take a nap if Carla will let us."

"I'm sure Judy will be happy to entertain her for us."

After nightfall, Diego started up the trolling motor and quietly guided the Robalo out of Pirate's Cove. Jon had no idea if Miguel might be watching them, but he decided he didn't want to alert anyone with sounds of a motor starting up this time of night. Fortunately, Diego had a small battery-operated motor he used when fishing the shallows, and he was happy to loan it to Jon. When they were about half a mile out into the ocean, Jon started the dual 250 horse power motors and sped toward the waiting shrimp boat.

Diving off of Coral Cay in the middle of the night was not something he had anticipated just a few days ago. He figured that by now, he and Meg would be elbows deep in chores around their home at Pirate's Cove. He had also considered taking a little family vacation to somewhere far from the ocean, like the Rocky Mountains. That would have to wait.

After all of these years of diving, he still felt excitement as he anticipated donning his scuba gear. He tried to remember the cave from the night he and Jose swam through the tunnels to rescue Lacy. He envisioned an intersecting tunnel, but he thought he remembered noting that the tunnel on the left was only about ten feet long. He distinctly remembered the beam from his flashlight dancing over a coral wall. He wasn't confident they would find any treasure because that tunnel was under water most of the time. Still, he was excited about giving it a shot. He had dived a number of caves through the years, and each dive was always an adventure. Meg, however, had never been in a cave like this one. She seemed to be a little anxious.

"We're coming up on your starboard side," Jon said into his cell phone. "We don't have on our lights, so don't let us spook you."

"I hear you, Uncle Jon. I've got a rope ready to secure your boat."

Jon quietly handed up the scuba gear to Kerrick while Meg busied herself with gathering up the bags of clothes and food she had packed. Once Jon and Meg were safely aboard the *Misty Dawn*, Diego turned the Robalo toward home.

"How was your trip?" Jon asked as he joined Kerrick in the wheel house.

"We've had a great time, though I think we were both about half dead yesterday."

"I had hoped you'd be able to sleep a little on your way over to Nassau," Jon said.

"I encouraged Lacy to, but she refused. We pretty much ate dinner last night, and then we both collapsed in our rooms. So much for a romantic evening in Nassau. We walked around the Straw Market for a little while this morning, but romance doesn't come to mind when I think of the market."

Jon grinned and slapped Kerrick on the back. "I have a feeling you'll have the opportunity for another romantic night out. Let's go toward the shallows out from Georgetown marina and drop anchor. We need to look over a map and figure out our strategy."

Meg made some coffee, and they gathered around the table in the cramped kitchen area of the boat. Jon showed them the printout of the map of the island that he brought along. He mentioned the idea of the two dirt roads intersecting and wondered if the treasure may not be in the tunnel at all. He also told them that he thought he remembered the tunnel to the left being quite short.

"If nothing else," Kerrick said, "we'll have a fun night dive. If we don't find the treasure, then maybe we should go ashore and follow the dirt roads you're talking about. Getting ashore may be a trick unless you think we can use the dock on the south side."

"We have a row boat, but there's no motor on it," Meg added.

"We're going to find it," Lacy insisted. "My medallion says 'beneath,' and we are definitely about to be beneath the island."

"Yeah," Jon maintained, "but what if Miguel's medallion says something like turtle rock formation."

Lacy grinned. "I've got a hunch,"

"Jon, I'm counting on you being right," Kerrick interjected. "If Lacy's wrong, she has to cook dinner for me for 30 days."

"You probably should hope she's right," Jon suggested. "I don't think Lacy can cook."

Jon and Kerrick laughed, and Jon saw a little smirk cross Lacy's face. She was a good sport, but he had a feeling that treasure or not, she was going to prove him wrong about her kitchen skills.

Jon looked south in the direction of Coral Cay. "I'm a little concerned about not having someone aboard the boat while we're diving, but I'm sure not going to leave one of you ladies up here alone. On top of that, I don't think anyone wants to miss out on this adventure."

"We could circle the boat several times under water when we return to make sure we don't see the bottom of another boat nearby," Kerrick suggested.

"Meg and I were surprised a few years ago when a guy boarded our boat while we were diving off of Conception Island. His boat was gone by the time we surfaced, and we had no idea we were in danger."

Jon noticed Meg shiver and realized that she probably still had difficult memories of that experience. It was a miracle that the creep who had her didn't really hurt her. Jon had always marveled that the two guys chose not to kill him.

"Okay. Here's what we'll do," Jon decided. "I'll come up first while you guys stay at fifteen feet beneath the boat. I'll check things out and then I'll drop a line over if it's clear. If I don't drop a line over, then get back to the island and call for help."

"Jon, you do remember that the cliff is at least 100 feet up," Kerrick added. "I'm sure I can climb up the skull, but it would take a while, and I'd be spotted. You also know that there's nothing on this end of the island. I mean there's no houses or people. Swimming around the island is quite a task."

"I know," Jon agreed. "You'd have to get around to the little community on the south side. We don't have any choice."

Jon looked at his wife and wondered if it was a good idea to bring her and Lacy out here into possible danger. He thought back to their experience nearly three years earlier when they had been kidnapped by Alvaro Lopez's men. Meg was tough and brave, and she was also stubborn. There's no way she would have agreed to Jon and Kerrick diving the tunnels by themselves.

She must have sensed that he was looking at her because she caught his eye and winked. Jon's heart raced. She was beautiful, but she was as tough as his old work boots.

Meg got up to refill everyone's coffee. "Maybe we should at least pull the row boat along with us and tie it to something at the bottom of the cliff. If anything happens, we'll at least have a boat."

"Good idea, honey. Hopefully, Kerrick will be able to just swim back and get it when I give you the coast is clear sign." Jon stood and kissed Meg lightly. "Kerrick and I are going back to the wheelhouse and getting this boat to Coral Cay. Why don't you two ladies work on something for us to eat. I have a feeling this is going to be a long night."

Chapter Fifteen

Girl Talk

"Hey, Miguel," Andrew shouted from the back room. "The little boat is leaving the cove."

Miguel rushed in and looked at the computer screen. "Are you sure that tracker is right? I mean, that thing is nothing more than a tiny magnet. Is it accurate? It's nearly 10:00. Why would they be going out at night?"

"To do a night dive?" Andrew wondered aloud.

"Maybe. At least it's the Robalo and not the yacht. They won't be going far in that little boat."

Andrew turned toward Miguel. "Do you want me to go out to Roker's Point?"

Miguel sat down beside the desk and rubbed his chin. "No. By the time you got there, the boat would be long gone. You can monitor it just as well from right here in front of your computer. Just let me know when it comes back."

Miguel walked back into the living room of the small house they had rented just south of Georgetown. He wondered if they should have found a place closer to Roker's Point.

He picked up his coffee cup and headed into the kitchen for a refill. He thought about how his work had changed. Just a few years ago, he had stationed Fernando out to spy on the Davenports, and the idiot nearly blew it. Now, all they had to do was place tracking devices on the Davenport's boats and vehicles and just watch them from the comfort of their home. Life was good, and if things went like they were supposed to go, it was going to get even better.

He pulled the gold medallion out of his pocket. He used to keep it stored in a box under his bed, but he began carrying it with him after the debacle on Coral Cay. He traced the lines etched into the gold. *Island of the skull.*

Miguel thought back to the years of study and travel he had put into finding the one place that could fit this description. He had no doubt that Coral Cay was the right place. There was treasure somewhere on that island, and Lacy Henderson had the clue where it could be found. Now, thanks to Fernando's screw up, she knew the medallion had some kind of value, but she probably didn't know anything more. She wouldn't know anything about treasure and certainly wouldn't know the treasure was on Coral Cay. He just needed to somehow get her medallion. He may just have to go to their compound and kill them all.

He smiled as he thought about the possibility of getting rid of the people who had caused him the greatest trouble. He might have to solve his problems once and for all. *I need to relax tonight. Tomorrow night could be busy. I think I'll go back to the club. What was that girl's name? Cherry. Yeah. Cherry. She'll be working tonight.*

"I'm going out," Miguel called back to Andrew. "Text me when the boat comes back. Call me if anything else happens."

"Got it, boss. My prediction is that Jon and his beautiful little wife are having some fun. They'll be back in a bit. I'll keep my eye on things here."

* * * * * *

Lacy walked over to the small refrigerator and pulled out four bottles of water as she watched Meg dig through one of the bags she had brought aboard. Lacy thought about what it must be like to have someone special like Jon to love you, but then her aunt was quite special too.

"Are you missing something, Meg?"

"I thought I put a bottle of hot sauce in here, but I can't seem to find it. Jon likes it on just about everything."

"No worries," Lacy said as she opened a cabinet under the sink. "It seems that Matt likes Texas Pete. He's got two bottles. I assume that if he doesn't mind us using his boat, he won't mind letting us have a little hot sauce."

"Wonderful," Meg said as she reached for the bottle that Lacy offered.

"Meg, I don't get it."

"You don't get what?"

"You and Jon! I mean, every person that I know who is married is miserable. Up until a couple of months ago, I was going to skip the whole thing."

Meg chuckled. "How many married people do you really know? Surely all of them can't be miserable."

"Okay. You're right. I don't know many. Of course, you know my parents were miserable. I used to babysit for the Judsons. They argued with one another with me in the room, and when Mrs. Judson wasn't around, her husband hit on me all the time. He was a creep."

"It's true that a lot of people have problems, and a lot of marriages are in trouble, but that doesn't mean marriage itself is the problem. It's the people and their understanding of marriage."

Meg took her coffee cup over to the table and sat down, so Lacy joined her. Lacy decided that if Meg wanted to talk, she wanted to listen.

"People by nature are selfish," Meg continued. "When two self-centered, self-absorbed people get married, it is an equation for disaster."

"Which means that marriage is a disaster," Lacy interrupted.

"Not exactly. If two people really love each other, they learn to put the other person and his or her needs above their own needs. You see, true love gives and serves. It doesn't take and demand. The problem with most marriages is that people enter the relationship thinking about what they're going to get instead of what they're going to give. They see marriage as a contract."

"I thought it was like a contract. I know people who have even signed prenuptial agreements. That's a contract, isn't it? I thought that was normal."

"It's a lot more normal than it used to be," Meg agreed. "Whether a couple signs a prenuptial agreement or not, marriage is not supposed to be a contract. I see it as more of a covenant instead of a contract."

"What's the difference?"

"Contracts are about getting what you want, but marriage is about giving. If you go into marriage as if it were a contract, then you're going to be disappointed if your needs aren't met. You may eventually end up in divorce court. If you go into marriage thinking about how you can serve your husband, and if he focuses on how he can serve you, then you have a marriage that will not only survive, but it will also thrive."

"Right," Lacy laughed. "Husbands who want to serve instead be served are found only in fairy tales."

"Then call me Cinderella," Meg grinned. "Jon is the most giving man I know. It's like he wants to out serve me."

"You're lucky, Aunt Meg," Lacy said as she got up from the table. "I think you got the last one like that."

Meg stood and put her arm around Lacy's shoulders. "Oh, I don't think so. There's still plenty of them out there. You just have to be patient. Kerrick seems to be pretty focused on you instead of himself, unless I'm just not seeing something."

"Maybe. I'm amazed that he even likes me when you consider how I was when I first met him. I was a real jerk. Selfish doesn't even describe me."

"I'd say Kerrick loves you, and love waits and gives. It gives time and grace. You've got to admit that Kerrick sure does seem to put your needs above his own."

"Okay." Lacy laughed again. "Here goes the grace talk. You may be right, but I don't know. I feel like deep down, every guy is going to be service oriented until he gets what he wants. Then, the real beast comes out. It's kind of like the opposite of what happened in *Beauty and the Beast*."

"Don't count him out," Meg urged. "He may surprise you. I'm sure you'll know in time."

"Speaking of time," Lacy tapped her watch, "your servant husband is probably starving. We'd better get him some food."

Chapter Sixteen

Liam's Cave - 1871

Liam left his cave first thing in the morning and walked out to the shore where he had been dropped off the previous day. He looked out to sea hoping to see his cousin's boat approaching, but there was no sail in sight. They had agreed to arrive on Conception Island on the first Monday of August, and today was Monday, August 7. Hopefully, Ludvig would be along soon.

Liam had awakened during the night with chills and perspiration pouring from his body, which he thought unusual considering the nights were quite warm. He'd also been sick at his stomach during the night. He'd decided a walk around the island would help him to feel a little better.

As soon as he reached the shoreline, a wave of abdominal pain hit him again, and he wretched as he bent over. *What is wrong with me? I've got to get back to the cave.* He picked up a few shells from the beach and formed an arrow that pointed toward the cave. *Hopefully, Ludvig will come find me.*

Liam walked back to his cave, pulled off his shirt, and drank from his diminishing supply of water. He saw that the red spots on his chest had more than doubled. *How is that possible? There are no fleas on this island.* He sat down and leaned against the wall of the cave, and his body ached from head to toe.

Sometime later, Liam was awakened in a fog when a crab crawled across his hand. He looked toward the back of the cave and saw movement. A woman walked toward him who looked just like his teacher from school. He thought back to her dead body lying on the ground. She had been his first.

"Why did you kill me, Liam? I was only trying to help you."

"I didn't really mean to kill you, Mrs. Olmstead. It was an accident. I only meant for you to be unconscious."

"I know what you intended, but you killed me, Liam. You'll pay for that soon."

"I didn't mean to."

Mrs. Olmstead suddenly changed, and the woman was now his mother. "Liam. I tried to help you, son, but you refused to listen."

"I listened, Ma."

"No. You grew up to be a very bad man. I tried to raise you right, but you were determined to be a killer. You are a killer, my boy. I know because you killed me."

"I didn't kill you, Ma."

As quickly as these visions appeared, the cave became dark again.

"I'm seeing things," Liam said aloud. "I've got to get out of this cave. My fever is messing with my head."

Liam pulled himself to his feet and stumbled out of the mouth of the cave into the twilight. The wind howled around him, and he instantly became drenched in the buckets of rain that fell from the sky. Lightning flashed across the black sky, and he fell back into the cave. He dragged himself deeper into the darkness where it was at least dry. He lay down on the ground and drifted off into a fitful sleep.

Throughout the night, his muscles spasmed, and he moaned uncontrollably. He vomited so many times that he lost count. At one point during the night, he crawled outside into the violent storm and sat in the rain for a while in an attempt to cool off from the fever. Something was definitely wrong. He continued to dream crazy things, and at one point during the night, he thought he saw Father Vincent in the cave with him.

The next morning, he considered his situation. He had to leave the island. *But what if Ludvig comes, and I'm not here?* He considered the possibility of writing a note for his cousin, but he had no paper. If someone else found the note, that could mean trouble, too. He considered carving his note in the side of the cave and leaving something that might point Ludvig to the carving, but how could he do it so no one else could read it? *Runic! I'll carve it in Runic. The cave walls are soft, so it shouldn't be too difficult.*

Throughout the day, Liam continued to lay around the cave and found it impossible to keep anything on his stomach. He decided to carve some clues in the cave wall for Ludvig, and he would finish by just including the word *Nassau*.

If I can get off of this God-forsaken island, I'll go back to Nassau. Maybe he'll come find me. Though he intended to start with the carving, he couldn't seem to keep his mind on the message he wanted to leave on the wall. He also didn't have much strength left. Why hadn't the fisherman come back to get him? He thought back to the man staring at the rash on his chest. *He knows I have the fever. He's not coming back.*

The night was filled with insane thoughts. Liam imagined himself carving Runic letters into the wall, and at times, he wondered if he had really done it. His mind slipped in and out of consciousness and delirium as he feared for his life. Several words kept rolling over and over in his mind: *Trelleborg, Bluetooth, diary,*

He had to find Bluetooth's diary. The priest told him that the King had a diary that explained everything, but Liam had not been able to locate it. He was on a fool's mission with only one medallion and one clue. Even when Ludvig came with the other medallion, they may still not have enough information to find the treasure. *I shouldn't have been in such a hurry to leave Sweden. We may have to go back.*

As the front of the cave was lit with the morning sun, Liam lay on the floor far back in the darkness. The light hurt his eyes, and the back of the cave was cooler. He reached for his medallion and found it was still dangling from his neck. He pulled the chain from around his neck and held the medallion close to his face. He couldn't make out the clue in the dark, but he knew the writing was there all the same: *island of the skull.*

His throat was parched, but his water was near the opening of the cave. He was so thirsty. He closed his eyes and another bolt of pain wracked his body. He suddenly felt a strange calm come over him. He had the strangest feeling of floating. He looked down and saw his body lying on the floor of the cave. *Why can I see myself sleeping? What's happening to me?*

Slowly, the heat began to grow. It first felt like the normal heat of a hot, summer day, but it became increasingly hotter. He couldn't take it anymore. He was burning. It felt like his clothes must be on fire. He began to hear moans and screams as he shot out of the cave and through the air into a strange blackness. He screamed in terror, for he felt like his body was going to burst into flames.

Chapter Seventeen

Beneath the Skull

Jon guided the *Misty Dawn* around the northern part of Coral Cay as the huge skull cliff loomed over the boat. He stared up at the place to where Fernando had pulled Kerrick just about a month earlier while holding a knife to Kerrick's throat. He felt a shiver run down his back as he pictured Kerrick pushing backwards so they both fell from the edge of the cliff. Jon knew he had seen a slight trace of blood on Kerrick's throat just before Kerrick drove his body backward. The scar the young intern would wear for the rest of his life would remind him of that night. Thankfully, Kerrick had cleared the rocks.

Jon decided to make a slow pass to the north of the island to make sure no one was keeping watch. He doubted they could know for certain that they were unnoticed, but he had to take every precaution possible. He placed Kerrick at one window with binoculars while Meg engaged her video camera at the back of the boat. He didn't put it past Miguel to have someone posted somewhere on the grounds of his old compound. *I should have brought Diego with us. He could have kept the shrimper moving while we made the dive.*

Guiding the boat for another mile past the island, Jon set the automatic pilot and slowed the boat. He wanted to watch the video and compare notes with the rest of the group. "So, does anyone have any hesitations?"

"I didn't see a thing," Kerrick acknowledged.

Jon saw Lacy's head shaking back and forth, and Meg shrugged her shoulders. He disengaged the boats automatic controls and manually turned the shrimper back toward the island. He turned off the motor and slowly drifted into position just beneath the gaze of the empty eye sockets of the cliff. He pushed the button to release the anchor, and the large metal hook dropped seventy-five feet to the ocean floor.

Once the anchor was set, Jon turned toward the other three. "Okay. If no one has any reason to head home, we'll make the dive."

"I'm good," Kerrick said. "I say we go for it."

"I'm in," Lacy nodded. "I've thought about this moment non-stop ever since I got on the plane for home over a week ago."

Jon looked at Meg. "Honey? Do you feel good about this?"

"I say let's do it before I lose my nerve."

"All right. Get your gear on and let's get in the water. I'd guess that the cave should be dry about now, but the tide will be starting its turn any time. While we may crawl out on dry ground, we need to carry our gear with us as we explore the tunnel."

"I didn't think about that," Kerrick admitted. "Carrying our gear through the cave is going to be fun."

"Just keep your tank on your back and carry your fins," Jon suggested. "We don't need to lose anything in the rising tide. Also, let's not turn on our lights until we're under the cliff. If anyone is up there, I don't want them to see our lights. I'll cover mine with my hand and flash it a couple of times once you're all in the water. Swim to me and let's stay together."

In less than ten minutes, Jon slipped into the water from the back of the boat. He felt the cool water seeping into his wetsuit, and a shiver ran up his spine. Thankfully, the thin layer of water would soon warm to his body temperature and serve as an insulator. He was pumped. The old thrill of being under water never got old.

He studied his dive computer and saw that he was ten feet from the surface. He looked up to see Meg swimming toward him as Kerrick and Lacy entered the water. He hoped Kerrick remembered to pull the small boat along. He flashed his light once and then grabbed Meg's arm. Once they were all together, they began swimming toward the island.

Jon felt the rock wall of the cliff with his hand before his body collided with it. He had hoped to be able to feel the rock in time to keep himself from crashing into something that might cut him, but no such luck. He turned on his light in time to spare the other three from getting hurt. Fortunately, the rock had not drawn blood, but he noticed his wetsuit was sliced open. He knew the opening to the cave was about fifteen feet beneath the surface, so he motioned to the others to follow him.

He saw Kerrick switch on the headlight that he wore and loop a rope through an opening in the rock. *Good. He remembered the little row boat.* In minutes, Jon's head popped out of the water within the protection of the cave. Meg surfaced beside him and inflated her BCD vest.

The light from Jon's LED flashlight danced around the cave walls, but nothing looked familiar. The last time he swam through this cave it had been full of water. Now, he saw a tunnel that went off to the left, but it was not completely dry. As he swam forward, he bumped into a rock with his shin and realized that he was at the intersection of the two tunnels. He pulled off his fins and stood to his feet in water that came to his knees. Meg, Kerrick, and Lacy soon joined him.

"Everything looks so different," Jon whispered. "I'm not sure why I'm whispering. There's no way anyone can hear us."

"When I was in here," Kerrick said, "I didn't have a flash-light, so I for sure don't recognize anything. It seems to me that this tunnel to the left is going up a bit."

Jon turned the light toward the tunnel and could see that it was eight to ten feet long. He remembered from the last time thinking that the cave ended in a stone wall. He pictured himself pausing with Jose at his side, though last time, they were fully submerged. He had shown his light into the short tunnel to the left before proceeding toward the tunnel that led to the pond behind Miguel's house. "Well, let's check it out. Maybe the tunnel turns."

They sloshed forward slowly trying not to bump the cave walls with their scuba tanks. Jon saw that he had been right about the tunnel ending, but he had not been able to see that the tunnel went straight up at least six or seven feet. He found rocks to step on and was able to climb up a few feet before the tunnel opened up before him again. He turned and helped Meg crawl up behind him. Kerrick offered his hand to Lacy once he climbed up to the next level of the tunnel.

The tunnel was now bigger than the one below them, and the floor of the tunnel was definitely rising in elevation.

"Everyone okay?" Jon asked.

"We're fine," Kerrick said.

Lacy came up beside Jon. "I'm just so excited I'm about to bust."

"Well. Nothing to do but to do it," Jon said. "Follow close."

After another 100 feet, the tunnel took a turn to the right and opened to a large room. Jon's eyes scanned the large room as he shown his light around the sides of the cavern. When the beam came down to the floor on the far end of the room, Lacy gasped. A small chest sat atop a pile of coral rocks.

"Oh, my God," Lacy whispered. "I'm not going to have to fix you dinner, Kerrick."

"I don't know if I should be happy or sad," Kerrick acknowledged with a laugh. "I was kind of looking forward to home-cooked meals."

Jon stepped toward the chest as it grew larger in the focused beam from his light. "Sure looks like treasure to me."

Chapter Eighteen

Bluetooth's Stash

Miguel pulled Cherry close and kissed her solidly on the lips. He knew he was breaking the rules by doing so, but he had given a lot of money to this joint. If the owner couldn't handle a little kiss, then Miguel would take his business elsewhere.

"Miguel," Cherry cooed. "You know you're not supposed to do that." She pressed her body against his and kissed him again. "But I've never been one much for rules."

Just as Miguel began thinking that things were starting to look up, his cell phone rang. He checked his caller ID and saw that it was Andrew. "Hold on a minute, baby. I've got to take this."

He turned his back on the beautiful brunette. "Hey. This better be important."

"I don't know if it is or not, boss, but I figured you'd want to know."

"Know what?"

"Well, the little boat did something kind of weird. I should have called you fifteen minutes ago, but I just didn't think about it until now."

"What are you talking about, Andrew. Spit it out."

"It seems that the Davenports went out a little over a mile from the cove. I was afraid they might go out so far that I'd lose signal. They sat there for about ten minutes and then came back.

They didn't go back to the cove, though. They went to the marina."

"Maybe they decided to go get something to eat."

"Maybe, but it sure seems strange that they went a mile out before going back to the marina. It's probably nothing, but I thought you should know."

"Okay, Andrew. I'm not far from the marina, so I'll just go check it out."

Miguel looked at the beautiful girl beside him and slipped his fingers into her hair. "I've got some business to tend to, baby. I'll try to come back after a while."

"Oh Miguel. I thought we were going to have some fun."

"Later. I said I'd be back."

He stuffed a wad of bills in the girl's hand and hoped he'd be able to come back. He left the club and drove to the marina parking lot, reminding himself that he'd have to be careful not to allow Davenport to see him. He surveyed the cars and didn't notice the F-250 he'd seen the boy driving, but when he looked out at the dock, the red Robalo was tied up in the third slip.

He sat in his car for a few minutes eying the Half-shell restaurant on the south end of the parking lot. He couldn't risk being seen, but he had to know what Jon Davenport was up to. He drove forward to an open parking space that he hoped would give him a good view of the building. *I'll at least be able to see the front door, and maybe I can see through the window.*

In just a matter of minutes, he spotted the Davenports' maintenance guy through the front window. He was eating dinner with a woman who was probably his wife. Where was Davenport? Maybe he and his beautiful little wife were back at the compound. Miguel started up his Camry and headed north toward Roker's Point.

He walked a half of a mile to edge of the Davenports' property and looked toward the main house. He paused behind a tree and turned his back to light up a cigarette. Smoke filled his lungs, and he relished the smell and taste of the tobacco. When he looked back at the house, there was no doubt that someone was home. The shadow of a woman passed behind the curtain, and he felt his heart race a bit. Meg Davenport was the most beautiful woman he'd ever seen. He'd give up five years with Cherry just to be with Meg for one hour. The thought crossed his mind to go in and teach Meg Davenport a lesson. He could tie Jon up or maybe even just shoot him. Then, he could have Meg all to himself.

Are you an idiot or what? You've got too much at stake here to go in and blow it over some beautiful woman. Your time will come, Meg Davenport.

Miguel began the walk back to his car and opened his phone. "Hey, Andrew. I don't know what the maintenance guy was doing, but he went out for a spin before going to eat dinner at the marina. The Davenports are home. I wish we knew if the yard guy met another boat out there. He may have a little side business running some dope."

"You think the Davenports are into drugs?"

"No. That guy is squeaky clean, but his little yard man could be a different story."

"Boss, do you want me to slip into the Davenports' house and install some cameras? If we'd had cameras, you wouldn't have had to waste your time driving out there tonight."

"Let me think about it, Andrew," Miguel said as his mind went back to Cherry at the club. "I'll be back in a little bit. I have some unfinished business that needs my attention."

****

Lacy ran her fingers over the edge of the ancient chest. The leather hinges had rotted long ago, and she wondered if they'd even be able to open the lid without the whole thing falling apart. She couldn't believe she was actually standing in front of a Viking treasure chest. She had been so confident they'd find treasure, and she had been right.

"Go ahead," Jon said behind her. "You're the one who found it."

"We found it, Uncle Jon. It's not like I came in here by myself."

"True, but you're the one who had the idea where to look. Go ahead and lift the lid."

Lacy's hands trembled as she placed them on both sides of the chest, and she felt like her heart was going to beat right out of her body. She tried to raise the lid, but it was stuck. Kerrick handed her the knife that he kept sheathed to his leg while scuba diving. With just a little effort, she pried the lid off.

She stood speechless as reflective light danced around the ceiling of the cave. "I've never seen anything so beautiful in my life," she said as she bent down to take a closer look at a necklace made of emeralds and diamonds. "Is that gold, I mean under the necklace?"

Jon stepped up, and Lacy pointed to five rocks that glimmered in the light. "I'd say so, but that on the bottom is not gold. It's some other kind of stone." He pulled the necklace and gold out of the chest to take a closer look.

"Yeah, it's a stone, but it looks like there's a carving on it," Lacy noted.

"Or part of a carving," Kerrick said as he stepped up to the chest. "It's broken on the end."

"Look at that scroll," Meg said as she slid beside Jon. "It kind of reminds me of the journal the little girl had from Sweden. I bet it used to be a note telling us how to find the city. I suppose the chest protected it somewhat."

Jon pulled out his camera and took pictures of what was left of the animal skin scroll and the treasure chest. The cave lit up with flashes of light from his camera. "I brought a water proof bag with me. Let's put this stuff in the bag and get back."

"Isn't it weird that the treasure is in here?" Lacy mentioned. "I mean, Bluetooth's guy would have had to take the chest underwater to get to the cave."

"Maybe there used to be another entrance from above," Jon suggested, "or maybe the opening to the cave used to be accessible at low tide."

"I'm just surprised there's not more," Kerrick sighed.

"I'm sure there's more where this came from," Lacy insisted. "I told you that Viking guy wouldn't bring a bunch of treasure back. He brought just enough to tell the Bluetooth heirs where to find the city."

"Too bad they hated each other so much that they couldn't work together to find it," Meg pointed out. "Now, we may never find it. There's no way we can read the writing on that skin."

"Maybe," Jon admitted, "but Cindy can do some pretty amazing things."

"Good old Cindy," Lacy laughed. "How do you seem to have connections in just the right places Uncle Jon?"

"First of all, I won't tell Cindy you called her *old*. I went to school with her, and she went on to do research of ancient manuscripts in Spain. She's a linguistic expert who can probably help us out a lot. Let's bag this stuff and get out of here."

"Yeah," Meg agreed. "I'm starting to get the creeps."

Fifteen minutes later, Lacy adjusted her scuba gear and then spit into her mask to keep it from fogging up. The water swirled around her thighs, and she had no idea how much further before they'd find the hole that dropped to the lower tunnel. Kerrick stood beside her getting his gear together, and she could hear Jon and Meg splashing up behind them.

"You know we're probably getting close to where the tunnel drops down," Jon said.

"I agree," Lacy acknowledged. "I was kind of thinking it might be good to start swimming as soon as possible. Will it be tricky swimming against the rising tide?"

"Maybe a little," Jon guessed. "You'll definitely feel the push against you, but it shouldn't be too big of a deal. I once swam against the current of a spring in north Florida. We had to pull ourselves along the sides of the cave. If that happens, we'll be dependent on your light, Kerrick. Meg's going to have to hold mine, but she'll need both hands. It will be on, but it'll be dangling from the ring on her vest."

Lacy saw Kerrick's light bob up and down, so she assumed he was nodding in agreement.

"You going to be able to hold onto the bag okay, Jon?" Kerrick asked.

"I think so. It may slow me down a little, but I'll manage."

Lacy took a few more steps forward and stopped to slip on her fins. The water was now up to her waist. A shiver ran through her body as the darkness of the cave seemed to envelope her. She felt Kerrick's hand on her arm.

"Hey. You okay?"

Lacy smiled and wondered if her cheeks were glowing a little. She loved the fact that Kerrick seemed sensitive enough to realize that she may be a little frightened. "I'm fine, though it is a bit spooky. It's pitch black in here. I can't imagine how you felt when you came up in this cave that first time without a light."

"It's a wonder I came up at all."

"I thought you were dead. Well, you know that. I saw the jeep going off the cliff, and you were just gone."

"I was lucky. I was also fortunate in that the tide was lower. If this cave had been full of water, I would have drowned."

"Oh, my God, Kerrick. I've never thought about that before."

"I have a feeling the water won't be getting much deeper here, but I think we can start swimming. We've got to be close to our little drop."

Lacy slipped her mask in place and put the regulator in her mouth. She was surprised by the strength of the current and knew that once they were fully submerged, it would be worse. She was also shocked to discover that they were only about five feet from where the tunnel took a turn down, but she saw that another tunnel kept going straight ahead. *So, it's a hole in the floor.* If she had just taken a few more steps, she would have fallen through the hole under the water. *Now, that would have scared the crap out of me.*

She felt Kerrick's hand on her leg, and another shiver ran through her body. He held his hand in front of his light and motioned that he was going to lead, and she should follow. Lacy let him slip by her and saw that he was already pulling himself along by holding to the rocky floor of the tunnel. He turned a ninety degree turn and went straight down. She followed close behind making sure not to get too close to his fins. She didn't want to risk having him kick off her mask.

Lacy let go of a rock and felt herself being pushed backward. She dragged her hand along the floor of the tunnel until she grabbed hold of a protruding rock. She had lost at least five feet of progress. She noticed that Kerrick's light had stopped up ahead, and she decided he must be at the place where they'd have to drop down another five feet or so to get out of the cave.

She was right. The tunnel leading to the pool behind Miguel's house took a left, and Kerrick held onto a rock that was jutting out. *The tunnel to the pool must drop down a bit before ending at the pool.* They had to wait about five minutes or so before Jon and Meg arrived. Lacy figured carrying that bag through the current had been more difficult than Jon was willing to admit. Jon pointed to Kerrick's light, turned off his flashlight, and led them out of the cave. Kerrick turned his light off, and the eerie darkness squeezed them in its grip.

Chapter Nineteen

Night Visitor

Meg stepped out of the shower and toweled off her wet hair. She stumbled toward the sink as a large yawn slipped from her mouth. *I think I could sleep til noon, but I'm sure Carla's not going to cooperate with that idea.* She looked at her watch lying on the counter top and saw that it was just past 4:30 in the morning.

She slipped into her night gown and crawled into bed beside Jon. She felt his strong arms wrap around her body.

"That was quite an adventure," he whispered in the darkness. "Too bad Carla's going to be up and at 'em in just a couple of hours."

"That's for sure. I still can't believe we found the treasure, but I was sure thinking it was going to be more than just a necklace, a few pieces of gold, and an ancient carving."

"There's probably more to all of that than we know right now," Jon insisted. "I'm just sorry that Jose and Ann missed all of the fun."

"Yeah. Too bad. They won't be back for at least another week. If we talk much longer, I'm going to be talking in my sleep."

Jon chuckled. "You're right, sweetheart. I'm just a little excited."

Meg rolled over and kissed her husband. She snuggled against his shoulder and felt herself drifting away. The next thing she knew, Carla was calling for her.

Meg slipped out of bed in hopes of getting to Carla before she awakened everyone. "Good morning, sweetheart. Did you have a good sleep?"

"Boat? Mama boat?"

"Yes, sweetie, me and daddy went out on the boat last night. I missed you."

"Wuv you, Mama."

Meg felt her body tingle, and a big grin spread across her face. "I love you too, sweety. Let's go downstairs and play. Lacy's here, but she's still asleep. She'll want to play with you when she gets up."

"Wacy?"

Meg pulled Carla out of her bed and tiptoed down the stairs. She sat Carla down on the floor near some toys and started making coffee. She turned at the sound of Carla banging away on the little toy xylophone.

"Sweetheart," Meg said as she hurried over to Carla. "You're going to wake up Daddy. He needs to sleep. Let's go for a walk outside. On second thought, let's read a book until the coffee is ready."

Once Meg's tumbler was full of coffee with a touch of cream, she picked up Carla, and the two of them walked through the mudroom and out the side door. The morning air was fresh, and the smell of rain invaded her senses. Her little girl tried to wiggle free, so Meg sat her down on the beautiful green turf Jon had planted when they first renovated the house. Meg always teased him about trying to turn the front yard into a putting green.

She heard the waves lap against the side of the boats tied up at the docks in the cove, and Meg looked down toward the shrimp boat. She wished that Lacy and Kerrick didn't have to return it to Matt. It bothered her that Miguel was on the loose and was after Lacy again. She knew Lacy should stay with them at the compound, but Lacy would probably not want to hang around.

"Mama! Bird. Mama!"

Meg turned to see that Carla had toddled over to the edge of the yard and was heading off into the bushes. "Sweetheart. Don't go in the bushes. Wait, sweety."

"Bird."

Meg raced over to Carla, who had already made it about five feet into the small trees that lined the edge of their clearing. Once her little girl was safely in her arms, she looked up to see two beautiful Lory Parrots in the tree about ten feet further into the brush. Their little rainbow-colored bodies glistened in the morning sun.

"I see the birds, sweety. They're beautiful. Let's see if we can get a little closer."

Being careful not to make any sudden moves or make any sounds, Meg moved stealthily toward the parrots. The two birds seemed totally oblivious that a woman and her little girl were just beneath them.

Carla reached her little chubby hand toward the birds. "Tank u, God."

The two parrots took off into the air at the sound of Carla's voice. "Oh, well, sweetheart. They were beautiful, and yes, thank you, God for the birds."

Meg started to turn around, but she saw something out of the corner of her eye that caught her attention. Walking a little further into the trees, she dodged a palmetto bush and squatted in the sand, balancing Carla on her leg. It was a cigarette butt. "Now, where do you suppose that came from?" Her eyes scanned the sand around the tree, and she saw what looked like footprints leading off toward the road. Because the sand was soft under the trees, she could have been mistaken about the footprints, but the cigarette butt had nothing to do with her imagination.

The side door of the house opened, and Meg saw her husband heading for the gym. He wore only gym shorts and tennis shoes, and his broad shoulders and pecs already appeared flexed as if in anticipation of his morning workout. If he was one thing, he was consistent. She wanted to be consistent, but Carla sat on her hip as a little, welcomed appendage. Meg was so thankful for her little girl, but this little treasure caused her life to be far from consistent in any area.

"Hey gorgeous," Meg shouted across the lawn.

Jon stopped in mid stride and looked at his bride. A big grin spread across his face as he began moving toward her. "Don't you mean handsome? Men are handsome, not gorgeous."

Repositioning Carla, Meg stood on her tip toes and placed a kiss on Jon's lips. "You are the exception."

"Hmm. Is there something you want?"

"No. Not really. I'm just admiring my beautiful husband."

"So, now I'm beautiful too? You're starting to make me question my masculinity."

"Sweetheart. If there's one thing you'll never have to question, it's your masculinity. Actually, there is one thing you could do."

"I knew there had to be something. Have you started a new list?"

"No. Just come over here and look at something."

Meg led him through the trees to the cigarette butt. Jon reached over and took Carla off of her hip, and Meg gave a little sigh of relief. Carla was two years old, and she was getting too heavy to carry around.

"What do you notice?" Meg asked.

"Well. I notice my beautiful wife standing in the trees."

Meg grinned. "Anything else, Tarzan?

Jon looked carefully around until his gaze rested on the cigarette butt. "That's interesting. No one around here smokes."

"That's what I thought. Look carefully at the sand around it."

"I see them. Those could certainly be footprints. Someone has been here watching our house."

Meg felt a shiver run up her spine as words were put to the fear she felt growing in her gut. "Do you think it was Miguel?"

"Either him or some flunky he's hired. I'd better call the police."

"And what will they do?"

"Nothing right now, but we should at least go ahead and alert them that we could be having a problem. We know that Miguel is up to something."

Meg looked around as the thought that someone could be watching them at that moment streaked through her mind. "We're going inside. Is your pistol in the closet?"

"Meg, whoever was here is not here any longer."

"I don't care. I want your pistol."

"Mama?"

"It's okay, sweety. Let's go inside and fix breakfast."

"I'll look around a bit before I work out."

"Please do but get your pistol first."

The feeling of being watched was eerie at best. As Meg imagined some creep looking through their windows during the night while they slept, an involuntary shudder twitched her shoulders. *Of course, he couldn't have looked through our bedroom window. We're on the second floor.* The once pleasant morning had turned into a piece of a recurring nightmare. She hurried toward the back door and stepped into the house.

"Aunt Meg?"

Meg gasped at the sound of Lacy's voice. "Lacy. I'm sorry. You scared me."

"What's wrong? You look like you've seen a ghost."

"I wish it were a ghost. I'd feel more comfortable."

"What's going on?"

"Miguel has been watching the house. Well, it may not be Miguel himself, but I just found a cigarette butt out on the ground. No one around here smokes."

"Maybe Diego just started smoking."

Waves of fear filled Meg's mind. She suddenly remembered Philippe ogling and touching her when he and Luis grabbed her years ago aboard the *New Beginnings*. She couldn't let anything happen to Carla or to Lacy.

"You know Diego doesn't smoke. Miguel has been watching our house, which means he's here on Exuma. We can't just sit here and wait on him to attack us."

"Okay. Let's attack him. I'm really not kidding. Let's take the game to his court."

Meg sat Carla down on the floor in the den. "Only problem is that we don't know where his court is located."

"I'm sure Jon will come up with something. In the mean-time, I'm dying to look at our treasure."

Meg thought about the bag of treasure Jon hauled from the boat last night. They had all looked at the items carefully on the boat, but she wanted to see everything again herself. "Me, too. Let's get breakfast going, and then we can look at it again together. It's all a little odd to me."

Forty-five minutes later, all four of them sat down together at the table just as Judy walked into the kitchen from the wing of the house that contained her little apartment. "Looks like I'm just in time for breakfast."

"Join us, Judy," Jon said as he got up and pulled the extra chair out from the table.

"I can't tell if you're all smiling or frowning," Judy announced. "Does that mean you found the treasure?"

Meg laughed. "Oh, we found it all right. We just discovered something else that's a little disconcerting."

"Let me guess. It has something to do with Miguel."

Jon returned to his place. "It seems that someone's been watching our house, that is unless you've started smoking recently."

"Not on your life." Judy grimaced as she reached for the pitcher of orange juice.

"Pway, Mama."

"You're right, sweety. Go ahead and pray for us."

Carla bowed her little curly head and started jabbering. Meg opened one eye in time to see Kerrick grinning at Lacy, before Carla abruptly stopped.

"Amen," Meg offered.

Kerrick grinned as he grabbed the bowl of eggs beside his plate. "I didn't understand a thing she said."

"She wasn't talking to you," Lacy said as she took the bowl from his hand. "Ladies first."

Over breakfast, they related the night's experiences to Judy. Jon mentioned that evidently Miguel must have checked on them last night at the compound, and because the lights were on at the house, he probably thought they were all at home. Meg could tell that Judy wanted to suggest that they stop playing around with danger, but she kept her mouth shut. Meg was beginning to think the same thing.

Meg cleared her throat. "I've been thinking about our problem. I suggest we all just leave the island."

"And go where?" Jon asked.

"Mexico!" Lacy nearly shouted. "Let's go to Mexico. We know that the clues in the treasure have to point to Mexico. We don't have to actually hunt for treasure. We could just get a feel for the place and maybe visit some of the ancient sites."

"You've got a point," Jon agreed. "Meg's been wanting a vacation."

"And we have to take the shrimp boat back to Matt," Lacy continued. "We could all leave on the shrimp boat during the night, and Miguel, or whoever is watching us, would never know."

"Of course," Jon suggested, "we'd have to walk around and make sure the property is clear of anyone and then leave."

"What about school?" Meg protested.

Lacy got up and started clearing the table. "School doesn't start for over a week. That's plenty of time." Lacy stopped before she got to the sink with a stack of dishes. "Uh, well, there is one little problem."

"What's that?" Jon asked.

"I don't have any money for a plane ticket, or for anything else for that matter."

Jon laughed. "I'll take it out of your cut of the treasure. When we find the treasure, that is."

"Speaking of treasure," Judy said, "I've got to see what you brought up last night."

Chapter Twenty

Vacation Plans

Miguel put on some coffee and tried to scratch a spot in the middle of his back. He felt horrible. His days of sitting in the bushes watching people were done. Andrew's way was far better. He pulled a cigarette out of the pack that lay on the counter and lit it. *I've got to quit this stupid habit. It's costing me a fortune.*

He sat down in his chair to wait on the coffee and laid his head back in the recliner. The next thing he knew, someone was shaking him.

"What are you doing, boss? You trying to burn the house down?"

Miguel opened his eyes and smoke filled the room. Andrew stood beside his chair with a partially burned towel in his hand.

"You must have fallen asleep with the cigarette in your hand. It's a good thing I woke up when I did, or we'd have had cops all over us."

Miguel jumped up and opened the windows and doors. *There's another reason to quit smoking the stupid things.* He turned on every fan in the house and examined the carpet. A blackened spot about four feet across pointed to how dumb it was to fall asleep with a lit cigarette in his hand. He knew better than that.

He jerked the coffee pot off the hotplate and poured a cup. "Hey, Andrew. I've been thinking. I want you to go into the

Davenports' house as soon as possible and put in those cameras."

"Sure thing, boss. I'll do it tonight."

"Just don't get caught. You'll need to wait until everyone's asleep."

"I'll go over around 2:00, unless you know whether or not they go to sleep early."

"I have no idea. Two o'clock sounds fine. If that yard man sees you, just kill him. Don't use a gun, though."

"Boss, I didn't sign up to kill anyone. I've never done that before."

"It's about time you prove your worth to me. I'm not saying you'll have to tonight, but you just need to be ready."

"I've got to get my hands on some cameras," Andrew said.

"I'll make a couple of calls."

Thirty minutes later, Miguel walked into Andrew's room where the younger man sat looking at his computer screen. Finding the cameras had not been a big deal, but Miguel was not too happy about having to go to Nassau to pick them up. "I'll be back before night fall tonight. You just be ready to go at two a.m."

****

Jon left the table and climbed the stairs to the master suite. He turned the knob to the combination of the hidden safe in the closet of his bathroom and pulled out the bag he had placed there just a few hours earlier. The excitement of the adventure flooded his mind as he felt the weight of the treasure. He knew that most of the weight was the stone, but the carving was sure to reveal some helpful information. He just hoped Cindy would know where to go for help on getting an interpretation.

"I see Lacy was right," Judy said as Jon rejoined the group.

"I usually am," Lacy claimed.

Kerrick choked on his coffee. "That's probably debatable."

Ignoring the banter, Meg lay a quilt down on the table top and opened the waterproof bag. "Did you hear anything back from Cindy, honey?"

"No. I sent the pictures just a few hours ago, so I don't expect we'll hear anything for a while."

"True," Meg admitted. She pulled out the necklace and the gold.

"This is all you got?" Judy seemed shocked as she reached for one of the chunks of gold. "I figured treasure meant mounds of diamonds and emeralds."

"There's also a piece of animal skin that had some writing on it, but I'm afraid the years have made it illegible," Jon sighed. "I took a picture of it and sent it to my friend in Spain, along with a picture of the carving on this stone. I've also sealed the skin up in a bag to hopefully preserve it." He pulled the stone out of the bag and laid it carefully on the table. "We figure the writing on the skin gave a lot of detail, but this carving must point to something as well."

Everyone gathered around the end of the table and stared down at the stone. Judy fingered the necklace.

"The necklace is beautiful," Judy acknowledged. "It must be priceless."

"I'm sure," Jon agreed. "I'm curious about this carving. It looks like the body of a man with the head of some kind of creature, maybe a bird."

"Oh, my God," Lacy exclaimed. "Is he doing what I think he's doing?"

Jon saw that Lacy's face had turned a little red. He couldn't ever remember seeing her embarrassed. "Let's just say he's cutting himself."

"That's insane," Lacy insisted.

Jon nodded. "They would probably have said devoted and not insane. I once read that some of the ancient cultures would cut themselves as an act of worship to their gods."

"Isn't it amazing what people did to appease a god that didn't even exist," Meg said.

"I think I hear a sermon coming," Lacy teased.

"It does make you stop and think," Meg admitted. "It seems like every ancient culture created deities to explain the source of their existence. It's just sad that their version of God was so far off from the truth. If this civilization practiced self-emasculation, they probably practiced human sacrifice too."

"Okay," Lacy quipped. "When I have to start bringing out the dictionary to know what you're talking about, and I don't think I want to know what you're talking about, it's time to change the subject."

"Look at how all of the people on this carving have bird like heads," Judy pointed out.

Jon pulled out his phone and took several more pictures of the stone. "I think I'll send Cindy a few more pictures. Hopefully she'll call back today. For now, we need to get ready for our vacation."

Kerrick leaned back in his chair. "Why don't I do a little walk about to see if I can find anyone watching us. If we're going to start loading luggage and stuff in the shrimp boat, we sure don't want anyone to see us do it."

"Good point," Jon agreed. "That would give away our surprise departure. Let's plan to get everything aboard the boat by dinner, and we'll leave as soon as it's dark."

"Uncle Jon, what are you going to do about our little stash?" Lacy asked as she pointed toward the gold and necklace on the table.

"I'll take the gold and the necklace to my safety deposit box at the bank. I'll have to hide the carving somewhere here at the house where no one would think to look."

Thirty minutes later, Jon stood in the doorway to Carla's room watching Meg put their little girl down for her nap. His heart warmed as she tended their little miracle. Meg was the most wonderful mother. He loved the little dimple that showed when she grinned down at Carla. She reached up and slipped her hair behind her ear as Jon eased up behind her.

She jumped as Jon wrapped his arms around her waist. "You are the most beautiful woman on the planet," he whispered in her ear. "Will you marry me?"

Meg turned around with a beautiful smile spanning her face. "I already have, but I'd marry you a thousand more times." Jon pulled Meg into his arms and gazed down into her angelic face. "I treasure you." Their lips met, and Jon once again felt as if his heart would explode with the joy of having Meg as his bride.

She gently bit the lobe of his ear and whispered, "We need to pack, but I've got some other ideas on my mind, too." He felt Meg's hand slip into his, and she led him out the door.

Nearly forty-five minutes later, Jon bounded down the stairs with an armful of dirty clothes. He dumped them into the washing machine and added some soap powder. He looked out the window toward the bay and saw Lacy push Kerrick off the dock into the water. He smiled as he thought of the love that was growing between them and wondered how long it would be before they started talking about marriage. When she reached down to help him out of the water, he pulled her in. *She had to see that coming.*

He sensed Meg's presence before he felt her body press against his back. "It looks pretty serious," Meg suggested. "What do you think?"

"I was just standing here wondering how long it was going to take for Kerrick to work up the nerve to ask her to marry him."

"Oh, Jon. They're too young. Lacy doesn't need to even think about marriage yet."

Jon looked back down to the water and saw that Kerrick held Lacy in his arms. He looked away as their lips met. "I don't know. They look pretty connected to me."

Meg laughed after she looked back toward the water. "Cute. Kissing in the bay is one thing but spending your lives together in marriage is another. Lacy has some growing up to do. I wish she could graduate first."

"If things keep moving along, I think her last name will be different when she gets her diploma." Before Jon turned around, he saw Lacy push Kerrick down under the water. "Do you care to make a wager?"

Meg laughed. "You know that you usually lose our bets."

"I know. That's why I want to bet. I need to improve my record, and this one's a sure thing."

Meg hummed slightly. "Let me think about something I really want, and I'll let you know."

As Jon walked back toward the kitchen counter, Judy came toward him lugging a bag. "Hey, Judy. I'll get that for you. You should have called me."

"Thank you, Jon. I have another one in the room that's a little bigger. I think I'm all packed, assuming that we're only staying for a week or so."

"Kerrick and Lacy have to be back for school, so I think a week will do it," Meg offered. "I'm also more than ready to spend some time at home. The truth is that I really hate to go away again. I was ready to stay put for a while."

"I'm sorry, honey," Jon said as he grabbed Judy's bag. "I'm planning to get the police out here to catch whoever is spying on us. Hopefully, they'll arrest Miguel while we're gone, and then we can come home for a while. I kind of hate waiting to get back to our treasure hunt in Eleuthera. I feel like we were onto something over there this summer."

"Maybe," Meg agreed, "though that will give us something to work toward with our boys next summer."

"I've thought about that. I'd say that we should at least do a little work on it between now and then so we'll have some better ideas on where to start next summer. It sure would be nice to be able to bring up something of value with the boys."

"We found the arquebus," Meg reminded him.

"I know. That is valuable, but you know what I mean. I'm carrying this stuff down to the boat."

"Okay. As soon as we can get these clothes clean, I'll get our stuff packed."

Jon went back into Judy's apartment and grabbed the other piece of luggage. While struggling to get both suitcases down the stairs, he wondered how in the world anyone would need this much stuff for just one week.

"Hey, Jon," Kerrick called up as he ran up the stairs toward him. Water dripped from his clothes and puddled around his feet. "Do you need some help?"

"Sure. I think Judy has hidden her boyfriend in this luggage."

"I didn't know Judy had a boyfriend," Lacy laughed as she joined them on the steps.

"I didn't either," Jon admitted. "Let's meet him when we get to the boat."

After Kerrick climbed aboard the shrimp boat, Jon handed him Judy's luggage. Kerrick hauled the bags below to the small cabin beneath the wheelhouse while Lacy and Jon leaned against the rail of the boat.

"Uncle Jon, I know that we said we'll go to Mexico, but where exactly in Mexico do you think we should go?"

"Good question. I intend to get online and figure that out this afternoon."

"Well, while you and Meg were..., uh taking a nap?" Lacy paused and grinned at Jon. "While you were taking a nap, I got on Google to check some things out. I found an ancient city in Mexico that I think would be a great place to start doing some research for our lost city."

"Where is it?"

"It's called El Tajin. It's located north of a city called Veracruz, which is right on the coast. Did you know that the reef system off of Veracruz is the largest reef system in the Gulf of Mexico?"

"No. I've never heard that before."

"I was thinking we could visit some of the ancient ruins of the Mesoamerican people and do a little diving while we're at it.

There's at least three different areas of ruins in that region, so we can get a feel for what a city like this might look like."

"I like it. Does Veracruz have a good airport?"

"Yep. Sure does. They have an international airport. I checked and saw we'll have to fly to Mexico City and then over to Veracruz. There's nothing direct to Veracruz from Miami."

"Sounds like a plan. Let's get back to the house and get our tickets. We can try to fly out of Miami tomorrow."

Lacy pulled wet hair out of her eyes. "I'll have to go back by the house in Miami to get more clothes."

Chapter Twenty-one

Back to the Mainland

Lacy's eyes popped open when she felt the boat bump against something. She was a bit fuzzy as she tried to orient her mind. She rolled over on her back and went right off the narrow bench onto the floor of the boat with a bang.

"Lacy?" Kerrick's voice resonated in the dimness. "You okay?"

What in the world is going on? Lacy felt Kerrick's hand on her arm, and everything came racing back into her mind. She remembered going down with Kerrick into the hold of the shrimp boat during the night to get some sleep. Fortunately, the cushioned benches were too narrow for two bodies to lay side-by-side, or she and Kerrick would have surely slept together. *Oh, my God. I have dried up drool on my face, and my breath smells like something died in my mouth last night.*

Before she could turn her head away, Kerrick's mouth was on hers, and she suddenly didn't care about her bad breath any more. Lacy's heart beat wildly in her chest as Kerrick pulled her close. She ran her hands through his hair and kissed him like a starved woman eating dinner for the first time in a week. She felt his hands sliding down her back, and suddenly, he rolled her over to the side and stood up. The door to the room opened as light flooded the hold. Lacy sat up rubbing her eyes and leaned against the bench.

"Good morning, guys," Meg cooed. "Hope I'm not disturbing you."

"No," Kerrick replied. "Lacy rolled off the bench."

Lacy squinted in the morning light coming through the door. "My mind was a little messed up. I guess I thought I was at home in my bed."

"I checked in on you last night," Meg admitted. "I didn't realize you were sleeping together, I mean, in the same room."

"We didn't really mean to," Lacy confessed, "but there wasn't anywhere else to sleep. Judy and Carla had the only bed in the place."

"I figured that out, too," Meg said. "I appreciate you two sleeping on different benches."

Lacy laughed. "It's not like we had much choice. The benches are a little narrow."

"Well, we're back at Matt's dock in Hollywood. Jon thinks we should go by the house at South Beach and shower before getting some breakfast and going to the airport. We don't fly out until 2:45 this afternoon."

Lacy ran her hand through her hair and thought about how horrible she must look. "That sounds like a great plan because I have to pack anyway. Kerrick's truck is here. We can all squeeze in it."

Meg left the small storage room, and Kerrick turned toward Lacy. "We almost got caught, Sleeping Beauty."

Lacy unconsciously wiped the side of her face. "We weren't doing anything wrong."

"Not wrong, but you've got to admit that would have been a little awkward. Come on. We've got to get the luggage to the truck."

Kerrick pulled Lacy up, and she straightened her hair. She looked down at her feet. "I must look like a fright."

"You look like a beautiful fright," Kerrick said before he pulled her into another kiss. "Maybe we can pick up where we left off later."

We'd better not pick up where we left off.

The sun nearly blinded Lacy as she followed Kerrick up the few steps to the top deck of the boat. It was not quite 7:00 in the morning, but the day was definitely started. She thought about poor Jon having to pilot the boat all night, and Meg must have stayed awake to keep him company. They had to be wiped out.

By 8:00, they were headed toward the house in South Beach. Lacy looked in the back seat and saw that Meg had her head on Jon's shoulder.

"Maybe you guys should take a nap at the house before we go get something to eat," Lacy suggested. "We can watch Carla. I imagine you could get two or three hours of sleep."

"I think we're going to have to," Meg admitted. "I don't believe I'll make it through the day without a little sleep."

"Sweep, Mama," Carla piped up from her car seat.

"Kerrick and I will whip up a late breakfast," Lacy offered. "Y'all can sleep til 11:00. Then, we can eat and leave by noon."

Jon yawned loudly. "That's perfect. Our trip today is going to be exhausting. We won't fly into Veracruz until tonight about 10:00."

"I'm so excited," Lacy said. "I've never been to Mexico. I spent all of those years studying Spanish, and now I get to actually try to speak it in a Spanish-speaking country. This is really going to be fun."

Kerrick guided the truck into the driveway of the house, and Lacy noticed the bicep in his right arm flex as he turned the steering wheel. Heat filled her core as she once again thought about how she had started her day. Feeling her cheeks glowing, she turned to look out of the window. *I've got to quit looking at him. Now that's a stupid thought. I can't quit looking at him.*

Jon grabbed his and Meg's carry-on out of the back of the truck, and Lacy watched Kerrick pull out his backpack. She began going through her mind about the clothes she had in her bag in the bed of the truck. Most of them were dirty.

Kerrick put his hand on Lacy's bag. "Do you want me to grab your bag?"

"I can get it. I've got to do some serious packing, if we're going to be gone for a week."

"Okay. Why don't you go look in the kitchen to see if we need to go to the store to get anything for breakfast. I'll carry your bags up to the room."

"I can get it," Lacy insisted again. "I'm not a weakling."

"I know you can get it," Kerrick argued. "Don't be so bull-headed. Just let me help you."

Lacy's mind went back to the conversation she had with Meg just two nights ago about Jon serving her. "Sure. Uh, I mean, I'd like that." She placed her hand on Kerrick's cheek and stared into his beautiful, blue eyes. She felt like she could fall into those eyes and spend the rest of her life in his gaze.

She turned and headed toward the house as she heard her suitcase scraping across the bed of the truck. The kitchen looked just like it did when they left—clean and bare. She opened the refrigerator and saw what was left of a gallon of milk and a near empty carton that only contained two eggs. They would have to go to the store. Since shopping was on the agenda, she decided that she would fix a breakfast they would long remember. She might even try to make her grandma's chocolate biscuits. Of course, she didn't have the recipe for chocolate biscuits, so that might not be a good idea. Eggs, bacon, biscuits, and grits might have to be enough. She stopped as she thought about grits. *I'm sure Kerrick will make fun of me if I say we're having grits. I think we'll do hash browns instead.*

"What's the verdict?"

Lacy jumped at the sound of Kerrick's voice. "Oh, well, we're going to have to go to the store. Why don't we take a shower first and then…I don't mean…"

Kerrick laughed. "I know what you mean. You sure are jumpy this morning."

"I'm not jumpy." *I'm just madly in love with you, and I can't even think right with you in the room.* "I'm going upstairs. I'll be ready in about thirty minutes."

"There's one more reason I love you," Kerrick grinned. "You don't spend hours getting ready in the morning."

Lacy walked into her bedroom and closed the door. She saw that Kerrick had placed her luggage on the bed, and the skull necklace was no longer on her dresser. *Kerrick must have taken the necklace. He is so thoughtful.* She pulled her dirty clothes out of the bag she normally used as a carry-on and threw them into the hamper in the bathroom. She pulled off her shirt and added it to the heap and decided that her shorts weren't dirty enough to need to be washed. Of course, she had slept in them all night, but how dirty could they be?

When she looked into the mirror, she gasped. Her hair looked like a rat's nest, and her eyes made her look like a raccoon. *I look so terrible. I cannot believe that I've looked like this all morning, and Kerrick saw me. He must love me for sure.* The mushy feeling returned to her stomach, and she felt as if a family of butterflies had just hatched from their cocoons deep down in her belly.

She stepped under the hot water of the shower, and her body shivered with delight as the water ran down her back. *Thank you, God, for showers. I don't suppose God really made showers.* Thinking about God making showers struck Lacy as an odd thought. Hanging around Meg was really starting to affect her. That wasn't a bad thing. Hanging around Kerrick was doing a number on her too. *He's the one. I know he's the one. I want to marry him. I want to have his babies. Woah. Now wait just a minute, Lacy. What are you thinking. I don't want to have babies.* Carla's little chubby face popped into her mind. *Well, maybe one baby.*

Once out of the shower and dressed, Lacy began filling up a larger suitcase with clothes. She included a couple of days of clean clothes in her carry-on bag, along with some other personal items.

She began calculating how long she had actually known Kerrick. She met him near the end of May, which means she had not even known him for four months yet. How could she be thinking about marriage? *I'm obviously mentally deranged. If we got married now, I'd end up divorced just like my mother. I can't imagine ever wanting to divorce Kerrick, and Meg says that the "D" word shouldn't even be in my vocabulary. Slow down, Lacy. Kerrick hasn't even mentioned marriage, though he has told me that he loves me. Loving me and marrying me are two different things. He's probably loved other girls.*

Lacy sat stiffly down on the bed as that thought filled her mind. She didn't know anything about girls from his past. It had just been a couple of months ago that she saw the picture of his sister on his phone and thought it was a picture of his girlfriend.

Should she ask him about other girls in his life? Surely, it was okay for her to know about any other girls he may have dated. Had he really loved anyone else before? She jumped up and quickly finished packing.

As Lacy entered the living room, Carla toddled to her and wrapped little arms around her leg. "Wacy." She began jabbering something, and Lacy wished Meg was around to interpret. She bent down and picked up her little cousin. She rubbed noses with her and kissed her slobbery cheek. She was so beautiful and was the sweetest child Lacy knew. *I'll take one just like you.*

"You ready to go?" Kerrick asked from the recliner, a newspaper lying in his lap.

"Sure. Judy, do you want us to get anything for you? We're going to the store."

"Are you sure you don't want me to fix breakfast?" Judy asked.

"Judy, I insist. Your vacation just started."

"In that case, I'd love to have some of that French Vanilla cappuccino mix."

Lacy smiled. "I had no idea you liked that stuff. I like it too. Anything else?"

"Nope. I think that will do it."

Lacy grabbed her small purse. "Alrighty. We'll be right back."

Chapter Twenty-two

Ready for an Adventure

Andrew pulled Miguel's Toyota to the side of the road and wondered if anyone would notice the vacated car. As his headlights lit up the tracks in the sand in front of him, it looked like he was not the only one who had used the little pull-off as a parking place. He got out of the car and eased the door closed.

Adjusting the bag that hung by a strap on his shoulder, he slipped through about three-hundred feet of brush and small trees and saw the Davenports' plush home looming before him. Though everyone seemed to be asleep, he noted a few lights were on around the place. *That's sure going to help.*

He paused at the edge of the tree line to make sure he didn't see any signs of movement before hurrying across the yard to the side of the house. He looked up and saw the side window of what must be the master suite. *I imagine that's probably the bathroom window, and Jon and Meg are sleeping in the room just beside it.* He pulled out a lock pick from his pocket and was inside the mudroom in no time.

Miguel had already told him that there was no alarm service on this part of the island, but just because there wasn't a service didn't mean that the Davenports hadn't put in a stand-alone alarm. He looked for a control box just in case and bingo! It was just inside the kitchen. With a few squirts of a liquid compound, the keys to the code lit up under infrared light - 1, 2, 8, 0. *Meg's birthday. That was simple.* He was glad that he had done his home-work, or he wouldn't have recognized the numbers. He punched in 0,2,1,8 and the red light turned green. He'd have to remember to turn it back on when he left.

The small night light plugged into a kitchen outlet provided just enough illumination to keep him from bumping into chairs and the table. He looked around the kitchen and saw that it was perfectly clean. He had already imagined Meg to be a neat freak, and evidently, he was right. Now, he just had to find the perfect place to hide a camera. His eyes scanned the kitchen and the den, and he noted several air vents in the wall near the ceiling. He'd rather use the one in the den, but the ceiling was too high. This one in the kitchen would have to work.

Andrew picked up a chair without a sound and sat it on the floor beneath the vent. This spot would give a perfect view of the dining area. He wondered what he might get to see that happens in the Davenport house in the kitchen. He quickly placed the small camera inside the duct and screwed the vent cover back into place. He used his lock pick to situate the camera so as to avoid as much of the grill as possible.

Setting the chair back in place at the table, he looked toward the stairs that led to the master bedroom. He eased over to the bottom step and looked up to the second-floor landing. His eyes followed the path that would take him to where the Davenports slept. Meg was beautiful and had to be ten years younger than her husband. *Maybe late twenties? That's how rich guys are. They ditch their first wife and marry some beautiful younger woman.* An article Andrew read came to mind. He had done a lot of research on Jon Davenport, and he recalled that his first wife had died. *Wasn't that convenient? He didn't have to divorce her to marry a beautiful, young woman.*

The house creaked, and Andrew's mind snapped back to the job at hand. *I've got to get out of here. If Jon catches me, I'm dead.*

* * * * * * *

Meg rolled to her side and looked at the clock beside the bed. She could have slept another five minutes. Reaching over to the bedside table, she curled her fingers around the clock to stop the alarm before it sounded. That act alone exhausted her. She was always amazed that her body somehow knew how to wake up just before her alarm sounded. *How in the world am I going to make it all the way to Veracruz without collapsing? Maybe I can sleep on the plane.*

Jon moved a little, but he was still comatose. Meg propped up on her right elbow and stared over at her husband. Dark hair and ripped body. He complained to her about his abs getting soft, but she couldn't tell it. The best thing, however, was that his heart was as big as the world. Nothing hard about that part of his body. She reached her hand out and placed it on his chest. Up and down, up and down. It was amazing that he could sleep right on without even being disturbed by her hand. She slowly traced the definition of his chest and up the curve of his neck. *Come on, you beautiful man. Wake up.*

Pressing her body against his, she placed her lips on Jon's neck and tenderly kissed him. She planted a row of kisses down to his chest. *He is really out.* Passion began stirring in her body as she willed him to open his eyes. In one quick motion, Jon grabbed Meg and rolled her on her back, as she screamed out in alarm before she giggled. He covered her mouth with his, which caused her heart to beat even more wildly.

"I thought," Meg panted, "I thought you were asleep."

"How can a guy sleep when a beautiful goddess is kissing him? Especially when she's his goddess."

Just as Meg pulled Jon's head back down toward hers, an abrupt knock sounded at the door.

"Wake up, sleepy heads," Lacy's cheery voice sounded on the other side of the door. "Brunch will be served in twenty minutes."

"We're not asleep," Jon whispered in Meg's ear, "but we were quite rudely interrupted."

"Thanks, Lacy," Meg called out. "We'll be out shortly."

Jon kissed Meg's neck again and placed his lips against her ear. "Not too shortly."

Twenty minutes later, Jon stepped out of the shower. "I've never known you to take a three-minute shower."

"You're pretty fast too, Romeo."

"Food is a great motivator."

Meg pulled the brush through her hair. "You know, I wish Jose and Ann were going with us to Mexico. What do you think about calling them and suggesting they fly down to Veracruz at the end of the week? They could at least spend the last few days with us before we all have to come home."

"That's not a bad idea," Jon agreed. "I'll call them after we eat."

When Jon and Meg walked hand-in-hand out of the master suite, the smell of sausage and home-made biscuits greeted them. Meg's stomach growled a few times.

"I think you're a little late," Lacy beamed up from an open oven door, "but I'm glad you are. Biscuits just finished."

"I'm impressed, Lacy," Jon admitted. "Are you sure Judy didn't help you?"

"I sure didn't," Judy offered, "but it's not like I didn't try."

"She's got beautiful eyes, a knock-out body, an awesome personality, *and* she can cook!" Kerrick announced. "I think I'll keep her."

Lacy grinned. "Go ahead. Flattery will get you everywhere. It's amazing what a little YouTube can do for you."

Judy pulled out a chair and sat down. "I hate to be a party pooper, but we're going to have to hurry. It's almost noon, and I took the liberty of calling a limo service to pick us up and take us to the airport. The driver will be here by 12:30. Even at that, we're going to be a little late getting to the airport."

"We'll be fine," Jon assured her.

They devoured an outstanding meal, and Meg couldn't help but be proud of Lacy. She had no idea how her niece had learned to cook like that. She was sure that Liz hadn't taken the time to teach her anything except how to hate people.

Once they were done, Kerrick led the group in setting a record on cleaning up breakfast dishes while Jon hurried back into their bedroom to gather up a few items. He began hauling suitcases out the door, and a black limo pulled into the driveway just as he sat the last piece of luggage on the porch. With the house secured and everyone in the vehicle, the limo pulled out of the driveway and headed to the airport.

Meg watched the south Florida neighborhood whiz past her window as she processed the craziness of the last few days. She marveled that she and Jon could be relaxing in their home on Great Exuma one minute and then zipping to the airport in Miami to fly out to Veracruz, Mexico the next. She used to live such a predictable and boring life. Now, it seemed like every day was filled with a new, sudden twist or turn that no one could have imagined. Would this mad dash to Mexico show them anything about their search for the treasure? She didn't really think so, but it would be kind of fun. After this trip, however, the "fun" had to stop for a while. She just wanted to be in her home doing normal things.

Thinking through the mad rush to get everything packed, Meg suddenly felt like something had been overlooked. She turned to Jon. "You sure we've got everything? Luggage and passports?"

"Check, check," Jon said. "At least we have our passports. You guys have yours, too. Right?"

"I'm good," Lacy and Kerrick said in unison before laughing.

Reaching over Carla's car seat, Judy tightened the seatbelt that held the little girl in. "How long is this flight?"

"Three hours and forty minutes to Mexico City," Lacy answered. "Then we'll have about three hours before we fly out to Veracruz."

"Let's hope Carla will make it," Meg groaned. "Did she sleep any this morning?"

"No," Judy confessed. "I tried to get her to go down, but she wouldn't sleep."

"Oh, well," Meg sighed. "Maybe she'll sleep on the plane."

"Pwane, Mama."

"Yes, sweetheart. We're going to fly on a plane to Mexico."

"Okay, Miss Tour Guide." Jon winked at Lacy. "What's on our agenda for tomorrow?"

"Well," Lacy put on her official tour guide voice. "Tomorrow morning, we'll awake at 07:30 and eat breakfast at La Parroquia de Veracruz. It's one of the premier restaurants in the old town. Then, I thought we should check out a dive shop. You told us to pack our snorkeling gear, so maybe we can make a dive on Wednesday. I found a website for a place called Dorado Buceo. I think they provide scuba gear for each dive."

"Sounds like a great plan," Meg beamed and then turned to Jon, "though we're going to be wiped out in the morning. Are you sure we should start up at 7:30? Of course, we'll be up, thanks to Carla, but you guys could sleep in."

"We only have seven days," Lacy reminded her, "though Kerrick should have planned to be back in Miami on Monday."

"It's just a meeting," Kerrick said. "I won't even be missed."

"If you say so," Lacy sighed. "Well, we only have seven days, so we don't have time to sleep in tomorrow. Besides, we should be able to be in bed tonight before midnight. Getting up at 7:30 shouldn't be a problem."

"Where are we staying?" Meg wondered. "I am so clueless about this trip."

"I found a beautiful villa on the north side of Veracruz through Homeaway," Jon said, "but unfortunately, it won't be available until Wednesday night. Creating a website to rent out vacation homes sure was a great idea. They must be making a killing."

Meg winked at Jon. "I'm surprised you didn't come up with that idea, honey."

"Yeah." Jon grinned. "Too bad. Lacy and I looked over some of the hotels in the historic district of Veracruz and thought it would be fun to spend a couple of nights near the tourist section of town. We found the perfect place that will meet our needs for a couple of nights."

"Are you sure it's safe?" Meg asked.

"We'll all be together," Lacy insisted. "What could happen?"

Chapter Twenty-three

Herocia Veracruz

Andrew staggered into the kitchen to get a cup of coffee. Of course, Miguel had left the pot empty. He pulled out a filter, and soon the machine was spitting and spewing out the midnight black liquid shot in the arm. He rummaged around in the cabinets for something to eat before pulling out the last piece of cold pizza from a box lying on the stove. He checked his watch for the third time and saw the minute hand tick past the six. *8:30. They're got to be up by now.*

He went back to his room, where he had already booted up his computer. After a few clicks of his mouse, he stared at the empty table in the Davenport's dining area. "Okay, Meg baby. Where are you?"

"You talking to me?" Miguel said from the doorway.

Andrew nearly fell out of his chair as he spilled coffee on his lap. "AAAWWW! Look what you did! You burned me."

"I didn't do anything. You're the one who's got a problem. What's going on?"

"Nothing, yet. I guess they're not up yet." Andrew wiped the hot coffee from his leg with a dirty tee-shirt that was balled up on the floor beside his chair.

"Seems kind of strange, don't you think? I mean, it will be 9:00 pretty soon. How long you been watching?"

"About an hour or so," Andrew lied.

"You idiot. You should have been in here by 6:00. They could have already left for the day. I don't want you to move from that screen until they come back. Got it?"

"Sure thing. You're the boss."

"I've got some business to take care of, and I won't be back 'til later this afternoon. You have sound on that camera too, right?"

"Yep. I can hear everything. I'll make notes and let you know if anything important happens."

****

The red and white taxi raced through streets that were still quite busy even though it was getting close to midnight. Of course, to Lacy's body clock, it was almost 1:00 in the morning. Her body screamed for a bed, but she was giddy with excitement to be in a foreign country. The thought crossed her mind as to exactly which room would be hers. She and Jon had reserved two rooms at the Meson del Mar hotel. The picture online had shown a full-size bed on the main floor and then a loft above it. She placed her hand on Kerrick's knee and lay her head on his shoulder. *Kerrick and I will take the bed in the loft of Judy's room. On second thought, we'll just get our own room.* She smiled as she imagined Meg's expression if she really told her aunt that they were going to room together.

The lead taxi carrying Jon, Meg, and Carla slowed down. Lacy peered through the front windshield and saw the road was blocked. *They must be doing some road construction.* The driver took a right turn, and Lacy couldn't believe her eyes. *That's the biggest McDonalds I've ever seen. Is that a parking garage under the restaurant? Oh, my God. KFC. You'd think I was back in Georgia.* A chill ran down her spine as she felt Kerrick's hand on her leg. *If Judy weren't in the front seat, I'd… You'd do what, Lacy. Don't be stupid. If Judy weren't in the front seat, you'd sit right here with your head on Kerrick's shoulder and your hand on his knee.* She sighed with contentment.

The taxi slowed as Lacy noticed a dead end ahead. The driver pointed to a large white building in front of them. "Museo Naval." *Museo. I think that's museum.*

"What did he say?" Kerrick whispered.

"That building is the navy museum," Lacy answered as she saw a huge anchor on display behind a fence.

The taxi turned left and came to a stop beside another white building with multiple small balconies on the second floor. She recognized the building from the picture she had seen on the Internet. "This is it. Meson del Mar."

"Si, senorita. Este es Meson del Mar."

"I assume that means this is Meson del Mar?" Kerrick raised his right eyebrow in such a cute expression that Lacy wanted to eat him up.

"Yeah. Let's go to our room. I'm about to drop."

"So, we're rooming together?" Kerrick chuckled.

"Oh, yeah. I didn't tell you? Meg thought that would be the best arrangement."

"Right. If you believe that, I'll sell you some Atlanta Falcons tickets to the Super Bowl."

"Hey. The Falcons might make it to the Super Bowl. If not this year, maybe next year."

"I wouldn't hold my breath. Let's go."

Lacy leaned up to the driver and asked in Spanish how much the ride cost them. She reached in her pocket and pulled out some of the pesos Jon had given her before they left the airport. "Gracias. Buenas noches."

"Good night," the driver said with a long u sound on his accented version of the word good.

Kerrick got out of the cab and opened the door for Judy. He grabbed two of the suitcases from the driver and slipped his backpack over his shoulders. Lacy pulled out the handle of her large bag and carried her small one. She looked up at Kerrick. His face seemed to glow in the light from the corner street lamp. "Do you suppose that driver could understand English?"

Judy laughed at Lacy's question. "Whether he could or not, I could. No, you two are not rooming together."

Lacy laughed. "I was just kidding, Miss Judy."

"I know, sweetheart. You are so precious."

Precious? I don't think anyone has ever called me precious.

Jon tapped on the door to the hotel with his knuckle and turned to the little group huddled on the sidewalk. "Lacy, you can sleep in the loft of our room. If they have another room available, Kerrick, I'll get one for you."

"He can sleep in my room, Jon," Judy remarked. "I don't mind. That is, I don't care as long as he doesn't mind hearing an old woman snore and as long as there's a loft with an extra bed.."

"We'll see, Judy. Meg or Lacy, do you know how to ask if they have an extra room? Once I get past good morning and thank you, my Spanish is a bit limited."

Lacy thought back to her Spanish classes. She thought the Spanish word for room would be *habitacion*, but she wasn't sure how to say *extra*. She decided to just say *otro* for *another*. "I think I've got it."

A young man that couldn't have been any older than Kerrick opened the door. He smiled and greeted the group. "Dr. Davenport? Bienvenido."

"Thank you," Jon said. "Gracias."

Kerrick leaned over to Lacy. "I'm getting it. *Bienvenido* means *welcome*."

"You got it," Lacy grinned. She turned to the young man and told him they had reservations for two rooms, and she asked if he might have another room available. Then it occurred to her that he must have known they had reservations because he called Jon by his name.

The guy smiled at Lacy and seemed to appreciate her attempt at Spanish. She also didn't miss the once over he gave her when he thought her eyes were taking in the lobby and the large stair-case going up to the second floor. He probably didn't see too many blondes.

"Si, senorita."

Everyone stepped through the lobby to the small desk where the attendant fished out three room keys. He grabbed Lacy's lug-gage and told the others to leave their luggage in the lobby. He would bring it up shortly. After Lacy translated most of his words, Jon thanked him and grabbed two of the larger bags. Kerrick did the same and then followed the desk clerk up the stairs.

Lacy loved her room. Just inside the door, a metal, spiral staircase went up to the loft, where she found the most amazing bed. It was the cutest hotel room, and she had never seen a room where you had to put the plastic key card in a little slot on the wall in order to turn on the lights. Of course, she hadn't really seen that many hotel rooms. She spiraled back down the stairs and went to Kerrick's room. His door was cracked open. She sneaked in behind him as he looked out the curtains to the street. When she goosed him, he didn't even jump. Instead, he turned around, grabbed her, and wrapped his arms around her.

"Come on, Kerrick. You know I scared you."

"Actually, I heard you. So, Jon must have changed his mind? You going to be my roommate?"

"In your dreams."

"Don't encourage me," Kerrick said before he placed his lips on hers. "Oh, well. Too late."

"What do you mean?" Lacy looked up into his blue eyes.

"There's no keeping you out of my dreams." He kissed her again.

"We better get some sleep. I'm exhausted."

"Yeah. It's nearly two o'clock in the morning back in Florida. I'll see you in the morning, beautiful."

Lacy blushed as she turned to leave the room. She stopped at the door and turned to look at Kerrick one more time. They just stared at one another for a moment before she slipped into the hallway.

Once in her bed, Lacy imagined curling up in Kerrick's arms and staring into his beautiful, deep blue eyes. What would it be like to be married to him? She couldn't imagine how wonderful it would be to fall asleep in his arms every night for the rest of her life. She closed her eyes and could almost feel his hot breath on her face as she snuggled up in his warmth.

Breakfast at La Parroquia the next morning was an experience. Lacy was grateful that Meg could help her translate the menu for the rest of the group, and then the waiter offered an English version. All of the waiters wore brown pants and white serving shirts that made Lacy think they all looked like chefs.

The large restaurant was packed with people. It was an open and airy place with little square tables that sat four people. Large, glass windows lined three of the sides. Thankfully, the waiter saw the group of Americans coming and pulled two tables together. He even brought a highchair for Carla.

While Jon and Kerrick were content with cafe Americano, Lacy wanted to try the lechero, and Meg followed her lead. Lacy loved how the guy with the pot of milk came by and poured it into the cup. He started the flow near the rim of the cup and then pulled the tin pot of hot milk up into the air about two to three feet. The show was quite impressive. *If I tried to do that, milk would be all over the place.* While Kerrick loaded up with hot cakes, Lacy was content with a bowl of fruit and yogurt. She looked around and decided that she really liked this place.

While Lacy drank her lechero, she scanned a tourist brochure. "There's an old fort out in the bay. Maybe after checking in with the dive shop, we can take a tour of the place. It's called Fort San Juan de Ulua."

"There were some serious battles around here back in the 16th and 17th centuries," Jon told them.

Lacy imagined Jon standing before his history class at Emory University lecturing years ago. She decided being in his class would have been fun.

"I believe Francis Drake got cornered here around this fort," Jon continued, "but he escaped."

"It's going to be real handy having you around," Kerrick said. "It will be like a history lesson on location."

"I don't know," Jon admitted. "Mexican history has never been my focus. I suggest we finish up here and head over to the dive shop. It would be nice to get to the store before they go out for a dive today. Judy, do you want to go with us or would you rather go back to the room?"

"I believe I'd like to go. You never know. I might want to get into scuba diving."

Lacy laughed and loved that Judy was so much fun to be around. Lacy's life had been full of stuffy, self-absorbed people. It was refreshing to be around the part of her family that actually knew how to be happy *and* selfless. *Maybe the two issues are connected.*

Chapter Twenty-four

Dive Plans

The taxi ride to Dorado Buceo was short, and Meg was impressed with the cleanliness of the city. Although the driver had to take them around a few blocks, they eventually ended up on a busy street that ran beside the ocean. The scenery was beautiful, and people scurried down the sidewalks seeming to head somewhere important.

Rolling the window down, Meg inhaled the fresh smells of the sea. She noted a lot of families walking together down the sidewalk and was surprised to see an outdoor gym on the walkway next to the beach. A number of people were exercising individually, and a young, healthy looking guy led a class of mostly young women. The group made Meg think about the Zumba class she took years earlier at the gym near her home.

The thought of trying to speak to the people at the dive shop crossed her mind. Her Spanish was okay for getting around, but she didn't think she could carry on a lengthy conversation about scuba diving. She figured they'd at least have pictures with explanations of the different dive locations this shop serviced. Years ago, she had been quite good with Spanish, but she seemed to have forgotten a lot of words.

Dorado Buceo was located on the main street, just across from the bay. As they climbed out of the two taxis, Meg looked out into the ocean and saw a couple of dive boats anchored about ten yards from the beach. Several workers wearing yellow tee-shirts were waist deep in the water and dragging scuba tanks behind them. "Looks like we're just in time," Meg observed as she pointed toward the water. "They're loading tanks on those dive boats."

To the left of the dive boats, Meg noted a couple of large navy ships and a tug boat docked at a wharf. She saw several larger private boats at a marina just a little way down the beach to the right. A small beach area stretched out straight across from the store that served as the launching area for the day's dive trip.

Jon held the front door open as everyone filed into the scuba shop. Meg took in the dive shop covered with gear and displays on the walls. An "L" shaped glass counter filled with knives and gauges lined the right side and back of the small shop. She smiled at two people sitting at a round table on the left side of the store that was just out of the way of the main entrance.

"Good morning," a young man behind the counter said in perfect English.

"Good morning," Jon replied. "I'm so glad you speak English."

"Welcome to Dorado Buceo. My name is Chucho. I'm the dive master here."

"It's a pleasure to meet you, Chucho. My name is Jon Davenport, and this is my family, except for Kerrick. He's a good friend. We wanted to find out some information about scuba diving."

"Yes, sir. Do you all dive?"

"I don't," Judy offered. "I'm just along for the ride. I'll take care of the baby while everyone else goes out tomorrow."

Jon stepped toward the counter and shook Chucho's hand. "We just flew in last night and thought about possibly diving tomorrow."

"We've got room on tomorrow's boat," Chucho said. "The water is great."

"Any idea what you'll be diving?" Jon asked.

"I'm not sure," Chucho confessed. "It depends upon several factors."

Meg saw a girl who looked to be around twenty-years-old walk out from the back carrying a bag with some gear in it.

Chucho looked toward the young lady. "Iris, do you have any idea what we're diving tomorrow?"

"Manuel said something about diving the C-50." She turned to Jon and eyed Kerrick. "Good morning. My name is Iris. If we dive the C-50, you'll really like it. We'll probably also dive the Cathedrals for a second dive."

Meg stepped toward Iris. "I'm so glad you speak English. I was trying to figure out how in the world I was going to be able to communicate with the little bit of Spanish I know. My name is Meg Davenport, and this is my husband, Jon. This is Lacy, my niece, Kerrick, our friend, and Judy, who may as well be our mother."

"It is so good to meet all of you," Iris said. Carla ran up and wrapped her chubby arms around Meg's leg. Iris knelt down and waved at Carla. "And who is this?"

"That's Carla," Kerrick said "She's actually the boss."

Meg noticed Lacy watching Kerrick. Iris was a pretty girl, and Meg wondered if Lacy might be feeling a little threatened. If so, she was going to have to learn to deal with that emotion. Meg made a mental note to talk with Lacy about the importance of trust.

"Good morning, Carla," Iris said. "You're beautiful."

Carla stood transfixed staring at Iris before Meg picked her up. "What's the C-50?" Meg asked.

"It's called the C-50 Riva Palacios," Chucho replied as he turned the pages of a book lying on the counter, obviously looking for a picture. "It's a ship from the navy that was decommissioned and sank about 15 years ago. It's a great dive."

"How deep is it?" Jon asked.

"The ship sits at about 28-29 meters, but the deck lies in about 21 meters of water. You don't usually deal with much of a current, and visibility is pretty good. We also provide any gear you might need along with lunch while we're out."

Jon turned and looked at everyone before returning his gaze to Chucho. "Sounds really good. What time will we need to be back tomorrow?"

"Just come around 9:00," Iris suggested. "We try to leave the bay by 9:30. You'll need to sign some paperwork and then go across the street to the water. You'll find the boat anchored out in the bay."

"Yeah," Meg said. "I saw it on our way into the store. What time would we be back?"

"Probably by 3:00 or so," Chucho said as Iris picked up the two tanks and headed out the door. "As far as we know, everyone that is going out tomorrow is experienced. We have a video crew that will join us. They're filming an ecological documentary on the health of the reef, but they shouldn't get in your way. They'll probably be diving at the reef while you dive the wreck. It will be a great dive."

"Sounds like it will be a lot of fun," Jon said. "I suppose we'll see you in the morning. We have a little girl that's going to get pretty sleepy in just a bit, so we better get back to our room. It's a pleasure to meet you, Chucho."

"The pleasure is mine, Mr. Davenport. See you tomorrow."

When Meg climbed out of the taxi back at the hotel, Carla was starting to get a little fussy. *Oh, well. I knew it wouldn't last.* She pulled her little girl out of the car seat, and Jon handed the seat out the door to Kerrick. The door to the hotel stood open, and the group strolled through the lobby, speaking to the lady who sat at the desk before climbing the stairs to the second floor.

Jon stopped at the door to his room and turned to the rest of the group. "Since we want to go to El Tajin on Thursday, why don't I go to the bus terminal and get our tickets. I assume it would be best to ride the bus."

"I want to go with you," Lacy announced.

"I'll go, too, if that's okay," Kerrick added.

Jon nodded. "Sure. Give me ten or fifteen minutes, and I'll meet you in the lobby. Judy, I assume you want to stay here?"

"Yes. I'll rest for a while so I can be ready for our adventure to the fort this afternoon."

Jon stuck the key card into the door, turned the knob, and slipped the card in the socket inside the room that controlled the lights. Meg noticed that the air conditioner seemed to work regardless of whether the room key was in the slot by the door or not. She was grateful because it was already quite hot outside. The room was perfect.

"Okay, missy," Meg said as she lay Carla down on the bed. "Let's put on a diaper for your nap."

Once the diaper was in place, Meg lay down beside her. Jon pulled a couple of chairs in place for extra protection in case Carla rolled over in her sleep, which reminded Meg that she needed to ask for a crib. She noticed that housekeeping had cleaned up the sleeping pad on the floor they had created the previous night. That idea had not worked very well anyway.

"Jon, would you ask the lady at the desk if she has a crib we can use for tonight? We'll be fine for now, but I don't want to have another night like last night."

"True. I love my little girl, but I'd rather not have her wanting to climb into our bed again in the middle of the night. I just don't know how to ask for a crib in Spanish."

"Oh, yeah. I didn't think about that. See if Lacy knows how to ask for one."

"So, are you going to sleep too?"

"I'll probably get up in a minute and read. I'll see you when y'all get back."

Meg turned her face up to her husband, and he kissed her gently. "I love you, sweetheart. Please be careful."

* * * * * * *

Jon headed down the stairs and saw Lacy and Kerrick looking through a rack of brochures located to the right of the bottom step. Lacy had a small backpack over her shoulder, and Jon assumed she was carrying it in place of a purse. When they saw him coming, they followed him to the door.

Lacy slipped a brochure into her pocket. "Jon, I asked the lady at the desk to call a taxi for us. She is really nice."

"Oh, that reminds me," Jon said. "Meg wanted me to ask you to see if you can get them to bring a crib up for tonight. Will you ask her when we get back?"

"I'll go back inside and ask her now. Our taxi's not here yet anyway."

Lacy went back inside while Jon and Kerrick leaned against the outside wall of the hotel. Jon noticed that if he had been driving the previous night, they never would have found this hotel. There wasn't much signage anywhere. To his left, he saw the naval museum down on the next block. He wondered if it would be worth going in to check it out. A red and white taxi pulled up just as Lacy returned to the sidewalk.

"She said she would have a crib for us later this afternoon."

"Great," Jon said. "Thanks, Lacy. Not sure what I'd do without you."

"Oh, you'd think of something." Lacy grinned before climbing in the back seat.

When Jon sat down in the front seat, he looked at the driver and wondered how to say "bus station" in Spanish.

Lacy leaned forward. "Estación de autobuses, por favor."

Jon looked to the backseat. "Por favor is please?"

Lacy nodded. "Yep. We're going to all be speaking Spanish before we go home."

"I doubt I'll master it," Jon sighed, "but I hope to pick up a few words. What's in your backpack?"

"I brought a bottle of water and my iPad. Not sure why I brought my tablet. I guess it's an old habit. I'm always afraid I'm going to be stuck somewhere and have to wait without anything to do."

"You could talk to us," Jon said with a grin. "Kerrick and I are actually pretty good company."

Jon saw a sheepish grin appear momentarily on Lacy's face. He watched the buildings pass as the taxi moved slowly through the streets of Veracruz. After traveling west for a few blocks, Jon inhaled the smell of meat on a grill before he saw the sign of the restaurant: El Asador.

Jon whistled. "Oh, my. That smells heavenly."

"You're not kidding," Kerrick agreed. "I say let's come back here for dinner."

"Deal," Jon said. "Remind me to ask the lady at the hotel if this is a good restaurant. Better yet, Lacy, why don't you ask her?"

"Glad to, Jon."

The taxi driver turned left onto a divided road that was quite busy with traffic. After several blocks, he took a left into the bus station and came to a stop. He turned to Lacy to tell her how much they owed.

"Fifty pesos, Jon."

Jon dug into his pocket and pulled out a fifty. "Lacy, can you ask him to come back to get us in about twenty or thirty minutes?"

Lacy rattled off a few words, hesitated, and said a few more. The man nodded, so evidently Lacy communicated adequately. Jon, Lacy, and Kerrick walked into the busy bus terminal and headed to a counter. People were rushing everywhere, and one little girl stood in the middle of the crowd crying. *What a mad house.*

Chapter Twenty-five

Thief

Jon stopped abruptly in the middle of the bus terminal, and Lacy ran into him. "Sorry, Jon. I didn't see your brake lights."

"My fault, Lacy. I'm just not sure which counter. It seems like different companies have their own counters, but I doubt they all go to El Tajin."

"I'll see if I can figure it out," Lacy offered.

She walked down the row of counters studying the signs. *El Tajin or...What is the name of that city? Oh, yeah. Papantla.* As her eyes scanned every available sign, she tried to remember a Spanish word for something like the word counter or...*what? I don't know how to communicate this in Spanish. I could just ask someone for a ticket to El Tajin.* At the end of the row of counters, she spotted a group of people standing in front of a picture of an ancient pyramid. *That's it.*

Hurrying back to the other end of the terminal, Lacy saw Jon and Kerrick. "Found it. Wouldn't you know it's all the way at the other end."

They worked their way through the crowd, causing Lacy to imagine that this must be what it's like to be a running back on a football team. She bumped against someone, and her backpack nearly fell off her shoulder. She thought about slipping it onto both shoulders, but that would have to wait. She felt more like a sardine squished in a can than a human being. The crowd parted slightly allowing them to wiggle up to the counter. Lacy sat her pack on the floor in front of her feet and was suddenly surprised to hear someone call her name. She turned and saw Iris walking up to the counter.

"Hey Iris," Lacy called back. She couldn't believe the girl remembered her name. "How did you manage to get away from the dive shop?"

"I only had to work until noon today. I'm scheduled to go out on the boat tomorrow, so I got to leave early today. I just had to pick up a bus ticket for Tuxtepec. I have to go there this weekend to meet my brother."

"Tuxtepec?" Jon raised an eyebrow.

"It's south of here about two hours or so," Iris replied. "Do you need any help?"

"Oh, yes," Lacy conceded. "I've been trying to remember Spanish words since I walked in this place, and I'm not doing a very good job. We just want to get bus tickets to El Tajin for Thursday morning."

"Oh, I love El Tajin. It's an amazing place. If you're going to dive tomorrow, you should get Chucho to tell you about it. He and his father seem to know a lot about Mexican history. If you want to ride a bus up there, I suggest you use ADO. Their desk is on the other side of the terminal. One of you will need to show them your passport."

"I don't have mine," Jon said. "I didn't think I'd need it."

"I have mine," Lacy said as she turned around to get her backpack. She looked on the floor by the counter, and her stomach twisted in a knot. "Oh, no! It's gone! My backpack is gone! It was right here. I mean, it was between me and the counter."

Lacy looked around the crowded terminal hoping to see someone rushing off with her bag. She clinched her fists and imagined grabbing the thief and punching his lights out. If she could get her hands on him, she'd wring his neck. Nothing. She didn't see a single person with her pack. She saw Jon and Kerrick searching the terminal with their eyes as well.

"Let's split up," Iris suggested. "What does your backpack look like?"

"It's black, but it has a yellow string on the front."

"Okay," Jon said trying to take control of the situation. "Let's meet back here in ten minutes."

Lacy hurried through the crowd toward the main entrance. Her eyes scanned everyone, and she once grabbed a black backpack on someone's shoulder only to discover it wasn't hers. "Lo siento, I'm so sorry." She thought the young boy was going to punch her. *Relax kid. I just thought you had my pack.*

She stopped at the door and turned around to face the crowded terminal. This was hopeless. Lacy felt tears starting to well up in her eyes. Wouldn't you know they must have chosen to come at the busiest time of the day. She couldn't believe how stupid she had been. Someone probably watched her walk into the terminal and then followed her to the back counter. *I can't believe I set my backpack down. My iPad! That's the only gift from my father that meant anything to me. How can I get another passport? I won't be able to go home.*

A young man hurried toward the restroom holding onto a black backpack. Lacy sprinted across the terminal and called to Kerrick. In her fury, she ran into the men's room without thinking, and Kerrick was close behind her. She stopped as a line of surprised men turned their heads and stared at her.

"Uh, you may want to let me handle this," Kerrick whispered.

Lacy's face burned with embarrassment as she hurried out of the bathroom. She stood by the entrance waiting for Kerrick to return with her pack. She felt as if she'd been sucker punched when he came out empty-handed.

"It wasn't it. I saw the pack on the floor under the door of one of the stalls. To start with, there was no yellow string. I waited for him to come out, and then I saw that it didn't say *L.L. Bean* on the front. Yours was from *L.L. Bean* wasn't it?"

"Yes." Lacy dropped her head into her hands and wanted to cry.

"You were pretty brave to run into the men's restroom. I wish I'd had a picture of your face when all those guys turned and looked at you."

"That's not funny, Kerrick. I just lost my iPad and my passport."

"I'm sorry, Lacy. You're right. I just think you're amazing not to let a men's room stop you."

"Right. I'll try to remember what defines amazing in your book." She grinned as she thought back to the looks on the guys' faces. She wasn't sure who was more shocked. "I've always wondered what a men's restroom looks like. Now I know."

"You've never seen a men's restroom?"

"Nope. Why would I have ever been in a men's restroom? So, do you spend a lot of time in the women's restroom?"

Kerrick laughed. "I used to help my mom clean the church, so I've been in one or two ladies' rooms in my lifetime."

"Well, that was my first experience like that, I don't think I ever want to see another one. It's a wonder we hadn't all suffocated in there. That place was toxic."

Lacy felt Kerrick's arm wrap around her shoulders as they turned to head back to the counter where they were to meet up with Jon and Iris. Jon was already waiting on them, and Iris walked up just after Lacy and Kerrick leaned against the counter. No one had spotted Lacy's backpack.

"I'm afraid that crime is common at bus terminals," Iris said. "I'm so sorry, Lacy."

"Thanks, Iris. I was stupid to set my pack down. I should know better."

Jon rubbed the stubble on his chin. "Iris, if this is common, then this person who stole Lacy's bag will more than likely be back."

"Probably so," Iris agreed. "He may even be part of a crime ring. There's a lot of that here."

"I guess it's gone for good," Lacy sighed. "What am I going to do about my passport?"

"We'll have to go to the embassy, I guess," Jon said. "Let's go back to the hotel"

"What about our bus tickets?" Kerrick asked.

"I'm thinking about renting a car," Jon answered. "Iris, what's it like driving to El Tajin?"

"It's no problem. The roads are good."

Jon nodded. "All right, then. That's what we'll do. Let's take a cab back to the airport. I saw a National car rental counter. I hope we can get a car large enough for our group. I don't feel like being confined to taxis and busses our whole time here anyway."

Lacy hugged Iris. "Thanks so much for helping us. We'll see you tomorrow."

An hour-and-a-half later, Jon pulled the SUV rental against the curb in front of Meson del Mar. Lacy looked at her watch and thought about how long they'd been gone, and she was starving. Although they had picked up a little something for lunch at the airport before getting the rental car, that chicken burrito was long gone. She began thinking about the steak place they had passed on the way to the bus station and decided that would be the perfect place for dinner.

The thought of some kid looking through her iPad crossed her mind, and she wanted to punch something. The kid couldn't get into her iPad without a password, assuming it was a kid. She closed her eyes and took some deep breaths.

As Lacy got out of the car, Jon leaned toward her. "How about asking the lady inside if I can park on the street."

"Sure."

She walked inside expecting to see the same woman who had been working the desk when they left the hotel, but this time, there was a girl working that had to be around Lacy's age. She wondered if the pretty Mexican spoke English. "¿Habla Inglés?"

"No."

Lacy thought for a moment and then asked her in broken Spanish if Jon could park on the street. The girl said that it was no problem, but then began to explain something about a garage. Evidently, they'd have to move the car to the garage later. *I wish I could really speak Spanish. I'd like to get to know this girl.*

Once she let Jon know he was safe to leave the car on the street for a little bit, Lacy decided she wanted to at least make an attempt to get to know the girl at the desk. Kerrick excused himself and climbed the stairs to his room. After five minutes of struggling with the Spanish language, Lacy learned that the girl's name was Ruth and her family ran the hotel. The lady who worked the desk early in the morning was Ruth's mother, and her brother worked the night shift. Lacy had no idea how to say the word *vacation* in Spanish, so she just told Ruth they were "turistas."

When Lacy asked about El Tajin, Ruth's face lit up. She described the place with reverence, and Lacy understood some of what she said. She kept saying something about ball courts and men on a pole, at least Lacy thought she was saying pole. *Does polo mean pole or is it like the sport?* To hear this girl talk, Lacy figured she went to El Tajin all of the time, but Ruth admitted that she'd only been once about five years earlier. Her family had worked at the hotel for years, so they couldn't travel that far from the city of Veracruz.

By the time Lacy returned to the room, Carla was up from her nap and Jon and Meg were into a deep discussion about something serious. It was apparent she had interrupted a moment.

"Uh, I'm sorry I interrupted you. I'll just go to Kerrick's room."

"You're fine." Meg smiled. "We were just talking about Jon's crazy plan to find your backpack."

"Jon, my pack is long gone. We don't have a prayer of finding it."

"I've been thinking about that," Jon said. "Odds are, your pack was stolen by someone in a theft ring. I think if we go back there tomorrow afternoon after our dive, we could catch the thief."

Lacy doubted that was possible. "You really think so? My iPad is probably already sold to someone else by now."

"It's possible, but wouldn't you like to catch the thief?"

"I sure would, and I want to be the one to break both of his arms," Lacy huffed.

Meg shook her head. "It's just not safe, Jon. You could really get hurt."

"Oh, sweetheart. We'll be fine." Jon winked at Lacy. "How could this guy hurt me when Lacy's going to break both of his arms?"

"You're incorrigible, Jon."

"Maybe, but you're still working on me, so that's always a good sign. Lacy, we'll talk about my plan over dinner."

Lacy's stomach growled as if on cue. "Speaking of dinner, I'm starving. What do you think about going to that steak place we passed on the way to the bus station? I think it was called El Asador? I'll go down and ask Ruth if it's a good place to eat."

"Who's Ruth?" Meg asked.

"She's the girl at the desk, and she is so sweet. She's my age. I hope to get to know her a little better."

"Maybe she could go with us to the restaurant," Meg suggested.

"She works 'til 7:00, but maybe she can go with us to La Parroquia to get dessert later tonight. She told me that they have an amazing cake called Pastel de Tres Leches. Let's go to dinner before I start gnawing on the dresser."

Chapter Twenty-six

Night in the Old Town

The smell of steak over a grill made Lacy's mouth water. A really cute waiter met them at the entrance of El Asador and escorted them to the back of the dining area near a big fan. The room was a little warm without air conditioning, but Lacy figured that most places that catered to local business wouldn't have air conditioning. She was a spoiled American and felt a little embarrassed that things she accepted as normal were considered luxuries in most of the world.

In broken English, the waiter introduced himself as Pedro and welcomed them to El Asador. Lacy noticed him looking mostly at her as he spoke to the group, and she felt a little heat rising up to her cheeks. He gave them each a menu, and Lacy wondered if it had been an accident when he touched her hand.

"Beauty is hard to hide," Kerrick said quietly, but it appeared that everyone at the table heard him.

"He's obviously enthralled with you." Meg agreed. "He probably doesn't see a lot of blonde, fair-skinned girls down here. He's a nice-looking young man."

"Y'all stop it. You know he's not looking at me."

"Go ahead and kid yourself," Kerrick teased, "but in the meantime, I'm going to hold your hand so he'll know he has a little competition."

Lacy cocked her head and looked at Kerrick. "So, you think you have some competition? Hmmm. He does have nice skin tone."

"See what I mean?" Kerrick sighed. "I can't even take you out in public."

Kerrick grabbed Lacy's hand and rubbed his thumb over hers. Electricity shot up her arm, and she couldn't imagine wanting anyone other than Kerrick ever to look at her for the rest of her life.

Lacy decided that even though the steak sounded like a good option, she really wanted a hamburger. When Pedro explained that the hamburger was a boneless steak on a bun and not ground beef, Lacy was sure of her order. She had never had a real steak burger. Everyone else got steak, but Meg ordered a bowl of beans for her little girl. Pedro asked for drink orders and suggested they try the horchata.

"What is that?" Lacy asked.

"It is rice milk. We add cinnamon and sugar. It's very delicious."

"Rice milk doesn't sound very good to me," Lacy admitted, "but I'm game. I think I'd still like a diet coke along with the horchata."

Pedro brought a pitcher to the table filled with a white liquid. It looked like watered-down milk, but when Lacy took a sip, it was quite tasty. She decided that even if the steak was horrible, coming back for the horchata would be worth it.

When Pedro sat her burger on the table in front of her, Lacy's eyes about bugged out of her head. "How am I supposed to even fit this into my mouth?"

Jon grinned. "I don't think you'll have any problem."

When Lacy acted as if she was going to throw her cloth napkin at her uncle, Kerrick squeezed her hand and leaned toward her. "I personally like your mouth just the way it is," he whispered.

The heat started at her lower back and rode all the way up to her face. She was confident that her cheeks glowed. For just a second, she thought she might just forgo the burger and place her big mouth on Kerrick's luscious lips that needed kissing. *On second thought, I'm starving. His lips will just have to wait.*

By the time Lacy had polished off her steak burger and french fries, she felt like she needed to unbutton her shorts to make a little more room. She leaned back in her chair trying to decide if she could fit another glassful of horchata in her bloated belly. A quiet belch slipped out. *That was the best hamburger I've ever eaten. I think I'll just order the meat next time without the bread.*

She looked over at Kerrick's plate, and it looked as if he had licked it clean. He had used the tortillas to sop up every drop of juice. Looking at the table beside theirs, she wondered about the purple drink in the pitcher.

Pedro walked up to see if they wanted anything else. "What's that purple drink?" Lacy nodded her head toward the other table. She looked around the restaurant and noticed several people had ordered it. "It must be good."

"Jamaica." Pedro grinned showing a row of pearly white teeth. "Though you pronounce it with an 'h', you spell it like the country. It is a typical drink in Mexico. Would you like to try some?"

Lacy's hand went instantly to her belly. The thought of adding one more drop of anything to her stuffed stomach was more than she could stand. "I'll have to try it next time. I'm really full."

Jon cleared his throat. "We'll take our check, please."

"Si senor."

It took another ten minutes, but Jon paid the bill, and Lacy felt like she waddled to the door. She considered going for a run, and then the thought of that cake at La Parroquia went through her mind. *If I eat anything else tonight, I'll puke. Oh, no. I've already asked Ruth to go with us.*

"What do you think about walking around Veracruz for a bit," Lacy suggested. "I've got to walk off this dinner, or I'll never fit a single bite of that cake in my stomach."

"We could wait until tomorrow night for dessert," Meg offered.

"True," Lacy agreed, "except we've already invited Ruth to go with us. She gave me her number, and I'm supposed to call her when we know that we're ready to go."

Meg sighed "Oh, dear. I don't need to eat anything else tonight. That's for sure. And I'm going to have to get Carla down for the night before too long."

"Lacy and I could go by ourselves with Ruth," Kerrick proposed. He elbowed Jon. "You know how it is with young people. We can eat as late as we want to and stay up half the night. You old folks will have to go on to bed."

"True." Jon's voice quivered like he was a little, old man. "I'll need to take my Geritol and hit the sack."

"Are you sure it's safe for you three to be out at night like this?" Meg wondered aloud.

"For starters, Aunt Meg, it's not late. It's only 7:00. By the time we walk around a bit, we could eat at La Parroquia at 9:00 and still be back at the hotel by 10:00. We'll be fine."

"It seems like I heard you say something like that on Eleuthera right before you went off and got yourself kidnapped."

Lacy felt a shiver run down her spine. "That's hitting below the belt, Meg. I've already admitted that I was stupid. I learned from my mistakes. Besides, Kerrick and Ruth will be with me the whole time. I promise not to go off by myself."

Jon dropped Kerrick and Lacy off at the square not too far from the famous La Parroquia. As they slid out of the back seat, Meg reminded Lacy for the 100th time to be safe. Kerrick's hand slipped into Lacy's as the SUV pulled away from the curb, and the crowd engulfed them as they moved toward the music. A lot of people gathered in front of a stage that was beautifully decorated with flowers, and dancers, dressed in typical costumes, performed for the crowd. Several boys crowded in behind them, and Lacy heard them talking about her. She didn't understand everything they said, but she understood *chica de Norte America*. She also understood another word that was totally unbecoming in any language. Unfortunately, some boys in her tenth grade Spanish class taught her that one.

Lacy felt a hand touch her inappropriately, and she knew it was no mistake. She whirled around to see a Mexican boy that had to be about eighteen-years-old grinning at her. She balled up her fist and hit the guy so hard that his nose instantly burst into a bloody mess. The crowd screamed, and Kerrick pulled Lacy away toward an alley.

"What did you do?" Kerrick shouted over the mayhem.

"I hit him. The creep couldn't keep his hands to himself. He'll think twice before touching a girl again."

They ran through the alley to the next block. Slowing to a walk, Lacy and Kerrick passed a line of stands where artisans sold crafts, and then they got enveloped in a crowd of people dancing in a courtyard that had a bar on each end. By the time they made it back to Meson del Mar, they were alone, and Lacy's knuckles were aching with every fast beat of her heart. When Ruth saw Lacy's hand, she hurried back upstairs to her apartment and retrieved a bag filled with ice. Though Ruth suggested they wait for another night to go for dessert, Lacy insisted on going ahead with their plans. She just kept the bag of ice on her swelling hand.

Lacy winced in pain as she reached for her chair at La Parroquia. She sat down, gingerly placed her hand on the table, and lay the ice pack over her knuckles. "Maybe it's best that we not tell Meg and Jon about our little incident at the Zocalo."

Kerrick raised his right eyebrow "Zocalo?"

"That's what you call the square of a town in Mexico," Lacy replied. She looked around the restaurant, and her mind went back to the brochure she had looked at earlier that morning. "We never made it to the fort today."

"Fort?"

"Yeah. Fort San Juan de Ulua. It's out in the harbor."

Kerrick nodded his head. "We'll just have to check it out later."

The hour-and-a-half at La Parroquia flew by, and Lacy loved spending time with Ruth. Between Google Translate and Lacy's Spanish, they talked up a storm. Ruth was so sweet. She and her family had moved to Veracruz several years earlier from a little village about two hours south of the city. It seemed that she was so happy. She was attending school hoping to one day teach at the university.

When Lacy slipped into the hotel room at 10:45, she was hoping that Jon and Meg would be asleep. No such luck.

"I started to come looking for you," Jon whispered as he got up from a chair by the bed.

Lacy looked at Carla sound asleep in her little crib. "I'm so sorry. We didn't realize how late it was getting. I didn't even think about calling you. We had such a good time with Ruth. She is one of the sweetest girls. I think we could easily become good friends."

"I saw you leave with Ruth and figured you'd be okay, but we do need to keep each other informed. We're in a strange place, and anything can happen."

"I know, Uncle Jon. I'm so sorry. I won't let it happen again."

Meg got up from the bed and hugged Lacy. "We're glad you had a good time. I wish I could speak Spanish well enough so I could get to know Ruth and her family."

"I'm pretty tired," Lacy whispered. "I'll see you guys in the morning. We're eating at 7:00. Right?"

"Right," Meg answered. "We'll go back to La Parroquia, unless you've got another place you'd rather go."

"No. That sounds fine with me. You've got to try Pastel de Tres Leches. It is wonderful."

Meg grinned. "Probably not for breakfast, so I guess that means we'll have to go back tomorrow night. You know we'll be moving tomorrow to the house we've rented."

"Oh, yeah," Lacy winked. "So, you two can have a little privacy. Good night."

Chapter Twenty-seven

New Friends

Andrew sat in front of his computer screen knowing that the next thirty minutes were not going to be pleasant. His head pounded, and he felt like his eyes were going to pop out of his head. He had been in this same position all day long, with the exception of a few bathroom breaks and a quick run to The Burger Shop down the street. As the day progressed, he waited for Meg to show up on his computer screen, but the house was empty. How had they managed to slip away? *The house must have been empty when I went in last night to put in the cameras. They're gone.*

He smelled Miguel before he saw him. The man reeked with alcohol, which meant he would be even angrier. "So, my fine computer geek." The slurred words rolled out of his mouth along with a little drool. "What have we learned today?"

"Well, Miguel. We've learned that they're gone."

The beer bottle nearly hit Andrew's head as Miguel's cursing filled the room. "What do you mean they're gone?"

"I mean that they're not in the house. They must have left before we got the camera installed."

"And why didn't you go check to make sure they were in the house while you were there?"

"Come on, Miguel. You know I couldn't go into the bedroom with them asleep."

"Why not?" Miguel bellowed. "You know you want Meg Davenport. You could have gone in there and…"

"You're drunk and stupid."

Miguel moved toward Andrew with such speed that Andrew didn't see the blow coming. His head jerked back so hard with the force from Miguel's fist that he fell back onto the desk. His body hit the computer monitor and sent it flying onto the floor. The screen shattered into a million pieces.

"Don't you ever call me stupid," Miguel growled. "I'll kill you. Do you hear me?"

Andrew stood to his feet with his hand on his jaw. He was afraid that his jaw was broken. "I'm out of here. This is not what I came down here for. You can find them yourself."

Miguel pulled a snub-nose pistol from the small of his back and pointed it at Andrew. "If you try to leave now, you're a dead man."

Andrew froze as he stared into the end of the pistol. He wondered if he could somehow move before Miguel could pull the trigger, but there was no way he could avoid being shot. "Uh, I didn't mean that I was leaving now."

After staring at Andrew for a good two minutes, Miguel returned the pistol to the place he normally carried it. "If you're not leaving, then find the Davenports. I want you to hack into their credit card account. Find out where they're spending money."

"I can't do that, Miguel. Hacking into a bank is against the law." Andrew thought about hacking into Lacy's email account and discovering a notice about a purchase she had made with her debit card in Miami. That was not the same as hacking into a bank's computer system.

Miguel doubled over with laughter. "Like you haven't already broken the law? You think going into someone's house at night and placing a camera in the HVAC vent is not breaking the law?"

"Hacking into a bank's secure site is a major deal. I'll go to jail for the rest of my life." Andrew watched Miguel's right hand moving back toward where he kept his pistol. "As long as I can use a computer with an IP address that can't be traced to me, I'll do it. Being that my monitor is busted, I'm going to need something else anyway."

"Okay. Fine. You can use my laptop."

Miguel stumbled to the back bedroom running into the wall several times before he got to the bedroom door. He disappeared for just a few moments and returned with an old HP laptop in his hand. "Here you go genius. See what you can find out."

Andrew opened up the laptop and began typing on the keys. Miguel sat down on the couch and laid the pistol on the cushion beside him. He closed his eyes and began breathing deeply. Andrew figured he was asleep. Almost forty-five minutes later, he leaned back in his seat. "Got it. They're in Veracruz, Mexico. Hey, Miguel. Did you hear me? They're in Veracruz, Mexico"

Miguel cursed loudly and sat up on the couch. "I heard you. Veracruz, Mexico?"

"That's right. They've used their card a few times. It seems that they're staying at a villa that was offered on Homeaway." Andrew pointed to the screen.

"Veracruz, Mexico? Why would they be in Veracruz?" He stood unsteadily from the couch and turned toward the living room window.

Andrew saw Miguel tuck the pistol inside his pants at the small of his back. He pictured himself grabbing the gun and shooting the thug. It would be one less detestable person in the world. "Maybe they went on vacation." He took a silent step toward Miguel.

"Why would they be on vacation? It has something to do with the medallion. I'm sure of it."

Andrew moved closer toward Miguel and lunged for the pistol. Miguel stepped to the side and clobbered Andrew in the head. The little table by the window broke as Andrew's body crashed into it. He lay on the floor looking up at Miguel, and he could feel blood flowing from the side of his mouth. He must have busted a tooth.

"Why did you do that, Miguel? I wasn't doing anything."

Miguel pulled the pistol from his belt and pointed it at Andrew. "Right. I saw what you were doing. You wanted my pistol."

"What are you doing, Miguel? We're on the same side. You need me. I want to help you find the Davenp…"

The shot rang out in the small confinements of the room, and Andrew felt a pain in his chest unlike anything he'd ever experienced. Blood spurted from his body as he struggled to maintain consciousness. Miguel raised the pistol again, pointed it at Andrews head, and pulled the trigger.

****

Lacy struggled into her wetsuit. She had at first decided not to wear the neoprene suit, but it appeared that she was the only one planning to dive without it. Jon certainly knew a lot more about diving than she did, and he was suited up, so she figured it wasn't worth risking being cold on their first dive.

Getting to the dive shop had been crazy. They were late getting to breakfast, and the restaurant was crowded. Meg had been pretty stressed out, but when Chucho welcomed them to Dorado Buceo, it was as if all of the stress drained away.

Leaving the bay, the dive boat bounced along, and the dive shop was now only a spot off in the distance. The boat was a little crowded with divers. In addition to her group, there was a camera crew aboard who was shooting a documentary about the reef. Lacy now remembered Chucho mentioning the film when they met the previous day, but she had forgotten about it. She looked across the boat to the beautiful girl who seemed to be in charge of the filming. Lacy couldn't quit staring at her. She had a captivating, exotic beauty, and she was so young to be in charge of shooting a film. She looked to be around her age, but Lacy knew she must be older.

The thought occurred to Lacy that the girl could be a famous actress. She certainly had the looks. When she smiled, her whole face lit up, and Lacy could imagine her picture on the front of some magazine. When she stepped out of her sweats, Lacy saw that she wore a black bikini that accentuated her body. Lacy looked over at Kerrick to see if he was looking at the beautiful Mexican girl, but he was looking out to sea. *That's interesting. She ought to be on the cover of some hot magazine, and he doesn't even seem to know she exists.*

The girl looked toward Lacy. "Good morning. Is this your first time to dive here?"

"Oh. You speak English. Uh, and yes. This is my first time to Veracruz."

"My parents had me attend a bilingual school, so I learned English when I was a little girl. My name is Andrea Luna." With an outstretched hand, she took two steps to cross the boat toward Lacy.

"I'm Lacy Henderson. It's good to meet you."

Andrea nodded toward Kerrick. "Is he your husband?"

Lacy laughed. "No. He's just my...my boyfriend. So, what are you guys doing? I mean, with the cameras and all?"

"I own a production company, and we shoot documentaries for people. We've been commissioned by a conservation organization to create a documentary on the health of the coral reef. We're worried about pollution affecting the coral and the other sea life, so we're going to do a campaign to save the reefs."

"You own the company?"

"Yes. I started it up just out of college."

"How old are you? Or...maybe that's rude."

Andrea laughed. "No. You're not rude. I'm asked that all the time. I'm twenty-four. I graduated from the university two years ago with a degree in historical anthropology and decided to get into the film business. I worked with a company during college, so I had a good bit of experience. Before I graduated, I teamed up with a couple of guys I knew from school, and we started Espora Producciones. We make documentary films, do video mapping projects, offer filmmaking workshops, and several other things. We've done work in Nicaragua, Panama, Argentina, the United States, and other places."

"That's amazing. So, do you do underwater films much?"

Andrea's lips parted into a mischievous grin. "Actually, this is our first. We had to get certified to scuba dive just so we could shoot this film. I'm a little nervous about this dive, but I guess being nervous is a good thing."

"Yes. My uncle says you should always be nervous a little. You don't ever want to take anything for granted when it comes to scuba diving. That's him in the front of the boat. He owns a salvage company in the Bahamas."

"A salvage company?" Andrea's eyebrow raised. "You mean like sunken ships and stuff?"

"Well, the fact is that Jon and Meg are treasure hunters. They found a sunken Spanish ship a few years ago and pulled up a bunch of gold and silver. They now use their money to help inner-city boys get away from drugs and gangs."

"That is so good," Andrea said. "I think I saw something on TV a couple of years ago about a big find somewhere in the Bahamas. It seems like it was buried treasure though, so that wouldn't have been him."

"It probably was them. Turns out they found the treasure in a buried cavern in their back yard. It was crazy."

The boat began to slow, and Lacy figured they must be getting closer to their first dive spot.

Andrea looked back at her gear. "I guess I better get ready. We have to shoot some before I get dressed for the dive. I'd love to hang out later if you're free."

"Sure. That would be great. Are you going to be around tonight? Maybe we could meet up for coffee."

"Sounds like a good idea. I want to hear all about your dive. Unfortunately, we don't get to dive the wreck you guys will dive. What's it called?"

"The C-50"

"Yeah. The C-50. That sounds so awesome. We have to dive the reef. All work and no play kind of thing."

"It's good to meet you, Andrea. I look forward to getting together later. Good luck with your filming. Let's swap numbers when we get back to the store."

Lacy watched Andrea walk to the back of the boat, and a young man with a camera filmed her as she stared out to sea. The camera guy was obviously going for the beautiful girl in a bikini look. *I suppose sex appeal can save a reef, too. I've got to get my act together or I'm going miss the C-50.*

Chapter Twenty-eight

The C-50

Lacy held onto the anchor rope about five feet beneath the surface while waiting on Kerrick to join her. Once he swam to her side, she turned and began to kick toward the bottom. She couldn't see the ship yet, but Chucho had told the group that the deck was about seventy feet down. The darkened shape slowly began to appear as she cleared the pressure in her ears several times. Nearing the ship, she discovered that the anchor line was actually tied to the C-50 instead of to an anchor buried in the sand.

The Mexican navy vessel sat upright on the sea floor and was covered with barnacles and all other manner of sea life. When Lacy looked behind her to make sure that Kerrick was there, he motioned for her to follow him. They moved toward the sand at the back of the ship to where Lacy figured the propellers would be located. She floated down to the sandy bottom on her knees and looked at her dive computer. They were at 98 feet. She knew they didn't need to stay this deep too long, or their dive would have to be cut short. She looked toward the bottom of the ship and noted that someone had removed the props. They were probably salvaged before the navy sank the ship.

Chucho had told them that the boat was decommissioned about fifteen years earlier and sunk in order to create a marine habitat. She remembered Jon's comments from months earlier when he told her this practice was not uncommon. There was always a point in which it took more money to renovate a ship than to sink it, and sunken ships were always a plus for marine life.

Kerrick was at the back of the boat shining his flashlight into a cavity under the hull. He motioned for her to come and pointed to something under the ship. Lacy followed the beam of the flashlight with her eyes and saw a huge manta ray resting in the sand. It had to be ten feet across. She had seen pictures of divers riding manta rays, and she imagined herself grabbing hold of this one. *Nope. I don't think I want to do that.*

They swam up the side of the C-50 and paused at a small opening. Kerrick pointed at a little centipede-like creature that was attached to the metal, and Lacy noticed several of the little worms. Kerrick shook his head and made a slicing motion at his neck. *Is he telling me that thing will kill me? Maybe he's just saying it could hurt if I touch it.*

Lacy avoided the little creature and grabbed hold of the side of the ship. She took the flashlight from Kerrick's outstretched hand and peered into the darkness of the ship's interior. She saw the movement of a big fish inside and figured there must be a larger opening somewhere else. She couldn't see the fish clearly enough to determine what kind it was, but it caused her to remember being in the barge the day Randal was injured back during the summer. She pictured in her mind the tiger shark swimming toward her like a bullet, and a shiver ran down her spine.

Feeling a tug on her arm, Lacy saw Kerrick pointing to a huge angelfish swimming above them. With a couple of kicks, they made it to the deck where she saw not just one angelfish, but two. They were amazing. They looked exactly the same—

dark blue bodies with yellow splatters of color on their sides. They looked like they wore white lipstick on their swollen lips. She had never seen one that large. The fish just hung there, suspended and staring at the divers. They didn't seem to be afraid. Lacy figured they lived around the ship and were quite used to seeing divers from another world.

The superstructure stretched up twenty feet toward the surface with openings where the ship's captain must have stood to direct the operations of the vessel. Lacy swam up to where she imagined a gun must have once sat just above what she determined was probably the control center. Directly in front of her, she saw a cross. *Is that some kind of mast? It must be metal because it's all corroded.* She followed the long base of the cross all the way down to the deck. She saw Kerrick snap a picture of her, and then he pointed to his pressure gauge. She looked at hers and was surprised to see that she was below 1000 psi. It was almost time to surface.

Kerrick joined her, and they circled the superstructure. It was so beautiful and eerie at the same time. Once back at the rope, they began their slow ascent toward the fifteen-foot mark, where they took a five-minute safety stop. After surfacing, Lacy inflated her BCD and began to slowly kick toward the back of the boat.

"So, what did you think?" Kerrick asked as he swam up beside her.

"It was amazing. I felt like we didn't have enough time, though."

"Yeah. Time flew by."

Lacy stopped kicking her feet and looked at Kerrick. "What was the bug? I mean, what was the worm-looking thing?"

"It's called a fire worm. It stings like heck, so you don't want to touch it. You haven't ever seen one before? They're usually all over the place."

"I guess not. Thanks for the warning." Lacy's stomach growled. "I guess I don't have to tell you that I'm starving."

Kerrick laughed. "Good for you that Dorado serves us lunch. I'm guessing we'll eat something while we take a little break, and then we'll make our next dive. I think I heard Chucho say we were diving a reef called The Cathedrals."

Two hours later, the dive boat motored toward the beach area near the dive shop. The dives had been awesome. Lacy thought back to the coral reef and couldn't remember ever seeing anything quite like it. The coral covered the seafloor and periodically formed a shape that looked a lot like church steeples. It was quite interesting.

Lacy was shaken out of her thoughts when she heard Meg's voice. "So, did you like it?"

"It was really unique. I loved the C-50 and want to dive it again. The reef was really interesting, too. Is that common for coral to grow like that?"

"I don't know," Meg admitted. "I've never seen anything like it. Maybe we can make another dive before we go home. Lacy, I don't feel good about you, Jon, and Kerrick going after those guys at the bus station."

"What could happen, Aunt Meg?"

"Well, you could be killed, for starters. These people are professionals."

"They're professional thieves, not murderers." Lacy heard her own words, but she couldn't help but wonder if she really knew what she was talking about. "We'll be careful. Jon said that if the thief looks scary that we would just drop the whole thing.

He thinks the thief is a kid, anyway. What could a kid do except bite us?"

Jon sat down beside Meg and put his arm around her. "So, what are you two beautiful women talking about?"

"About trying to keep you from getting killed," Meg said. "I just don't feel good about this plan."

"We don't have a plan yet, sweetheart. We're just going to the bus station today to scope it out. We'll come up with a plan and go back sometime this week and get those little creeps."

"Just promise me that you'll alert the police before you do something foolish."

"Me do something foolish?" Jon winked at Lacy. "Since when have I ever done anything foolish?" Jon kissed his wife on the cheek. "We've got to get to the villa as soon as we get back. The lady at the hotel agreed to let us check out a little later, but we don't need to take advantage of her generosity."

Lacy looked up and saw Andrea bend over to pick up her fins. "Hey, Andrea. When are you leaving Veracruz?"

"We have to leave tomorrow. We're going south to Catemaco for a few days and then back home on Sunday."

"Catemaco?"

Andrea nodded. "Yeah. It's a resort area about two or three hours south of Veracruz. A lot of movies have been filmed down there around the lake. It's beautiful. There's also a waterfall near there that looks kind of like your Niagara Falls."

"Actually," Lacy conceded, "I've never seen Niagara Falls. It's way up north. I hope to go there one day."

"Are you still up for coffee tonight?" Andrea asked.

"Sure. That would be great. Is La Parroquia okay? That's the only coffee place I know about around here."

"I like La Parroquia," Andrea admitted. "I'll get your number and call you tonight to work out a time. I assume I'll be available around 8:30 or so."

Lacy looked at Meg, who nodded in agreement. "That will probably work for me, too."

A couple of hours later, Lacy picked up her luggage and climbed the steps from the parking garage to the main level of the villa. She took in a sharp breath when she saw the beautiful swimming pool surrounded by rock walls with a rock staircase leading up to the second floor of the villa. Two levels towered above her with balconies overlooking the pool, and Lacy figured the view out into the bay must be beautiful. Jon walked behind her and headed into the house.

Lacy felt someone press against her back and knew it had to be Kerrick. "Hey beautiful. Let's go find our rooms."

They walked into the large, tiled foyer, and Lacy stared at herself in a large mirror hanging on the wall. *Oh, my. That looks scary. How could I let anyone see me looking like this? I look like...like I've been scuba diving and haven't showered yet.*

The kitchen and dining room were beautiful with tons of room. This place could handle another ten people if needed. Kerrick pulled Lacy's hand toward the stairs. They found four more bedrooms upstairs, two on each side of the house. Lacy walked through a bedroom that opened up to the balcony overlooking the bay. She stood at the sliding glass door mesmerized by the view. Since the villa sat on a hill to the northwest side of the city, she could see the old town of Veracruz along with the bay and some small mountains that rose up south of the city.

"Beautiful," Lacy breathed.

"You sure are," Kerrick said as he wrapped his arms around her.

Lacy turned and put her arms around his waist. "You're after something, and you know what I've said about flattery."

"True. It will get me anywhere. In that case, you're the most beautiful woman in the world, and I can't believe that you're my girlfriend."

He placed his lips on hers, and Lacy melted into his body. He was firm and tender at the same time. His muscular body was like a rock, but his heart was as soft as a rose petal. She felt his passion like electricity shooting through her body as her heart raced uncontrollably, and she knew that she wanted to spend the rest of her life in his arms.

"Here's the plan," Jon said as he pulled the SUV against the curb across from the bus station. "Lacy, you walk in with your backpack to the same counter we were at yesterday and set it down on the floor. Act like you're reading the sign, or something, but make sure that it's obvious you're not paying attention to your bag."

"Uh, Uncle Jon. I thought Meg was pretty adamant about not taking this situation into our own hands. Aren't we supposed to be scoping out the place and then getting the police involved? This plan feels like a little more than just scoping."

Jon thought back to the conversation he had with Meg before they left the villa. He had no plans to do anything stupid. He figured that as long as they kept their activities inside the bus station, they'd be safe. "Sure, Lacy. That's what we're doing. We're going to scope out whoever steals your bag. If I can get a policeman to stop him, I will."

"And if you can't get a policeman to stop him?" Lacy queried.

"I won't have any choice but to stop him myself."

"And Aunt Meg will be royally ticked."

"She'll be just fine. It's probably a good thing she had to stay back with Carla, though. I don't think she would fully understand our level of surveillance."

Kerrick laughed. "So, you call this surveillance? If you say so. It sounds to me like engaging the enemy."

Jon grinned as he looked at Lacy and Kerrick through the rear-view mirror. "Since we think the guy went into the bathroom last time with Lacy's pack, I'll stand near the bathroom. Kerrick, you stay near the door. Lacy, you can try to watch your bag out of the corner of your eye. Let us know when you see it disappear. We'll all communicate through our cell phones, but use your blue tooth ear pieces."

They jumped out of the car and moved to get into position in the bus station. Jon suggested they enter the building separately, for he knew that three Americans would stick out like a sore thumb.

Jon headed toward the restrooms located on the side of the main lobby. He saw Kerrick pick up a newspaper from a bench near the main entrance and sit down. Lacy, on the other hand, was not walking toward the counter. She was just walking around the station looking at different signs. *That's probably a good idea, Lacy. Walk around a bit so you'll get the attention of the bad guys, not that you have to do much to get any guy's attention.*

Jon knew that Lacy was right about Meg getting royally ticked, but they weren't going to get into any trouble. Catching these guys was at the top of his list. He watched Lacy move across the lobby to the counter where they had stood the previous day. Several men were staring at her. She sat her bag down, and Jon saw her turn to look at the sign advertising bus trips. He remembered from yesterday that this service went to El Tajín, Mexico City, and even Playa del Carmen. *I can't imagine riding on a bus all the way to Playa del Carmen.*

A young boy walked up to Jon and started saying something in Spanish. Jon couldn't understand the boy, but he was evidently selling pens. "No gracious," Jon said in the best Spanish he could muster. The boy continued rattling on. "No gracious," Jon repeated. He looked back across the lobby toward the spot where Lacy had been standing, but she was gone. He quickly scanned the terminal for his niece, but the place was covered up with people.

* * * * * *

Lacy turned to read the sign she had looked at the previous day. Of course, nothing had changed. She saw the familiar trip to El Tajin, Mexico City, and Catemaco. Had Catemaco been on the list the day before? It probably had been, but since she just heard Andrea say the name of the city earlier, it was fresh on her mind. She turned back toward the bag she sat on the floor, and it was gone. She looked up in time to see a teenage boy hurrying through the station toward the front door. The red pack was in his hand. She couldn't believe it. He had been so sneaky. Anger boiled up from deep within her, and she felt like a volcano about to explode. She sprinted after him.

Dodging left and right, Lacy kept the boy in sight. "He's got my bag, and he's heading toward the front door. Do you hear me, Kerrick?"

Nothing. What was wrong with everyone. She chanced a look at her phone, and the screen was blank. *My battery! I can't believe my phone picked now as a time to die.* Lacy waved her arms wildly as she saw Kerrick up ahead. He looked at her as the boy ran past him.

"Kerrick. My bag. He's got it!"

As the door to the outside closed, Kerrick ran after the boy. By the time Lacy was outside, Kerrick was a little over a block away sprinting after the thief. Kerrick leaped through the air and made a diving tackle. The teen tumbled to the ground, and the red backpack rolled up against the wall of a building. Kerrick landed on top of the boy and grabbed hold of his flailing arms. To Lacy's horror, a big man stepped out from behind a beat-up van with a gun in his hand. Lacy's world spun into slow motion as the huge man raised the gun toward Kerrick's head.

"Kerrick!" Lacy screamed as she ran down the street.

Out of the corner of her eye, she saw a blur of movement in the street, and Andrea appeared on the sidewalk behind the man. In a burst of speed, Lacy's new friend jumped into the air, twisting her body in flight, and landed a roundhouse kick to the man's head. The gun flew from his hand, and he fell to the sidewalk like a sack of rocks. His head bounced on the concrete with a sickening thud.

"Andrea!" Lacy shouted. "Oh, my God. Andrea!"

Lacy ran up beside her friend and saw a pool of blood forming around the gunman's head. It seemed to be coming from his nose, so he had probably fallen flat on his face, but the man was out cold. Kerrick pulled the teen to his feet as a policeman from the bus station ran up, and Jon was a couple of feet behind him.

"Andrea! I can't believe what I just saw. You were like…like Jackie Chan." She wrapped her arms around her friend. "Thank you for showing up when you did."

"I'm glad I had to come to the bus station," Andrea said without even appearing to be winded. "I was here to make arrangements for our travel tomorrow."

"You were amazing," Lacy gushed.

The policeman began rattling off something so fast that Lacy couldn't understand any of it. Andrea replied and was evidently explaining to the officer what had happened.

"This kid stole my backpack yesterday," Lacy interjected. Andrea began translating for her. "We came back today to see if we could catch the thief. We had no idea someone would pull a gun on us."

The policeman explained through Andrea that they had been trying to catch this crime ring for a while. They knew the crooks were dangerous, and people had lost their lives while chasing the thief.

"You mean someone else ran after the kid and was killed?" Lacy asked in shock as she felt something like a rock fall into the pit of her stomach.

"Yes," Andrea replied. "He's saying that your boyfriend is lucky to be alive."

Lacy felt the blood drain from her face. Meg had been right. Why had they been so foolish? "Thank you, Andrea." A tear rolled down Lacy's cheek. "You saved Kerrick's life."

"I'm glad that I came along. This could have ended much differently."

The police officer asked for Lacy's name and phone number, and Jon stepped forward to introduce himself. He took the officer's pad and scribbled down his name and number. He added Lacy's name under his. As other policemen arrived to take control of the scene, the officer told Andrea that he would be in touch with Jon soon, and he thanked them for their help. He shook hands with everyone and turned to assist with the arrest.

Jon reached out to shake Andrea's hand as they stepped away from the commotion. "We can never thank you enough, Andrea."

"I'm so glad I was here to help."

"I'd like to somehow express my thanks. Would you and your whole crew go to dinner with us tonight? That's the least I can do."

"You don't have to do that," Andrea insisted.

"I know I don't have to do it," Jon agreed, "but I would like to."

"In that case, we'd be honored."

"My wife mentioned that she would like to have seafood tonight," Jon continued. "What's the best seafood restaurant around here?"

Andrea thought for a minute. "Someone once told me that a place called Villa Rica Mocambo is the best. It's down in Boca del Rio, which is the city on the south side of Veracruz."

"Sounds good to me," Jon said. "I'll have a car pick you and your guys up at around 7:00. Will that work?"

"Perfect." Andrea's smile spread across her beautiful face. "It will be a wonderful evening."

Jon pulled a pen out of his pocket and wrote down the name of Andrea's hotel. Lacy hugged Andrea again before heading back to the SUV.

A few hours later, Lacy and Kerrick walked hand-in-hand into the restaurant behind Jon, Meg, Carla, and Judy. The large restaurant was covered with a thatch roof and located right on the beach. The back was open to the ocean, so it seemed as if the restaurant was one huge thatch-covered pavilion. They walked past a small stage where a woman and a man were singing. The two singers were accompanied by two guitarists and a young guy playing the conga drums. Lacy looked around the vast seating area and saw that the waiters and waitresses were dressed in white. The women wore beautiful white dresses that were obviously typical to this part of the world. She already loved the place, and she hadn't even ordered her meal yet.

The hostess sat them at a large table that would provide enough room for everyone. Lacy figured that Andrea should sit in front of Jon and Meg, so she suggested to Kerrick that they leave two seats open. Kerrick pulled out a chair for Lacy so she could be sitting next to Andrea, and he sat beside her.

"You look beautiful in this candle light," Kerrick whispered in her ear. "I think I'll order you for dessert."

Lacy blushed, though she was sure no one heard him. She reached under the table and grabbed his hand. "You sure know how to flatter a girl. No doubt you've used that line a hundred times."

"Nope. That was my first, and it wasn't a line. I love you, Lacy Henderson."

Lacy lowered her eyes as she felt her heart beat quicken. She wanted to cry, melt, shout, and sing all at the same time. She turned and looked into his beautiful blue eyes that seemed as deep as the ocean. "I love you, too, and you can have me for dessert...uh, I mean, within reason...if you know what I mean."

She felt as if the whole room became totally empty, and she was alone with the man she loved. Kerrick grinned at her and squeezed her hand. She sensed a hunger deep inside of her that craved something greater than food.

"Lacy!" a voice cried out from several tables back.

Lacy turned to see Andrea and three guys walking toward her. Lacy stood to meet her friend and hugged her when she walked up.

Andrea turned to the man standing next to her who looked to be in his mid-twenties. "This is my co-worker, David, and these two guys work with us. This is León and Joaquin. Thank you so much for inviting us to dinner. This place is amazing."

Everyone sat together and poured over the menu. Lacy explained the food options to Kerrick, and she heard Meg reading the menu to Jon. Lacy ordered blackened grouper, and Kerrick decided to try octopus. The thought of eating long tentacles with little suctions on them nearly turned her stomach. She heard Jon ask for lobster, and she wondered if she should have gotten that instead.

The waitress spoke some English and was extremely gracious. She served tortillas and chips along with some really good salsa. Andrea told everyone about her experience at the university and how she and David met while in school. They shared their dream of starting a film production company, and it seemed that their company was quite successful.

Jon leaned toward the group. "Lacy, I haven't told you, but I got a phone call from the police just before we left. They found your backpack. Your iPad and passport are safe. We have to go by the station and pick them up."

"I can't believe it," Lacy gushed. "I didn't think I'd ever see that iPad again."

The evening was enjoyable, and Lacy hated to see it come to an end. The food was outstanding. She even tried a bite of the octopus, and it wasn't bad. She had expected rubber, but it was actually a little like chicken. She tried not think about the slimy part on the outside, but the inside was pretty good.

After telling Andrea and her crew goodnight, Jon drove the SUV by the police station and then back to their villa. Lacy was so relieved to have her iPad and passport back. She began feeling extremely exhausted and couldn't wait to go to bed. Once inside their beautiful vacation home, she told Jon and Meg that she had to go to sleep. She couldn't keep her eyes open. She climbed the steps to her room on the third floor and expected Kerrick to come up behind her, but he sat in the kitchen talking to Jon.

Once alone in her room, Lacy showered and dressed for bed. She was just about to slip under the blanket when she heard a faint knock at the door. She had no doubt who was at her door and wondered why it had taken him so long to come tell her goodnight.

"Hey," Lacy said as she leaned dreamily against the door jam. She suddenly felt a little self-conscious about Kerrick seeing her in her long tee-shirt. Even though her shirt was longer than some of her dresses, she still felt a little naked.

"Hey yourself. You look exhausted."

"I am," Lacy agreed as she grabbed Kerrick's hand and pulled him into her room. She wrapped her arms around him and pulled his face down toward hers. Her kiss was long and passionate. Splaying her hands across his strong back, she squeezed his body firmly against hers. A few moments later, she pulled away breathlessly.

Kerrick smiled down at her. "So, was that dessert? If so, what can I do for seconds?"

Lacy traced his stubbled jaw and ran her finger down his neck and to the strong slabs of his chest. "You'll have to come back tomorrow night for seconds," she cooed.

"Is that right?" Kerrick leaned toward her parted lips, and they kissed again. "Well, since the dessert buffet is closed for the night, I better go to bed. We do have to get up early in the morning to leave for El Tajin."

Lacy opened her mouth to a large, unguarded yawn. "I hate to agree with you, but I'm so exhausted. I'll see you in the morning."

"Good night, Lacy. I'm sure tomorrow is going to shed some interesting light on our search. There's no telling what we may discover."

Chapter Thirty

The Dance of the Flyers

Miguel walked through the terminal at Lynden Pindling International Airport in Nassau with a ticket to Miami in his hand. He sat down near the gate where his plane would be loading in less than an hour and carefully scanned the crowd. The last thing he needed was to be recognized by a cop, though he knew that was unlikely. A year earlier, he had stolen the identity of a terminally ill guy from Milwaukee, so there was little risk that anyone would suspect him to be anyone other than Mr. Jose Rodriquez.

He opened his laptop and began scanning the area around three homes in Veracruz where the Davenports could be staying. Miguel considered the possibility that Andrew could have located the proper address, but the boy had to be killed. Now, Miguel figured he'd have to find the Davenports' vacation home on his own. Most of the houses on Homeaway were eliminated as possibilities because of either their size or location. Miguel felt like Jon Davenport would prefer something with at least four or five bedrooms. Out of the three options, one of them stood out as the most likely place. It was large and plush and located on the south side of Veracruz in Boca del Rio. This area was definitely a place where rich people would go on vacation. He spotted the Real de Boca hotel a few miles away from the house and decided to go online and make reservations for one night.

The second most likely house was north of the city. Davenport could have chosen this place because it was certainly fancy enough for a rich guy. It wasn't in a wealthy community like the other one, however, so Miguel decided Boca del Rio was the best place to start. He looked at the map showing the location of this second house and saw that the community was called Nueva. *Why would they just call an area New? It must be a newer neighborhood, but when was it built? It could have been new thirty years ago and be run down by now.* He spotted a Walmart nearby and decided the area must be populated and possibly more affluent. If house number one didn't work out, he'd check out house number two.

He leaned his head back and thought about his strategy. He needed that medallion, so his only option was to take the girl. If she didn't have the medallion with her, Davenport would just have to go and get it. This would mean that he would have several days with the beautiful Lacy Henderson. She was gorgeous—bright blue eyes, long blonde hair, and a sexy body. He had already decided that he wanted Meg instead of Lacy, but the younger girl might just have to do. He could take both of them. Meg was a knockout. It just wasn't right for rich men to always get the beautiful women. The more he thought about taking both of them, the more he liked it. Now that would be a vacation to remember. *That will make Davenport get the medallion for sure, and I can have double the fun.*

****

Meg crossed her arms, sat down on the bed, and glared at Jon as he walked into the bedroom and closed the door. She didn't know if she should cry over what could have happened at the bus station or laugh with joy over what did happen. She had told Jon not to take matters into his own hands, and his actions could have gotten all of them killed.

"I know you're upset with me, honey, and I'm sorry," Jon began. "I didn't intend for that to happen."

"What did you think would happen, Jon? If you set up a trap to catch a thief, you're probably going to catch a thief. What then? Did you process what you would do in response to someone stealing Lacy's bag?"

"You're right. I didn't think everything through very well. I thought we'd just grab a kid in the bus station and hold him for the police."

"Jon, even that is dangerous. You can't just grab someone and hold him. What if he had a knife?"

Jon lowered his head, and Meg felt like steam must have been coming out of her ears. She had been sitting in their bedroom alone for at least ten minutes, and the longer she sat there, the angrier she had become. She stared at her husband and felt a ball of confusing emotions welling up within her. She put her head in her hands and began to cry.

Sitting down beside her, Jon wrapped his arms around her quivering shoulders. "Honey. I'm so sorry. I know what I did was stupid. I just wasn't thinking."

Meg sniffed loudly and tried to talk through her tears. Her words were muffled and nonsensical until she got up to get a tissue. She finally got her emotions under control. "It's just...Jon, it's just that I can't bear to lose you. I need you, and Carla needs you. I love you, Jon. I don't want anything to happen to you."

"I know, sweetheart, and nothing's going to happen to me."

"You don't know that, Jon. You could have been killed. Kerrick could have been shot."

"I'm sorry, Meg. I know now that I shouldn't have done it. I'll be more careful next time."

"Let's don't let there be a next time." Meg wrapped her arms around Jon and buried her head in his shoulders. She felt tears coming again, and she became a blubbering mess as Jon held her while she cried. "I'm sorry I'm so emotional. I went through losing Steve. I can't lose you, too."

Just mentioning Steve's name brought back to her mind the night when the death officers came to her house years earlier to tell her that her first husband had been killed in action in Afghanistan. Just being held in Jon's arms brought her comfort and gratitude for the marriage she now had with him. They had somehow gotten tangled up with some really bad people from the very beginning of their relationship, and it seemed like everywhere they turned, someone else was out to hurt them.

"I'll not let that happen again, Meg. I can't promise that bad people won't be after us in the future because our world is filled with bad people."

"And we seem to attract them like metal drawn to a magnet."

"True," Jon agreed. "It's kind of weird. It all started with the gold beneath the floor of my boat. We couldn't help that. I think that there's always going to be someone after any gold that we find. That's just how it works. It may take the form of legal battles in a courtroom or bad guys in an alley."

Meg wiped her eyes and leaned her head back to look up at her husband. "I get that we're involved in a dangerous profession, but let's not help the bad guys out by putting ourselves in their cross hairs."

"I won't, honey. I promise. I won't."

Jon pulled Meg into his arms and kissed her cheek and then her neck. Their lips met, and a surge of passion swelled up from deep within her. She felt Jon's strong arms pulling her down onto the bed, and the joy of being married to such a wonderful man consumed her.

The drive north to Papantla and then to El Tajín the next morning was beautiful but a little rough for Carla. Meg loved the variety of scenery, but the first speed bump they hit nearly jarred her brain out of her head. Kerrick actually bounced up and hit the ceiling of the SUV.

"What was that?" Judy gasped.

"I guess it was a speed bump," Jon assumed. "Oh, no. The hubcap is rolling down the street."

Lacy jumped out of the car and Meg watched her run after the rogue wheel cover. It rolled off the street into a pasture, and Lacy charged barefooted after it. Meg heard her yelp in pain and then saw her stop to pull something out of her foot. She grabbed the hubcap and limped back to the car.

"What happened?" Meg asked as she got out of the car.

"We hit a speed bump," Jon replied with irritation. "This sign beside it says *Tope*. It must be called a tope."

"I think it's pronounced *to-pay*," Meg corrected. "Lacy, are you okay?"

"Cactus," Lacy stated emphatically. "I stepped on a dang cactus."

Meg looked at the bottom of Lacy's foot as she held it up to be inspected. "Did you get all of the needles out? It might get infected if something is still in there."

"I think I got it out. It's just sore as rip."

Meg grinned as she thought about Lacy's word choice.

"What? What's so funny?" Lacy wanted to know.

"It's just that a few months ago, you wouldn't be 'sore as rip.' You'd be sore as something else that's not mentionable. I like the new Lacy, even though you had to step on a cactus to reveal your new identity."

"My new identity?"

"Yeah. Everyone is kind of like a cream-filled donut. You don't really know what's on the inside until you get squeezed. You just got squeezed by a cactus, and I really like what I'm seeing on the inside of you."

Lacy smiled. "You're my inspiration, Meg. I really mean that. You don't even know it, but you're helping me become the person I've always wanted to be."

Meg hugged her niece and saw Jon walk around the back of the car.

"I hate to end the hugfest," Jon said with a grin, "but we've still got a lot of driving to do. Give me the hubcap so I can put it back on." Jon hammered the wheel cover back into place and told Meg and Lacy to get back into the car.

After three-and-a-half hours of driving, Jon pulled through the entrance of El Tajin. Meg thought it felt like driving down the main street of a market as little booths lined both sides of the road. Artisans sat in the booths, and their crafts were displayed for sale. Meg saw a beautiful, hand-made dress hanging in one of the booths. *I'll have to come back and check that dress out.*

Jon parked, and two vendors met the little group as they began crawling out of the car. Jon put Carla into a baby carrier and slipped it onto his back.

"No gracias," Jon began to say immediately, and everyone else repeated the words.

"Don't they see that we all have sunglasses and don't need another pair?" Lacy asked with exasperation.

Kerrick reached down and took her hand. "You have to see it as people working real hard to feed their families. They don't care that you have sunglasses. They just desperately need to sell you another pair."

Meg saw a crowd of people hurrying past the booths to a sidewalk up ahead. Six men in colorful costumes were walking out of a small building while one of them played a tune on a wooden flute. Meg turned toward the rest of the group. "Come on. It looks like they're about to do some kind of dance."

They all watched in fascination as the men stretched out four ropes from a huge pole in the center of the courtyard. The flautist continued to play and another man beat on a small drum.

Meg saw a young couple standing near them who looked very English. "Excuse me. What is this?" she asked them.

The cute, petite brunette turned to look at Meg and spoke with a British accent. "It's called the Dance of the Flyers. An ancient Totonac myth tells the story of a great drought, and the villagers created this dance as a way to appease the gods. The flute player is supposed to represent a bird singing, and I think the four guys represent earth, air, fire, and water. The whole ritual is somehow supposed to be their way of praying to the gods to bless them. One thing is for sure, though."

"What's that?" Meg asked.

"Before they officially began, the big guy will walk around with a bucket so *we* can bless them. You're supposed to put twenty pesos per person in the bucket."

"Oh. Thanks for the warning."

Once the man collected the money, the large group stood mesmerized as the flautist climbed the pole while continuing to play his instrument. The pole had to be at least sixty feet tall. Once at the top, the man stood on a small platform performing a dance while he played. Meg couldn't believe the guy didn't fall. Finally, the other four men joined him, and they wrapped their ropes around the pole fifty-two times. Meg's new British friend explained the rope was wrapped one time for every week of the Totonac annual calendar. The men tied the ropes to their ankles and leaned back from the top perch. Once free of the top rail, they began spinning around slowly upside down to the sound of the flute as the rope unwound from the pole. It reminded Meg of the swing ride at the county fair she attended as a kid. The whole show was really amazing.

The men completed the dance and stood to their feet on the ground to the applause of the crowd.

Lacy looked at the rest of her group. "That was the most unusual thing I've ever seen. It makes me wonder what awaits us inside El Tajin."

Meg saw Kerrick reach for his phone and marveled that he had signal here to take a call. *I wonder who would be calling him.* Moving away from the group, Kerrick walked toward the main entrance of the ancient city.

Chapter Thirty-one

El Tajin

The crowd formed at the ticket counter, and Lacy looked further down the hallway to the museum. Her pulse quickened when she saw part of a display that was visible through the open door. Out of the corner of her eye, she saw Kerrick step up beside her and put his phone into his pocket.

"Important man," Lacy teased. "You can't even go on vacation and get away from people."

"It was my mom. She said that someone from school was trying to get in touch with me."

"That's weird that they called your mom to find you."

"Yeah. I thought the same thing. She probably just wants to borrow a book or something."

"She?" Lacy raised an eyebrow.

"Some girl. I don't really know her very well. I don't mind loaning out a book, if that's what she wants. I'll call her later."

Lacy pointed to the door on the right of the passageway. "Did you see the museum up ahead? The door's open. Do you notice anything inside that might be of interest?"

Kerrick peered through the door, and his lips spread into a big grin. "Oh, my. I need to see it up close, but I'd say that carving has a familiar ring to it."

After they had their tickets to go into the ruins, Lacy decided she had better visit the restroom before going to explore. "I read on Trip Adviser that there's no restrooms once you leave this building, so you guys may want to make a pit stop."

When Lacy came out of the ladies' room, Kerrick was leaning against the wall waiting on her, and Carla was sitting calmly in her little carrier waiting on Jon to come out. Kerrick was reading a text on his phone. *Man. He sure has gotten popular all of a sudden. A phone call and now a text.* "Hey, handsome. You want to go exploring with me?"

Kerrick looked up and grinned. "Wow. Why would such a beautiful girl want to spend the day with me?"

"Your lucky day, I guess." Lacy grabbed his hand and pulled him toward the museum as Jon came out of the restroom and picked up Carla.

They walked through the open door and saw a large display on a wall that contained pieces of rock. Pictures had been carved onto the rock that looked nearly identical to the carving they found in the cave on Coral Cay in the Bahamas. Lacy stared at the carving of the man who had a human body with what looked like a bird's head. She thought back to the men on the pole. *Didn't that British girl say the flute player was supposed to be like a bird?*

Jon walked up behind them. "Well, that sure looks familiar."

"Do you think the rest of the treasure is hidden here in El Tajin?" Lacy almost whispered.

Jon turned from the carving and lowered his voice. "We should be careful about talking about it in public. I doubt that it's here. If it were in El Tajin, surely someone would have found it by now. It's surprising how similar the carving on that stone is to ours we found."

Lacy leaned in to view the carving more closely. "Maybe El Tajin is the lost city Bluetooth's men found."

"It's possible," Jon agreed, "but I hope not."

"Amazing, isn't it?" Kerrick said. "Look at the detail of that carving. What does it mean?"

"It's all a part of their worship," a deep, accented voice said from behind them.

Lacy saw the large Mexican man take another step toward their little group as Meg joined them. He was dressed in an official looking uniform. She hoped he had not heard her earlier comments about the treasure.

"The Totonac people worshipped different gods," the man continued. "Just the name of this place says that this city was a religious center."

"What does El Tajin mean?" Lacy asked.

"Most people think it means *of thunder,* and it represents twelve gods of thunder who live in this place. Another possibility is *place of invisible spirits.* You'll see through the museum and out in the ruins that this was a religious center for the Mesoamerican people. You may want to pay special attention to the ball courts."

"Ball courts?" Kerrick marveled. "They played ball?"

The man laughed. "It seems to have been an early form of soccer, and it was connected to their worship."

"Kind of like football in the United States," Meg joked. "Men worship that game every weekend of the fall."

"While there's a debate on who actually built this city, many think it was either the Totonac people or the Huastec. Regardless, we know that they practiced human sacrifice to their gods. They used the ball courts to determine who they'd sacrifice."

"They played a game, and the losers were sacrificed." Jon restated. "I remember reading something about that somewhere."

"Yes. Sometimes, they would go to war with another tribe and bring the defeated tribe back to El Tajin. The defeated warriors played the game, and the losers were sacrificed."

"So, they played a soccer game, and the losers lost their heads," Lacy concluded. "Sure would be an extra incentive not to lose."

"Sometimes, it was just the residents of El Tajin playing the games, and the winners were sacrificed. The ancients saw it as an honor to be sacrificed to the gods."

"Unbelievable," Kerrick marveled.

"I said it was like soccer. The players hit a small ball made from rubber. It seems that they usually hit the ball with their hips and tried to get the ball through a ring on the side of the court. A similar game is still played in some remote villages today. We have a replica of the city on the other side of the museum where you'll be able to see the location of the ball courts. I suggest you study the replica before going out into the ruins. It will help you to be able to understand the layout of the entire city."

"Thank you so much for your help," Jon said as he shook the man's hand. He looked back toward Meg. "Well, let's check out the replica and then go see the ruins."

Jon lead the group up a bricked path that went away from the entrance building. Women lined the way selling drinks, snacks, and crafts. One lady had bottles of vanilla extract, and Lacy couldn't help but think about how pure that extract must be compared to the stuff her mother bought at the grocery store. *Too bad I wouldn't be able to carry some home.*

They left the brick walkway and headed along a dirt path through a field. The tall structures loomed in front of them. They stopped in what seemed to be a courtyard between two pyramids that faced one another.

Lacy squinted up at the structures covered with stone and grass surrounding the courtyard. "I wish we had a guidebook to this place written in English. I tried to find something online, but there doesn't seem to be anything available."

"I asked the lady at the counter back at the entrance if they had something in English about this place," Meg said. "They don't."

"I would just like to know what these pyramids were used for," Lacy continued. "I suppose you could call them mounds as well as pyramids." She looked at the towering structure behind the courtyard. "Now that's a pyramid."

"I've seen that before in pictures," Jon decided. "I can't remember what it's called, but it seems like there are 365 openings in it to represent each day of the year, best I remember. I think it's called Niches or something like that. That's right. It's called Pyramid of the Niches."

"So, was it mainly for keeping up with the calendar?" Meg asked. "It sure seems like an extravagant way to keep up with what day it is."

"The niches were actually seen as passageways to the underworld," Jon remembered. "Here's a sign in front of this mound. I bet there's one in front of the temple as well."

"If I were going to hide treasure in a city like this," Lacy thought aloud, "I'd hide it deep within a pyramid like this one."

"In Egyptian and Mayan cultures, pyramids were used as burial tombs for royalty," Jon replied.

Meg reached for her camera. "If they buried the tribal leader in that thing, it makes sense that they would bury treasure with him."

"True," Jon agreed. "I'm sure, however, that archeologists have already poured over this whole place and taken anything of real value."

"Look at the steps going up this pyramid," Lacy pointed out. "What do you suppose they did up on top?"

"Maybe sacrifices," Kerrick suggested. "This sign says that this courtyard we're in was like the city-center. They had a market here."

They walked around the first cluster of mounds and pyramids to get a better view of the Pyramid of the Niches.

"I don't know if they sacrificed on top of the temples or not," Jon said as he looked down at a sign in front of a flat structure. The structure was about five or six feet tall with steps leading up to a large, level area. "This was the altar where they performed the human sacrifices."

Lacy felt a shiver run down her spine as she thought about people being taken onto the altar to be killed. How cruel and senseless. "That's unbelievable," she whispered under her breath.

"What is?" Kerrick asked.

"That they actually killed people right here for some made up religion."

"It's quite different from Christianity," Jon said. "It seems that in a lot of pagan religions, people had to be sacrificed for their god. In Christianity, our God was sacrificed for us."

Lacy felt a lot of emotions swelling up inside of her and even noticed a tear about to slip out of her eye. The thought of people dying on this spot was getting to her. She walked forward to another sign and read the message. She was grateful that while the signs were written in Spanish down the left side, the right side offered an English translation.

"Here's one of the ball courts," Lacy stated.

She looked at the long, narrow court lined with stone walls. Carvings covered the walls from one end of the court to the other. Lacy walked up to the first carving and pulled out her cell phone to take a picture. The group walked quietly down the length of the wall until they were in the center of the court.

Lacy raised her phone to take another picture of the carving and then paused. "Oh, my God. Is that man doing what I think he's doing?"

"What man?" Kerrick asked as he looked around.

"The carving, I mean. Is that a carving of a man cutting off his...uh...You know. Just like our carving. Self...something. What was that word?"

"Self-emasculation," Jon stated. "It was a form of worship in a lot pagan cultures."

Lacy looked back at the carving. "It's amazing what a girl has to see to enhance her vocabulary."

"Do you remember the Bible story of Elijah's contest with the prophets of Baal?" Jon asked.

"I think I must have skipped church the day they talked about that story," Lacy said dryly.

"The contest was basically to determine whose God was real," Jon continued. "The prophets of Baal went first. They placed their animal sacrifice on the altar and prayed for fire to come down from heaven. When nothing happened, Elijah began to taunt them. The prophets danced around and cut themselves. Nothing happened. When Elijah's turn came, he poured water over the sacrifice and prayed. Fire came down from heaven and engulfed the whole altar."

"And that's supposed to be true?" Lacy asked skeptically.

"I believe it," Jon insisted. "Just recently, archaeologists uncovered Baal altars connected to an ancient gate in Jerusalem that King Hezekiah ordered to be torn down. The discovery corroborates the biblical account. It's fascinating that archeology has never uncovered anything to disprove the Bible. Instead, it's always the other way around."

"So, I don't guess archaeologists have uncovered the altar Elijah and the Baal prophets used," Lacy stated.

"The Bible says they were burned up with fire from heaven," Meg said.

"That's convenient," Lacy cracked. "I will say that any religion that leads a man to cut off his you-know-what has got to be one screwed up religion."

They walked quietly down the remaining length of the ball court and paused at the carving of a man being decapitated. Lacy couldn't get over how calloused these ancient people were. Life must not have meant anything to them.

They walked up behind the Pyramid of the Niches, and Lacy stared up at the seven-story structure in awe. It was masterful and must have taken forever to build.

She then looked up at a wooden platform on the side of a hill. "Let's go up there," she suggested.

"Jon," Judy wheezed. "I'm getting pretty tired. Y'all can go on up there, but I need to sit down. I saw a bench under a tree on the other side of those mounds. I'm going to wait there."

"Okay," Jon agreed. "We'll come back to get you on our way out."

Ten minutes later, Jon led them out on a platform that overlooked the main portion of the complex. The view was stunning. The temple to the right was certainly the dominant structure. Lacy couldn't quit staring at the altar. It really bothered her that these people killed human beings as a sacrifice to the god of thunder.

They spent another two hours walking around the complex looking at structure after structure. Lacy noticed a repeated design in multiple places throughout the ruins. It was usually made with stacked stones and resembled the letter "p." It seemed to come in pairs with one of the shapes inverted and turned on its side. Maybe it looked more like an upside-down capital letter G. She didn't know what it meant, but it must have had some significance to these people.

Lacy's stomach growled, and Meg laughed. "Lacy, girl, you must be hungry."

"I'm about to start eating these rocks," Lacy said as she pointed to a pile of stones.

"Well, you know that I brought a picnic lunch, and considering it's almost 3:00, I'd say we should go eat."

"I'm past ready," Lacy announced.

"I think I've seen enough of the ruins," Jon said. "Why don't we go eat and then start our drive back to Veracruz. "I'd love to stop by that archaeological site we passed on our way up here. I think that's the area where Cortez first landed in Mexico."

"Is that the place where he supposedly burned his ships?" Kerrick asked.

"Yes. It's somewhere in that area," Jon agreed. "Surely there will be a marker at the spot. If we hurry, we can get there before dark."

Chapter Thirty-two

Villa Rica

Jon got out of the SUV and walked to the locked gate. He looked at the sign strapped to the fence and tried to pronounce the name of the ruins: Quiahuiztlan. He looked at his watch and ran his hand through his hair before looking back toward the road leading to the ruins on the other side of the gate. It was only a few minutes after 6:00, but the sign clearly indicated that the archaeological site closed at 6:00 p.m.

"We did our best." Meg slipped her arms around Jon's waist. "Other than slowing down for the topes, I'd say you drove about as fast as you could possibly drive."

Lacy walked up to the gate and looked toward the tall mountain that was evidently a focal point of the ruins. "I'd agree with Aunt Meg. You almost killed us when you passed four vehicles at one time."

"I didn't almost kill us," Jon argued with a grin. "Staying behind that truck going five miles per hour would have killed us. That was a road hazard. Besides that, I only did what everyone else was doing."

"Let's see." Lacy placed her finger against her cheek. "What was the one good thing my mom said to me growing up? Oh, yes. If everyone was jumping off a cliff, should you?"

"Thankfully, we weren't confronted with a cliff," Jon acknowledged, "and your mom's advice is certainly worthy of remembering. I think every mom says that to her kids at some point in her life. It's in the *What Moms Should Say to their Kids* manual."

"I've never seen that manual," Meg quipped. "I suppose I better get a copy before Carla gets to be much older."

"We can come back here before we go home," Jon suggested. "Maybe we can return with Jose and Ann. It's only an hour from Veracruz. Lacy, what did you find out about the spot where Cortez landed? I know you were trying to find some information on your phone about it. It's got to be nearby."

"It is. A small peninsula juts out into the ocean just east of here in a little town called Villa Rica. That's where he landed. I pulled the map up on my phone, and that road across the highway will take us to another road that leads to Villa Rica."

"I didn't see a sign about Cortez's landing," Jon said. "It seems like such an important place would be memorialized somehow. Let's go check it out."

Jon pulled the SUV across the highway onto a small road that led toward the beach. He knew they weren't far from the water because just a mile back, they could see the ocean from the main highway. They came to a dead end and had to turn right or left.

"Left," Lacy instructed as she looked down at her phone.

A mile later, the road took a ninety degree turn to the right, and a small, beach-side village opened up before them. It seemed to be a hangout for families, and a number of kids were playing around in the ocean. Jon pulled the vehicle into a parking place in front of a small house that evidently served as a restaurant for the community, and everyone got out of the car. Meg pulled Carla out of her car seat, and they walked down the road to the beach. Jon looked just a little to the north at the rounded penin-sula that extended out into the ocean.

"That's got to be where Cortez landed," Jon said. "The story says that the men climbed a cliff and Cortez had someone burn the ships so they couldn't return."

"That's odd," Kerrick concluded. "It does seem like there are cliffs at the end of the peninsula, but why wouldn't they just land here on the beach so they wouldn't have to climb a cliff?"

"Climbing a cliff makes for better screenplay," Jon conceded and then laughed. "I have a feeling that they didn't climb the cliffs, and that no one set fire to the ships. Who knows? The peninsula is higher than anything else around here, however, so it would have made a great place for a protected camp. It almost looks like a natural fort."

"Can we go out on the peninsula?" Kerrick asked.

"I'd love to," Jon said, "but it's about to get dark. I vote that we come back up here when Jose and Ann arrive. I think they'd love to check out this place, too. Remember that Jose is from Spain, so I imagine he could tell us some things about Cortez. I'm especially interested in why there's no visitors' center here with tour guides and a short film."

"And a souvenir store," Lacy added.

"They could at least have a plaque," Meg concluded. "Maybe they're not proud of what Cortez did. It seems like I remember that he sort of betrayed the Aztecs."

"Yeah," Jon agreed. Sort of."

"I'm exhausted," Meg said. "Let's get back to our house."

"If we can stop by a grocery store, I'll cook us something for dinner," Judy suggested.

"I think it's too late for that," Jon offered. "Let's just go to that taco place downtown and have a real Mexican taco."

****

Lacy wrinkled her nose as she looked up three steps into the taco restaurant. She was sure the health department back in Griffin would have a stroke over this place. Flies buzzed around the grill where a man stood cooking meat for the tacos, but the smell of the food pulled her toward a table.

The waitress was very kind and patient with the group as they all tried to figure out how to order their meal. She explained that the restaurant offered beef and pork. Once the group decided on which meat they wanted, they could go to a bar and choose ingredients for their taco. Lacy looked at the bar and saw that the items were covered up with plastic. *Well, that's good. At least, there won't be any dead flies in the tomatoes.*

Dinner was outstanding. The green sauce from the bar was out of this world. Lacy tried to figure out how to ask for a recipe, but she was unable to communicate the idea of recipe to the waitress.

"We'll just have to come back," Meg suggested. "Even Carla liked this place."

Lacy looked down at Carla and couldn't decide if the little girl ate her dinner or chose to wear it. Carla reached for a bowl of salsa on the table, and Meg pulled it away just in time.

"We could go back to La Parroquia and have some more pastel de tres leches," Lacy suggested.

"If I put anything else in my already bloated body," Judy began, "I'm going to pop. You can do the pastel, but I'm going to have to pass."

"We should probably all pass," Jon recommended. "Let's just walk around the market for a little bit and then head back to the house."

An hour-and-a-half later, Lacy fell back onto her bed, and her wet hair spilled across her pillow. A belch slipped out, and her hands instantly went to her overstuffed tummy. If she ate like this the whole time they were in Mexico, she was going to return to Miami as big as a barn. She grabbed her sleep shirt and pulled it over her head just as she heard the door squeak.

"Kerrick! What are you doing? I'm not fully dressed."

He smiled at her. "I've seen you dressed for bed before, and you look beautiful to me."

She grabbed a pillow and threw it at him. "You shouldn't be in here."

"Your door was open a little. I didn't realize you'd be indisposed."

He walked toward her and placed his hands on both sides of her face. Lacy's heart beat wildly in her chest, and she desperately wanted him to kiss her. She reached up with her hand and pulled him toward her, and they fell back on the bed in a passionate embrace. His lips were like hot bolts of lightning, and she could feel his heart beating on her chest like someone pounding on a door desperate to come in.

After a few minutes, Kerrick pulled back and leaned on one elbow. "Lacy, I love you more than I can even say. Because I love you, I should probably go back to my room."

Lacy reached up to pull Kerrick back down to her. "Don't leave."

"I don't want to, and there lies the problem." He took her hand into his. "We have something really different, and I don't want to do anything to mess that up. On top of that, Jon and Meg trust us. We don't want to blow that trust."

"Then why did you come in here to start with when you knew I was half naked?" Lacy asked coyly.

"I couldn't help myself, and besides, I didn't know you were half naked, which you aren't."

He kissed her softly and got off the bed.

Lacy sat up and grabbed for his hand. "Kerrick." He turned back and looked at her with those two deep pools of blue. "I love you. You know that, don't you?"

Kerrick sat back down on the bed. "I know that, Lacy. I love you, too."

"You do know that you're really special."

Kerrick grinned. "I know that. Actually, I learned in my biology class that I'm in the top 15% of Americans. That makes me real special."

Lacy was a little confused and irritated that he was turning a serious moment into a joke. "What do you mean?"

"I have O negative blood. My biology professor chased a rabbit last semester in class, and I learned that not many people share my blood type."

"Kerrick, what does your blood type have to do with us right now." Lacy huffed.

Kerrick placed his warm hand on her cheek. "It's called a distraction, Lacy. You're the most beautiful girl in the world, and I have to do something to get my mind off of the fact that I'm in the room with the girl I love, who by the way is only wearing a flimsy gown."

Heat rushed to Lacy's cheeks as her face was surely glowing. She looked down at her gown and knew that she should be wearing more clothes if Kerrick was in the room. "I thought you said I wasn't half naked."

"Not half. Maybe three-quarters. I don't want to do something that will make you not be able to look your aunt in the face in the morning. You know she loves us and trusts us implicitly. While my blood is pumping pretty hard out of my heart right now, it helps me to focus on the fact that I'm pumping O negative blood and not on the fact that I really don't want to leave you right now." He leaned in toward her face and kissed her lips gently. "Good night, Lacy Henderson. I love you so much."

As her bedroom door closed, Lacy heard Kerrick's cell phone ring. She lay back in the bed still breathing hard and wanting him to come back. Maybe he was right but being with him tonight sure felt good for the moment. He was right, though. The last person she wanted to betray was Meg. Lacy knew that Meg would be so disappointed if she and Kerrick had sex. The truth was that Lacy had never had real sex before, and the more deeply she fell in love with Kerrick, she didn't ever want any other man besides him.

A shiver ran down her body as she thought back to what her cousin had done to her. That wasn't sex. That was a violation. She remembered thinking that she never wanted to have sex with anyone after that experience, but now, her feelings were quite different. Maybe saving herself for marriage was a good thing, as long as it was marriage with Kerrick Daniels.

Lacy got up and finished getting dressed for bed. She couldn't believe what had just happened and how badly she wanted Kerrick to stay. She had always wondered what being with a man for the first time would be like, and she wondered if she would even be able to go through with it. Now, she knew that if she were with Kerrick, she had no doubt of how the experience would turn out. It would be mind-blowing.

She hummed softly as she began the nightly ritual of brushing her hair. She smiled as she remembered telling her mother years ago that she was going to cut off all of her hair so she wouldn't have to brush it any more. It was a pain, but Lacy decided it was worth it. She imagined Kerrick's fingers in her hair and his mouth on hers.

Okay. Enough of that. I've got to go to bed.

* * * * * *

Jon sat down in the chair in his room as Meg finished getting ready for bed. He closed his eyes feeling as if lead weights held them shut. It was hard to believe that they left the house at 4:30 that morning, driven seven to eight hours, toured an ancient city, visited Villa Rica, and still ended the day with a Mexican taco dinner in Veracruz.

He watched his wife as she moved through her nightly routine. Even though he was exhausted, he felt the quickening of his heart and had the fleeting thought of not going straight to sleep. She was so beautiful. Somehow, she had managed to stay in top shape even with her full schedule of being a mother and a wife. She had already talked to him about going running in the morning.

Meg finished rubbing some cream on her face and turned out the bathroom light. "What are you looking at?"

"My beautiful wife. I could stare at you all night."

Meg walked over and sat in his lap. "Is that a fact? Is that what you were doing last night about this time?"

"Yep. I was staring. It's just that my eyelids were closed."

"That's what I figured." Meg bent her head toward his and kissed him. She stood up when there was a light knock on the door. "I'll slip back into the bathroom."

Jon went to the door and opened it and was surprised to see a very pale-looking Kerrick. "Hey. Are you okay?"

"I'm sorry to bother you, Jon. I know you've got to be tired, but can we talk for a minute?"

Jon looked back toward the bathroom door. "Sure. Let's go out to the living room."

Chapter Thirty-three

Murder in Veracruz

A large man bumped into Miguel, who reached for his knife only to remember that he didn't have it in his pocket. He had tucked it into his luggage that was probably in Mexico by now waiting on him. "Hey. Watch where you're going!" A woman with a baby stared at him as several curse words slipped easily from his mouth. He felt like his head was about to explode. If people from the airline kept saying that they were sorry and that there was nothing they could do, he was going to punch them.

How can this happen two days in a row? He thought back to the angry crowd of people that were forced to leave the plane the previous day when there was smoke in the cockpit. At least, the airline had put him up in a hotel and fed him, but this issue today was ridiculous. He should have been at the airport first thing that morning to catch the first plane out, but he had figured all of those people who were bumped the night before would be trying to get on that first flight. Now, he was just told he couldn't board the only other plane bound for Mexico City that day because it was overbooked.

There was no way he was spending another night in Miami. He headed to customer service where a little, wiry woman who looked to be about two-hundred years old stood behind a desk.

"May I help you?" the woman droned.

"I have spent two days at this freakin' airport trying to get to Mexico City, and I want to get out of this place."

"Yes, sir. I'm sorry, sir. I did hear of trouble with the plane yesterday." She paused and typed on some keys on her computer. "I see that the plane that just pulled away from the gate is full. Too bad you weren't here this morning. That plane had five empty seats."

"So, I wasn't here, but I want to get out of here now. Is there another way to get to Veracruz, Mexico?"

The woman typed some more on her keyboard. "Yes, sir. You can fly to Houston and then straight to Veracruz. We have a flight to Houston in forty-five minutes. Unfortunately, you won't make it to Houston in time to catch a connecting flight to Veracruz, but we can take care of your hotel bill and provide you with a food voucher."

"When will I get to Veracruz tomorrow?"

"You should arrive by 11:30 central time."

"Okay. That's better than staying in this rat hole."

The woman printed out tickets for both flights and gave Miguel vouchers for a hotel room and two meals. She explained the vouchers to him, though he tuned her out. He took the tickets and vouchers from her hands and headed to yet another gate.

Friday morning, Miguel finally stepped off a plane in Veracruz. He looked around the modern, international airport in surprise. He had expected a small building in a field, but what he saw was quite advanced. They were doing even more renovation on the place, so he imagined that it would soon rival any airport in the world, at least in services.

He wove through the crowd to the rental car counter, filled out the paperwork, and waited for the attendant to speak with someone over the phone. He pulled out his phone to check his messages.

"Senior. Rodriquez?"

Miguel continued looking at his phone until the lady's persistent voice registered in his mind. He nearly cursed when he realized she was calling him by the name he had stolen.

He looked up from his phone. "Yes. I'm sorry," he answered in Spanish.

"We have a car for you. Please meet our driver at the front door, and he'll take you to our parking area. Everything else is in order."

He walked toward the front entrance of the airport and wondered where he could buy a gun. He knew it would be expensive, but he had to have a weapon. If he could find the right part of town, there would be someone around willing to sell him a pistol for the right price.

Miguel saw the little Chevrolet pull up. A man got out and motioned for him to get into the car. After returning the attendant to the rental lot, Miguel pointed his car toward Boca del Rio. *Okay Lacy Henderson. Enjoy your last day of freedom. You're mine tonight, babe.*

Several hours later, Miguel walked passed the palatial vacation home in Boca del Rio where he had decided the Davenports would be spending their vacation. He stopped on the street as if to pick up something he had dropped. He set a bag down containing a roll of duct tape and a coil of nylon rope, and he tied his shoes. He had intentionally waited until dark to check out the home to see whether or not Lacy was indeed on the grounds. The beautiful home was surrounded by a concrete wall that had both broken glass and barbed wire along the top. Several key things caught his attention. One resource that would prove to be helpful was a tree growing next to the wall on the inside of the courtyard. If he could manage to get to the top of the wall, he could easily jump to the tree and climb down into the court-yard. Gaining access to the house would then be simple.

The other helpful resource was the two-story house that was just up the hill straight in front of the vacation home. The lights were out, and no one appeared to be home. Miguel imagined the view from the roof and felt confident he would be able to see into the vacation home with ease. He needed to determine whether or not this place was for sure the Davenports' lodging. As he turned to head up the street, the gate to the luxurious home opened, and a car pulled out of the courtyard onto the street and turned away from Miguel. *That's got to be Meg and Jon. The woman has shoulder-length hair. It's too bad I'm not a little closer.*

He hurried toward the two-story house and easily gained entrance. It was apparent that someone lived there, but no one was home at the time. He climbed the steps to the roof and positioned himself on the eastern side of the house. He pulled out binoculars and peered down the hill to the vacation home. All of the windows were covered by thin shades. While he couldn't actually see the people inside through the shades, the shapes of the individuals couldn't be mistaken. His gaze locked onto a girl with long hair in a room on the second floor. *Lacy!* He couldn't tell if the girl's hair was blonde, but he was sure it had to be Lacy Henderson.

He grinned as a taller male walked into the room and took the girl into his arms. It started with kisses and grew more inter-esting. *Oh, my. I didn't anticipate the show. This is brilliant. I can slip into the room, kill Kerrick, and have Lacy all to myself. He'll be distracted and never hear me coming.* He trained the binoculars on the front door and saw a small, Mexican man. *That's the Davenports' grounds keeper. I'm sure of it.*

Miguel found a bicycle parked in the hallway just inside the house. He rode back down to the vacation house, leaned the bike against the wall, stood up on the seat, and was in the tree within three minutes. He thought to himself that whoever designed the security wall didn't do it to keep criminals out. He decided to enter the house through the back door, so he hurried around the corner.

Turning the knob to the back door, Miguel was stunned to discover that the house wasn't locked. He slipped through the kitchen and up the stairs. He paused at the door to the middle room and listened. A grin spread across his face. No doubt what was going on inside of this room.

He stepped into the room, and through the dim light, he saw the couple in bed. The man started to get up to face the intruder. *Kerrick!* Miguel reached for his knife and hurled it through the air. As the man collapsed back into the bed with the knife lodged in his throat, Miguel leapt on top of the girl with his hand covering her mouth. Pulling out the duct tape, Miguel quickly ran tape around Lacy's head to cover her mouth. He also taped up her hands.

He had gotten in the room, killed Kerrick, and taped up Lacy's mouth so quickly that no one had made a sound, other than a few grunts. He wanted Lacy to clearly see his face again, and he found a growing desire to look at the beautiful girl. He reached over to the bedside lamp and turned on the light. He stared down into dark eyes of hatred. The girl's black hair covered the pillow that was splattered with the blood of...*It's not Kerrick, and this isn't Lacy.*

Miguel sprang from the bed, hurried down the steps, and entered the kitchen just in time to see a young man dressed in black walk in the back door. The man hadn't anticipated an intruder, and Miguel's strong fist caught him totally off guard. His limp body fell out of the door onto the walkway, and Miguel moved stealthily to the tree and over the wall. He rode away on the bicycle to where he parked his car several blocks away.

As Miguel watched his rear-view mirror, he cursed and hit the steering wheel with the palm of his hand. *That's the second time I mistakenly thought someone was Lacy. That cannot happen again.* He raced back to the Real de Boca hotel and locked himself in his room. *I'll work on Plan B in the morning.*

* * * * * * *

Jon eased into bed over an hour later hoping Meg was sound asleep. He felt a heavy weight on him as if someone had placed a boulder on his back. His mind went back to Harry Truman. Jon had just been reading about how Truman had reacted when he was informed that the Enola Gay had taken off from Tinian Island heading for Hiroshima with the atomic bomb. The president knew of the destruction that was about to be unleashed while everyone else went about their normal routines. *We're going to have an atomic explosion, and no one but me realizes what's about to happen.*

Looking at his beautiful wife, Jon hated to tell her the piece of information that would rock her world. He listened carefully to her breathe, as he had done many nights, and realized that she wasn't asleep.

Meg rolled over on her back, and Jon could see her smooth face in the light coming through the window. "What's wrong?"

Jon could tell that she had probably been awake the whole time. "Hey, sweetheart. I'm afraid we have a real problem."

Meg sat up and turned on the light from the bedside table. "What happened, Jon? What did they do?"

"Well, it's not what they *did*; however, we've got to be prepared to pick up the pieces."

Jon saw dread cover his wife's face like an icy mask and hated to tell her the whole story. She had to know, however. Soon, everyone would know, including Lacy.

Chapter Thirty-four

Vacation Surprise

Lacy's alarm buzzed on her phone, and her feet hit the floor the next moment. She sat on the edge of her bed thinking about her plan, and her lips broke into a smile that covered her face. She knew that it would be at least an hour-and-a-half before anyone awakened, so she had to be careful not to make any noise.

She quickly went through her morning routine and eventually ended up in front of the bathroom mirror with a brush in her hand. Her hair was a tangled mess. Normally, she would just brush through it and pull it into a pony tail, but not today. She did her best to remove the tangles and put every hair into place. She studied the long tee-shirt she wore, Kerrick's University of Miami tee-shirt, and wondered if she should paint her toenails. *He doesn't care about my toenails.* She pulled out her gym shorts from the drawer and stepped into them.

After a short time in the kitchen, Lacy tip-toed back up the stairs with a tray in her hands. She wanted to sing or at least hum, but she knew that any noise could ruin her little surprise. Kerrick liked his eggs scrambled and preferred sausage over bacon, so she had gone to great care to prepare the perfect breakfast. They didn't have much food in the house, but they did have eggs in the refrigerator. Fortunately, she had seen some precooked sausage in the freezer that only had to be heated up in the microwave, and she had managed to accomplish that task without allowing the oven to beep. She had even found bread for toast. She eyed the glass of orange juice, being careful not to spill a drop.

When she got to the top of the stairs and looked down the hall to Kerrick's room, she noticed that the door was slightly ajar. She slipped back into her room, set the tray down on her dresser, and stepped in front of the full-length mirror. She stared at her long, bare legs thinking that she was glad that she had chosen to shave them the night before. She used to hate her long legs when she was in middle school, but now being just three inches short of six feet tall was perfect for Kerrick's six-foot three-inch frame.

Her Miami jersey was technically not hers, but she claimed it. It smelled like her now instead of Kerrick, and she loved it. She stared at her blue eyes in the mirror and almost lost her nerve to go into Kerrick's room. She thought back to the moments they had been together before she went to sleep the previous night and felt heat rushing up from her gut to her face. Thoughts of her mother flashed in her mind and sent a cold chill up her back. *She's a selfish bimbo. I'm not selfish. I just want to…What do I want to do? I want to love Kerrick. I want him to feel treasured and special.* She imagined saying that to Meg and wondered what she would say about her plan.

Returning to the dresser, she grabbed the tray and eased down the hall into Kerrick's room. The sun had not come up yet, but the moon lit the room enough for her to see Kerrick asleep in his bed. His bare chest rose and fell as her heart beat faster.

She sat the tray down on the bedside table without making a noise. She could leave his room and forget her whole scheme. *Am I being corny?* While going to sleep the night before, Lacy had imagined slipping into Kerrick's bed and wrapping her arms around his strong body, though she knew that would be a risky move. She wanted to hold him, to hear his heart beating as she laid her head on his chest.

Pulling the sheet up, she quietly slipped into bed beside him, and the bed didn't even squeak. He rolled over on his side, facing away from her, but he didn't wake up. She slid up behind him and wrapped her right arm around his body. She could feel his body heat as if she were snuggling up next to the sun. Lacy thought her heart just might explode. Her hand slid slowly over his chest, and she suddenly felt a shyness consume her. *It's too late to be shy now, Lacy. You're already in too deep. No. I could get out of this bed, and he would never know I had been here. That's probably what I should do.*

She rested her hand on his chest and lay her cheek on his shoulder. While she might not have the chance to hear his heart, she could already feel it beating under her hand. Kerrick's breathing suddenly changed, and Lacy knew he was awake. Her body tingled with anticipation as he slowly turned in her direction. She wrapped her arms around him and their lips met. Fire swept from her heart to her mind as his strong arms wrapped around her body that nearly burst into flames under his touch.

After a few moments, Kerrick pulled away. "Lacy? I thought I was dreaming."

"I guess you're not," Lacy said with a tremble as she reached up to stroke his face. "I brought you breakfast."

Kerrick lay quietly, and Lacy began to feel awkward. This had not been a good idea after all. Meg would have a stroke if she knew they were in bed together. They weren't doing anything, but Lacy could imagine Meg's speech about not putting yourself into situations that could lead you down a certain path. They weren't going down that path, at least, she didn't think they were. She was strong, and so was Kerrick.

"Lacy, I didn't go to sleep for a long time last night."

"Really?" Her hand slid down his face, over the sexy stubble on his chin, and back down to his chest. "Were you thinking about me?"

"Actually, I was. I've got to talk to you."

Lacy felt something hard fall down to the pit of her stomach. Something wasn't right. "About what?" She heard a little tremble in her voice.

Lacy felt Kerrick's hand cup her cheek. "Lacy, I love you, and I always will. I think I'll get dressed."

Kerrick got out of bed and stepped into the bathroom. Lacy could see that he grabbed a tee-shirt off the chair just before closing the door.

The budding flowers of spring that had been bursting from her heart had suddenly turned to the chill of winter. This was not how she had envisioned this surprise. She rolled over and looked at the scrambled eggs on the plate and wondered if they had grown as cold as her body now felt. She glanced up as the bathroom door opened.

"I made you breakfast," Lacy repeated.

Kerrick walked over to the lamp on the opposite side of the bed and turned it on. Lacy squinted in the sudden light.

"You went to a lot of trouble," Kerrick said.

Lacy thought his smile seemed a little forced. She looked at his face and thought his cheeks looked wet. *Has he been crying? Maybe he just washed his face.* Kerrick sat down on the edge of the bed beside Lacy, and she wondered if she should sit up.

"Lacy, I...I don't really know where to start. Do you remember the phone call I got from my mom about the girl from school?"

Just to hear the words *girl from school* made Lacy feel insecure. "Yes. I remember." She pushed herself to a sitting position and leaned against the headboard.

"And the text messages. Did you know that I got several text messages yesterday?"

"I saw you texting."

"As I walked out of your room last night, my phone rang. It seems that my roommate gave Hannah my cell phone number. She's the girl who called my mom the other day."

Lacy thought back to Kerrick's phone call from his mother while they were at El Tajin. She tried to say something, but nothing came out of her mouth. A sudden overwhelming dread made her want to get up and run out of the room. She looked up at Kerrick and noticed that his cheeks were wet. *Those are tears.* Now, she really felt sick.

"Lacy. I told you how Miguel contacted me last fall and threatened to kill my father..."

"...and your sister. How could I forget that, Kerrick. You didn't mean to hurt Jon or me. I know that, now."

Kerrick looked down for a moment and then back into Lacy's eyes. "I was miserable, and I didn't want to go to Nassau to meet with Miguel over Christmas break. I didn't want to betray Jon, but I felt like I had no choice. They were going to kill Kelsey and maybe my whole family. I went to a frat party the Friday night before finals and decided that I was going to get smashed. We were at some rich guy's lake house, and there were probably one hundred students at the place. There was music and tons of booze."

"I didn't think you liked to drink."

"I don't, but I had the thought that I could somehow make all of the pain disappear. It was a stupid idea. Sometime during my drinking binge, Hannah came up to me. I think she went to all of the parties at the fraternity. We were in the living room, and people were everywhere. I can't remember everything about it because by that point, I was close to gone. She kind of came on to me. She kept getting me more to drink. I started the night with beer, but she began bringing me the hard stuff. I promise that I don't remember what happened, but the next morning I woke up in a bedroom."

Tears were flowing down his cheeks now, and Lacy wanted to hug him, to console him, but she couldn't move. She felt as if she were spinning in darkness and falling through the air. The conclusion of this story couldn't be good. She was going to hit the ground soon, and she was sure whatever he was going to say next would kill her. She had to ask a really important question, but she didn't want to know that answer. "Were you alone? When you woke up?"

Kerrick looked back down and sobbed. "I woke up in bed, and I was…" He paused. "I woke up when Hannah kissed me. She was dressed and about to leave. She just said, 'Thanks for a really good time,' and then she left."

Other than being raped by her cousin, Lacy had never had sex with anyone, and she thought that Kerrick hadn't either. This news was difficult to hear, but she could forgive him. She loved him, after all. "So, is that it, or is there more?"

Kerrick didn't look at her. "Hannah called me last night and told me she is pregnant. She says that I'm the father and that she will be having our baby any day."

Lacy felt the wind knocked out of her as if she had been punched in the gut. She must be dreaming. She was having a nightmare. She and Kerrick loved each other. They were probably going to get married. Tears stung her eyes and then flowed freely down her cheeks. "No. Kerrick. This can't be true! You can't tell me that you had sex with this girl and don't even remember it."

"I swear Lacy that I don't remember it. I was so drunk. When Hannah left, I got up and puked my guts out. I'm so sorry. I love you, Lacy. I'm so sorry to hurt you." Kerrick sobbed again and broke down with weeping.

After a moment, he collected himself and looked at Lacy. "I'm going to have to go back home, or at least go to Orlando. Hannah lives in Orlando and says she'll be having the baby at a hospital there. I don't know what I'm going to do after that. I need to talk to my parents."

Lacy felt a wall going up around her. She was torn to pieces. She wanted to reach out to Kerrick, to hug him and tell him everything would be okay, but her heart was bleeding and broken. Everything was not going to be okay. She felt cold and nauseated. She just wanted to get out of his bed and out of his room. She had to be alone. She stiffly got up and looked down at Kerrick through her tears. "I'll miss you, Kerrick, and I will always love you."

She turned and walked numbly out of the room. Nothing seemed real. She didn't notice the beautiful sunrise through her bedroom window. She just collapsed onto her bed and wept.

Chapter Thirty-five

Hopeless

Meg looked up from the kitchen table as Jon walked through the side door of the house. His face was grim, and Meg's heart fell at seeing his obvious pain.

"So, he's gone?" She asked, already knowing the answer.

"Yes. There was room on the plane to Houston, so he should be in Orlando by this afternoon. I told him to call to give us an update."

Meg couldn't believe Kerrick was actually gone. She was so concerned for Lacy. Her precious niece had been through so much and had made such progress over the summer. Meg just knew that Lacy's story with Kerrick was going to end happily ever after, but maybe that was only in fairy tales.

"Jon, is it possible to be so drunk that you can have sex and not even remember it?"

"Yes, I think so. I had a friend in school that did it more than once. He swore that he didn't remember a thing, and I don't think he was lying. This girl, however, insists that Kerrick is the father. He said that he would have a paternity test just to confirm it."

"Poor Lacy. I feel so bad for Kerrick, too. I've never seen anyone so broken as he was this morning before he left. He couldn't even look at me."

"He was pitiful," Jon agreed. "I hated to put him on the plane by himself, but I couldn't leave you and Carla here without me. Hannah told him last night that she was beginning to feel contractions, so she could go into labor at any time."

"Will they get married?"

Jon filled a cup with coffee and sat down across from Meg. "I told him not to make two mistakes. He's going to have to support his child, assuming it is his child, but he doesn't need to marry Hannah unless he really loves her."

"Jon, you know that child needs a mother and a father. I mean a full-time mother and father who live together and love each other."

"I told Kerrick that. I suggested that after Hannah gets home from the hospital, they should spend some time together. The best thing that could happen would be for him and Hannah to grow to love one another and get married, but I insisted that Kerrick must not marry her just because she had his baby. They need to date a while and see if marriage is truly the right step for them."

"Oh, Jon. I'm so concerned about Lacy. What are we going to do?"

"Is she in her room?"

"Yes. The door is locked, and she doesn't answer when I knock."

"Well, Jose and Ann are flying in today and should be here in a couple of hours. I suggest we pick them up and go do something to help Lacy get her mind off of her troubles."

"Lacy's friend was going to Catemaco today," Meg remembered. "What was her name? The actress?"

"I think she's more like a producer," Jon corrected. "Her name is Andrea. That's a good idea."

"I think I'll go up and try to talk to Lacy again," Meg said.

The top stair creaked as Meg stepped onto the landing of the second floor. Everything looked just as it had thirty minutes earlier when she came up to try to speak to Lacy. She felt so helpless and had no idea what to say to her niece. She started to knock on the door again but decided to go down the hallway to Kerrick's room. It was empty, just like Lacy's heart.

Meg sat down on the bed and tried to think back to the times her heart had been broken. Her worst nightmare by far was when the casualty officer came to notify her of Steve's death. She and Steve had only been married for two years. The news had devastated her; rocked her world. She remembered sweet people coming by her home saying some of the dumbest things. The truth was that nothing could have been said to make the pain go away.

Her mind drifted back to one particular visit that really helped her. The lady's name was Michelle Howard. Meg would never forget her. Meg didn't know her very well, but she had attended the same church Meg and Steve attended. The thing about Michelle was that her husband had been killed in an automobile accident a few years earlier. This precious lady didn't come in with comforting words or answers to why bad things happen to good people. She just sat with Meg and listened to her and cried with her.

Meg returned to Lacy's door and gently knocked. "Lacy? Can I come in? I know you're hurting. Sometimes it helps to be able to talk." Nothing. It was as if no one was in the room. She stood at the door for a full minute and then turned to head back down the steps. Just before she started down, she heard the lock on Lacy's door click.

Hurrying back to the door, Meg quietly turned the knob and entered the room. It felt like a parlor at a funeral home or maybe a tomb. Lacy lay on the bed with her head buried in her pillow. "Hey, Lacy." Meg sat down on the bed beside her niece. She placed her hand on Lacy's head. "I'm so sorry. It's all so hard to believe. Do you want to talk about it?"

"No," Lacy's muffled voice sounded from within the pillow.

"I can't imagine how you feel. I've tried. I thought back to the night I learned of Steve's death, but I know that it's not the same."

Lacy sat up with fresh tears streaming down her face. She was a wreck. "Why, Meg? Why did this happen to me?" She buried her head in her hands and sobbed.

Meg placed her arms around Lacy's trembling shoulders and held her. Lacy's grief was overwhelming, and Meg struggled with her own feelings of sorrow. Lacy's question was a tough one to answer. Why had this happened? One unguarded night of…of what? It wasn't even passion. It was alcohol and despair combined into one regretful night. Tears began to spill out of her own eyes as she felt Lacy's body shake from sorrow and fatigue that combined into one ugly foe. Meg just held her and cried with her niece.

She finally collected herself. "I don't know why, Lacy. I wish I could answer that question. I suppose we don't always know why."

"I love him, Meg. I really love him, and he's done this to me."

"I know, honey. I'm so sorry. From what I know about this situation, I can't say that Kerrick meant to hurt you. It's just one horrible mistake."

Lacy sat still on the bed with her head resting on Meg's shoulder. Meg could smell Lacy's hair—fresh and clean. Too bad this situation wasn't as clean. Why did life have to continue to dish out blow after blow to a precious young woman who was trying so hard to be an overcomer?

"What do I do, Aunt Meg? I feel so lost."

"I wish I had some great answers, Lacy. Maybe you shouldn't do anything right now."

"What do you mean?"

"Well, you just told me that you love him. We don't need to live tomorrow today. Do you understand? We have no idea what tomorrow holds. We can only live one day at a time. I think that's why we call it faith."

"I know you have faith, Meg. I just don't. Nothing has ever worked out in my life."

Meg thought about the events over the summer and started to disagree with Lacy. Many things had worked out in amazing ways, but she decided that Lacy didn't need to be corrected.

"I don't know why we have to go through times like this, Lacy, but I know that it always makes us better, if we'll let it. I once heard someone say that trials will make us either bitter or better. It's our choice."

"It's hard not to be bitter. Right now, I hate that girl."

"I understand those feelings. What they did was wrong, but you've got to remember that they are both responsible. What's growing inside of Hannah is a precious little life that had nothing to do with Kerrick's or Hannah's decision. I'm sure she is just as broken about what happened as you are."

Lacy snorted. "She stole him from me. I doubt she's too broken about that."

Meg tightened her arms around her niece. "I know that you're angry, and I really understand. At the same time, there's a lot about what's going to happen that we can't even begin to know."

"They'll end up getting married."

"Maybe, but maybe not. You can't know that. We're not 100% sure that Kerrick is the father. It's going to take a paternity test to figure that out. Besides that, if they don't love each other, they don't need to get married. I would suggest you wait and see."

"Wait? How can I just wait?"

"Do you really love Kerrick?"

"You know I do."

"If you really love him, then love waits. There's a familiar verse that's used in a lot of weddings. As a matter of fact, Jon and I had it read at our wedding. It says, 'Love bears all things, believes all things, hopes all things, endures all things. Love never fails.' I think that in this case, that verse is saying that love waits."

Lacy sat up, looked down at her hands, and was silent for several minutes. "I love him more than I can say, Meg," she finally whispered. "I really do. If love waits, then I'll wait."

Meg hugged Lacy tightly and kissed the top of her head. "I'll wait with you, Lacy. We'll all wait with you." Meg thought back to her conversation with Jon before coming upstairs. "Jon had a suggestion."

"What's that?"

"Well, you know that Jose and Ann are supposed to arrive shortly. Jon thought it would be a good idea to go down to Cate-maco and meet up with Andrea. He thought we might want to spend a couple of days down there."

"I don't know, Meg. Maybe you guys can go, and I'll just stay here."

"You sure don't need to stay around here moping. If love believes all things, then you've got to believe that somehow this situation will work out in the best way. I want you to come with us. I Googled Catemaco. There's a beautiful lake down there with monkeys and waterfalls. I think we'd all enjoy it and being there would help us get our minds off of this problem a little."

"I guess. I would like to see Andrea again."

"Why don't you pack a bag for possibly two nights. We don't have to be home until Tuesday, so we may want to take our time and enjoy the lake. You never know what kind of exciting things we'll discover."

Chapter Thirty-six

Reunion of Friends

Meg watched Lacy drag herself onto a stool in the airport coffee shop; she appeared to have the weight of the world on her shoulders. Judy sat across from her, but Lacy kept her head down staring at her cup of coffee. Meg had hoped that the prospects of seeing Ann again would brighten her spirits, but Lacy wasn't even interested in greeting Ann and Jose when they came through security. She opted to wait in the coffee shop by herself, but Judy insisted upon sitting with her. Lacy's world was dying a slow death, and Meg couldn't do anything about it except just love her.

"Come on, honey," Jon said as he grabbed Meg's hand. "They'll be coming through those double doors at the end of this hallway any minute. I'm sure Ann would like a little help with her luggage."

Meg adjusted Carla on her hip and smiled as she followed her husband through the terminal. He was always so thoughtful. Meg wanted to remind him that just because Ann was pregnant didn't mean that she was helpless. Though she was definitely pregnant, she probably wasn't even showing yet. Meg still liked the fact that Jon was so caring and selfless.

Ann's auburn hair was easy to spot, not to mention that she was taller than most of the travelers who had been on the flight from Mexico City. She was smiling as big as the world when she saw Jon and Meg leaning against the wall on the other side of a strap that secured the area. She and Jose made quite the couple. Although Jose didn't flaunt his fit body, anyone could tell that he was a strong man, and he walked with an air of authority where every move seemed calculated. While people might recognize his fitness, they had no way of knowing that he was once an elite soldier with the Spanish military who could kill a man as easily with his hands as with a weapon. Meg shivered at the thought and waved at her friends.

"Hey, girl," Ann said as she wrapped her arms around Meg. "We have missed y'all so much."

"We have missed you, too," Meg said as she pulled away to look at her friend's belly. "I think I see a little pooch there."

Ann leaned in to Meg's ear. "Is it normal to want to be fat? I look at my tummy every day wanting to be bigger than I was the day before."

Meg laughed. "I think that's normal at first. Then, you'll feel like the side of a barn and long for the days you can return to your jeans."

"Elastic-waist pants, here I come. Where are Lacy and Kerrick?"

Meg grew somber and looked back down the hallway toward the coffee shop. "Ann, something really terrible has happened, and Kerrick had to fly back to Orlando this morning."

Jose heard Meg's comment and leaned in a little so he could hear. Meg and Jon explained all that had happened the last twenty-four hours. Ann couldn't hide her shock and sorrow.

"What are we going to do?" Ann asked.

"All we can do is love on Lacy and try to encourage her. She's pretty broken right now and doesn't want to do anything except mope around her room behind a locked door. We thought it would be a good idea to take a little trip and get away from the house. Do y'all mind heading south to Catemaco for a day or two?"

"We have no idea what Catemaco is like, but if that's where you want to go, then we're on board," Jose said.

"Catemaco is sort of a resort area about two hours or so south of Veracruz," Meg informed them. "I don't know a lot about it, but I know there's a big lake and an island with a bunch of monkeys on it. Several movies have been filmed in the area. I saw a picture of a waterfall that looked like a miniature version of Niagara Falls."

"I'm game," Ann said. "Whatever we can do to help Lacy is going to be the right thing."

Jon picked up Ann's carryon bag. "Let's grab some lunch in Boca del Rio and then drive on down. It looks like it will be a beautiful ride along the coast."

When they came up the hallway to the coffee shop, Meg stepped in to get Lacy and Judy. As they squeezed through the travelers to get out of the shop, Lacy tried to talk Meg into taking her back to the villa, but Meg refused.

"Lacy, you can't mope around the house for the rest of our vacation. Besides that, we can't let you stay there by yourself. It just wouldn't be safe."

"Lacy!" Ann cried out and pulled the coed into a strong hug. "I'm so glad you're off crutches."

Ann put her lips up next to Lacy's ear, but Meg could easily hear her words. "I'm so sorry about what has happened. Meg told me. I know you can't see it right now, but things will work out. You just have to have faith."

Lacy's shoulders dropped, and tears began to flow down her cheeks. Ann held the sobbing girl for at least a full minute.

"Y'all should just take me back to the house. I'm not going to be very good company."

"We can't leave you here alone," Jon insisted. "Veracruz seems like a safe place, but it's like any other big city in the world. It just wouldn't be a good idea."

"It sure wouldn't," Jose added. "I just saw a report on the news while we were waiting for our flight in Mexico City. It seems that the son of the leader of the cartel was killed here last night. Someone broke into the house where he was staying in Boca del Rio. The intruder sneaked into his bedroom. He killed the man with a knife. What's odd is that the guy was with his girlfriend, but she wasn't harmed. The assassin taped up her mouth, but that was all."

"Assassin?" Jon raised an eyebrow.

"Yes. They think someone was sending a message to the cartel leader.

Meg put her arm around her niece. "That settles it, Lacy. We're all going to Catemaco together for a fun weekend. Let's see if we can all squeeze into the SUV."

The drive south offered brief glimpses of cliffs dropping down to the ocean, rolling hills, and sea-side villages. Although the map on Meg's phone made it seem as if they'd be able to view the ocean for much of the first hour, the sea was hidden behind hills and trees most of the time. They stopped in the little fishing town of Alvarado and walked around for a few minutes. Jon bought the group ice cream, and Meg noticed that everyone seemed to enjoy the little town except for Lacy. While they walked around the city center, they looked at the old Catholic church building and admired the ancient architecture. Lacy just sat by herself on one of the benches in the center of the park-like setting.

Meg turned to admire the beauty of this central part of the town and had to run over to grab Carla before she toddled down some steps. The concrete benches were covered with blue and yellow tile, and someone had gone to great pains to plant bushes and flowers throughout the square. The government offices were housed in a beautiful, old building with a clock tower reaching up toward the sky from the roof of the second floor. The building was highlighted with adobe red arches and columns. It looked like something you'd see in a movie. She was just surprised that not many people were around.

"This is so beautiful," Judy said as she walked up to Meg. "I feel like we're on a movie set in Hollywood."

"I was just thinking the same thing," Meg admitted. "Where is everyone? Other than a few people over there at the ice cream store, this place seems desolate."

"Siesta," Jose suggested as he and Ann walked up. "My guess is that everyone around here takes an hour or two break after lunch."

"Come on, Lacy," Ann called out. "I want a picture of all of us in front of the church."

Lacy trudged over to the group. Meg organized everyone for the pose, and Ann placed her phone into the grip that rested on top of a small tripod. She placed the tripod on the top of a short wall and set her phone to take a delayed picture, but the phone fell over. A man walked over and said something to Ann.

Ann turned to Jose. "I assume he's offering to take our picture. Is that right?"

Jose walked over to the man and talked to him for a minute in Spanish. He showed the man the camera and explained how to take a picture.

"He's a little drunk, but I think he'll be able to take a picture," Jose said with a grin. "Everyone get ready." Jose hurried back to the group.

The Mexican held the phone in front of him and grinned. "Todos digan whiskey!"

"My Spanish is not very good, but I understand the word *whiskey*," Jon mumbled.

"Everyone say whiskey?" Meg and Ann said in unison and then laughed.

The man snapped the picture and stood in place holding the phone.

"I guess it worked," Jose said with a grin before hurrying over to the man to retrieve the camera. He reached in his pocket and pulled out a few pesos for the man.

"So, that's how they say 'smile' down here?" Meg asked.

"Evidently," Jose responded as he returned to the group. "At least, that's how he says 'smile'."

Meg heard Jon's phone ring and saw her husband walk over to some shade to answer the call. She thought she could read the word 'Kerrick' on his lips. She turned back toward the group. "Maybe we should head back to the car. We need to get to Catemaco before dinner." She motioned for Jon to follow them, and they all began walking the several blocks back to where they had parked.

Jon caught up to Meg and leaned in toward his wife. "That was Kerrick. He's in Orlando heading to the hospital. Hannah has been admitted."

Meg sighed. "Sounds like he made it just in time."

Chapter Thirty-seven

Fatherhood

The antiseptic halls made Kerrick feel a little queasy. The last time he had been in a hospital was when his grandfather died a couple of years earlier. Now, he was here for the birth of his baby. Everything seemed surreal. He was still in shock over the whole ordeal, but he knew that he was in the right place. He'd evidently had sex with this girl, and she was going to have his baby. Or was it his baby? He knew that he had slept with Hannah that night, but did they really just sleep? Jon had urged him to get a paternity test. He had wrestled with the crazy situation during his entire flight. He'd get the test, but for now, he had to find Hannah.

Jon had said that just because Hannah was pregnant with his child didn't mean that he should marry her, but he couldn't let his child grow up without a mother and a father. The previous year, he had written a paper about the family unit in his psychology class, and he had read a number of studies about the negative consequences of a child growing up without a father. He knew having a father around full-time was critical to a child's development.

Could he learn to love Hannah? She was a pretty girl, but the truth was he didn't even know her. Why in the world did he have sex with someone he didn't know? It was ironic that he had chosen to remain a virgin, even though he had wanted to have sex on numerous occasions. Now that he had broken his commitment to himself, he couldn't even remember the experience because of his drunken state. He hadn't even known Lacy at the time, but now, he felt like he had betrayed her, too.

He didn't want to marry Hannah; he wanted to marry Lacy. How could he just leave his baby to marry someone other than his child's mother? Kerrick didn't think he could live with knowing that he had made a choice that scarred his child. He would just have to learn to love Hannah. They used to do that in Bible times. He remembered his parents joking with him that they were going to pick his wife just like people did in the Old Testament days.

Another thought occurred to him. Wasn't Hannah the name of the woman in the Bible who couldn't have a baby? Too bad his Hannah didn't have the same problem. His Hannah? What about Lacy? *I love Lacy not Hannah.*

Kerrick found the Labor and Delivery area, and a nurse pointed him to Hannah's room. He didn't know how to act or what to think. Should he just walk in and help her deliver their child?

He walked into the room expecting it to be filled with nurses and at least Hannah's mother, but no one was in the room except a very pregnant girl. Kerrick looked at her drawn face and recognized the girl from the frat parties. She moaned and panted with what Kerrick decided must be a contraction. Because her eyes were closed, she didn't even know he was in the room.

Kerrick waited until the panting stopped. "Hannah?"

Hannah opened her eyes, and tears spilled down her cheeks. "Hey Kerrick. I…I'm so sorry. I can't believe you're here."

"Of course, I'm here. We're going to do this together. I'm just…Well, I don't know what to say. I'm still in shock. Let's not worry about all of that right now. We have a baby to deliver."

Hannah began to sob, and Kerrick sat down on the stool beside the bed. He pulled a tissue from a box on the bedside table and wiped her tears with one hand while he took hold of her trembling fingers with the other hand. "Where's your family?"

Hannah snorted. "As far away from me as they can get. They hate me, but I'm glad they're not here. They're all a bunch of drunks anyway."

"Oh, Hannah. I'm sorry. We can do this, though I've got to confess that I don't know anything about having a baby."

"Well," a voice said from the door, "you're about to learn."

Kerrick turned to see a smiling nurse walking toward the bed. She looked to be in her early thirties, and she seemed to be all business.

"Last time we checked her, she was at seven centimeters, so she's probably getting close. Of course, it could still take a while. There's no telling. How are you feeling, Hannah?"

"I'm really tired, Ashley. You've been so kind."

"I'm glad your husband made it. I was beginning to get a little worried."

Hannah looked at Kerrick with pleading eyes, and he realized that she must have lied about being married to him.

"Yeah," Kerrick coughed as he slid his high school ring over to his left hand and turned it around to look like a wedding band. "I was out of town on business, and my plane was delayed. I'm so glad I made it."

Ashley looked disapprovingly at Kerrick. "Hannah tells me that you weren't able to go to childbirth class with her. That's too bad, but I'll help you through it."

"Yeah, well," he said as he squinted his eyes at Hannah. "This whole pregnancy thing was a bit of a surprise."

"It is funny how these things happen," Ashley teased. "You'd be amazed at the number of fathers who skip out on childbirth classes. It's sad, but it is what it is. I'm sure you meant to go."

Kerrick's mind raced through all of the possible excuses. "Having a baby is not cheap, so I've had to take on extra clients. I know that's not a good excuse, though. My...uh...my wife and baby should come first."

"Well, I'm sure you'll be a great father...uh, what's your name?"

Kerrick stood and reached out his hand. "I'm Kerrick,"

Ashley shook his hand. "Pleased to meet you." She turned toward Hannah. "Okay, sweetie. I need to check you again." She pulled up Hannah's gown without any warning, and Kerrick felt heat rising to his cheeks. He turned to look at the television.

"I'm sorry, Hannah," Ashley said gently. "I know this doesn't feel so good. You're doing good, sweetie. Yes...oh yes. You're getting closer. I'd say you're about eight now. You're doing so good."

Kerrick heard the nurse's rubber gloves snap as she pulled them off of her hands. He was so embarrassed, but he couldn't let his discomfort stop him from doing his part. After all, there was a really good chance this child was his child, or their child, and Hannah needed him.

"Kerrick," Ashley said from the other side of the bed. "Are you going to be okay? You look a little pale. We don't need two patients here."

"I'm fine. Thanks."

"Okay. I'm going to let the doctor know of your progress, Hannah. I'll be back in a few minutes. You call for me if you need me. Okay?"

As the nurse left the room, Hannah started panting again. Kerrick felt helpless as he watched her face tighten up in pain. He sat back down on the stool and took hold of her right hand. She squeezed his hands so hard that he thought she might break his fingers.

"Okay, Hannah. Just, uh, just breathe real good. You're doing great."

About a couple of hours later, the nurse came back into the room to check Hannah for the third time since Kerrick had arrived. This time, he squeezed her hand and wiped her face with a cold, wet cloth. He heard the familiar snap of the gloves.

"I've got to get the doctor, okay? You're doing great. Just don't push until the doctor comes."

Ashley had not even left the room before another contraction wracked Hannah's body. Kerrick realized that the nurse had placed Hannah's legs up in the stirrups, and it looked like part of the bed was gone. *Should I put her legs back down on the bed? I think Ashley forgot to do that. Hannah's got to be uncomfortable.*

Hannah screamed.

"Breathe, Hannah. You're okay. Just breathe."

"I can't," Hannah wailed. "I've got to push. I can't stand it. I have to push."

"No, Hannah. Ashley said not to push until the doctor comes."

"I can't…"

Her face pinched and turned as red as a beet. Kerrick looked down and saw the most incredible, unbelievable thing. He was sure it was the top of the baby's head.

"Hannah! You can't have this baby yet. The doctor's not in here."

Hannah screamed again and gripped the bed with her hands. Her face turned red again, and she began straining and trembling. Kerrick rushed to the end of the bed and figured he had to somehow catch the baby. He pulled the stool up and sat down just as the baby's head began to come out of Hannah's body. Kerrick couldn't believe what he saw. It was the most miraculous experience of his life. Tears flowed down his cheeks as he pleaded with Hannah to slow down. He reached out to try to support the baby's head.

"You're doing great, Kerrick," a male voice said as Hannah screamed again. Kerrick turned to see a man in scrubs. "I'm sorry I didn't get in here sooner. You can go back to Hannah's side, and I'll take it from here." The doctor reached out and took the baby's head into his hands.

Fifteen minutes later, the nurse laid a pink, naked baby boy on Hannah's chest and helped Hannah pull her gown back so the baby could nurse. The nurses had already cleaned the baby up, and the room was filled with the joy of new life. Kerrick stood frozen as he stared at this precious, little life. Was this his child? He couldn't believe it, and he didn't really know his child's mother. This situation was shameful. How had he let this happen? *This is supposed to be Lacy, not some girl I don't even know.*

On the flight back to the United States, Kerrick had pondered the fact that Hannah had chosen not to have an abortion. He wondered why, and he was so glad that she had decided to let his baby live. Life was precious. Their son was precious. *Is he really my son?*

"Hannah," Ashley said as she pulled the sheet up over Hannah's shaking legs. "I'm going to get you another blanket, and then we'll leave you and Kerrick alone with your baby for a little bit. Then, I'll need to take him for a short time, so we can get his measurements and blood type and all of that. We won't have him for long."

Hannah didn't say anything. She just stared at the little person trying to nurse at her breast.

"Thanks, Ashley," Kerrick said. "Thanks for everything."

"You're welcome. You did great, Kerrick. You almost got to deliver your son all by yourself."

Ashley closed the door and left the little family alone. Kerrick reached out his hand and touched the back of his son. He couldn't believe it. He was a father. "You did so good, Hannah. You were amazing."

"No, you were amazing. I couldn't have done it without you."

They stared at one another for a few moments, and Kerrick wondered if he could love Hannah. They had just shared the most intimate experience he could imagine. He would do his best to love his son's mother, but he didn't know if it was possible. Lacy Henderson had his heart. If he could ever learn to love Hannah, he was sure it was going to take a long time. Hannah smiled as another tear ran down her cheek.

Kerrick leaned over and pulled the blanket up to also cover the baby. "Do you need anything?"

"No. I have everything I need right in this room."

Chapter Thirty-eight

The City of Witches

Miguel sat on the edge of the bed watching the news on television. He was stunned to learn that the man he had killed the night before was the son of the leader of Los Unidos cartel. Pedro Escobar was a cruel man and would surely do everything in his power to seek revenge for his son's murder. Miguel had met the cartel leader a couple of years earlier, and he knew that he had been fortunate to escape the house the night before without being caught. He thought it was odd that the son of the feared Escobar didn't have more bodyguards, but then he heard the second part of the newscast. Javier Escobar had been in the popular vacation home of the daughter of Manuel Sanchez, the president of Mexican's Chamber of Deputies. Miguel knew that Sanchez had presidential hopes, and Javier must have been trying to accommodate his mistress' wishes to keep their affair quiet. *It's not very quiet now.*

The alarm on the bedside table began ringing. Miguel had set it to awaken him at 11:00, but he'd already been up an hour. Even though he had not gone to bed until nearly 5:00 a.m., he couldn't sleep because of the noise going on in the room next door. He should have gotten in bed sooner, but when he returned to Real de Boca hotel, a police car had been parked out front. Miguel drove around Veracruz for a while waiting on the heat to leave. It turned out that some old man drank himself to

death up on the third floor, so the presence of the police had
nothing to do with the murder of Escobar.

Reaching across the bed to the clock, Miguel silenced the
alarm and picked up his pistol lying on the table. He had managed to buy the piece from a drug dealer near the bus station in
Veracruz. He checked to make sure it was fully loaded and stood
to his feet. Since the Davenports had not been in Boca del Rio,
they must be at the second home he had chosen that was on the
northern side of Veracruz city. He pulled on his clothes and left
his room. After breakfast, or maybe it was lunch by now, he
would find out why the Davenports would stay in the Nueva
community. In keeping with the name of the neighborhood, he
decided he would spend his breakfast time coming up with a
new way to kill the Davenports, and a new way to show Lacy
how really special she was going to be to him.

Almost two-and-a-half hours later, Miguel turned left onto
Playa Ensenada and drove past the luxury home he had seen
advertised on the Internet. It was exquisite, and he realized that
this kind of home would be the Davenports' first choice. He
could kick himself for wasting precious time. He drove through
the neighborhood several times to work out a plan on exactly
how he would get into the palatial house without being spotted
by a neighbor. He finally determined that it would be quite easy.
He might need to kill the next-door neighbors, but he was confident that would be no big problem. They would just be collat-
eral damage.

He waited until after 11:00 that night when he figured Jon
and Meg would be asleep. Of course, they may not be asleep.
The thought of surprising the Davenports awake in bed excited
Miguel, but then he realized that he needed to just take the girl

and leave Jon a message. The message would have to get his attention. Blood. He'd leave a message written in blood.

After slipping into the neighbor's house, Miguel discovered that only an old man lived there. The man was asleep, and Miguel realized the old guy couldn't hear it if a freight train drove through his living room. He saw the old grandpa sitting in the chair asleep, and when Miguel accidentally knocked over a lamp, the man didn't even stir. The back yard was small and dark, which was perfect. Miguel easily climbed the wall and dropped down onto the property of the vacation home. A light was on in the upstairs room, but other than that, the house was dark. *I'm coming, Lacy baby. I know you've missed me.*

The back door was no match to Miguel's lock picking skills. He made it into the kitchen within thirty seconds and walked past the closed door to the master suite. *Hello Meg. I know you want me, baby. We'll have our time together soon.* He eased up the stairs, being careful to walk up on the edge as close to the wall as possible. He had learned the hard way that the center of a staircase was usually not very quiet. He thought back to the guy he had to kill in Columbia just because of a little squeak.

The first door on the right was slightly ajar and a beam of light spilled into the hallway. Miguel paused at the top of the stairs to listen. Nothing. He took four, careful steps toward the open door and paused again. Not a sound. *She must be asleep with the light on. That would sure make things easy.*

When he pushed the door open enough to slip into the room, the door groaned slightly. Miguel hurried inside ready to get his hand over the girl's mouth. She wasn't in the bed. He looked toward the bathroom, and the light was out. *Where was she? Were they even staying in this house.* He saw a pile of dirty clothes in the corner and started going through them one-by-one. They definitely belonged to Lacy. He could smell her. *A University of Miami jersey. Yep. It's Lacy all right.*

He eased down the hallway to the room at the end and opened the door. He hadn't expected to find her in bed with Kerrick because by now, he realized they must not be home. He went back downstairs, pulled out his pistol, and walked into the master bedroom. Empty! He kicked over a chair and cursed. How had he missed them? Maybe, they'd be home later. He straightened up the chair and climbed the stairs back to Lacy's room. He could wait all night, if he had to.

At 5:00 the next morning, Miguel stumbled back to the wall in the back of the yard, scaled it, and dropped into the neighbor's yard. He wondered if the old man would be awake, and to his surprise, he was still sleeping in the same chair he'd been in hours earlier. Miguel picked up a small mirror from the bathroom sink and went back into the living room. He held the mirror in front of the old man's mouth. No fog appeared on the glass. He reached out his fingers to check for a pulse, but there was none. His skin was as cold as ice.

Miguel laughed out loud. This couldn't get any better. He needed a place to hide out and watch the Davenports, and such a place was dumped into his lap. He took the stiff body into a back room and closed the door. He stuffed a blanket under the bottom of the door and walked over to the side window that faced the Davenports' vacation home. *So, I'm guessing you won't be home til tonight. That's good because I need some sleep.* He climbed the stairs to one of the rooms that looked like it hadn't been used in a while and went to sleep. His last thoughts were that he hoped no one came to check on grandpa. The last thing he needed was someone prowling around while he was trying to get some sleep.

****

Jon guided the crowded SUV over the final mountain, and they began making the descent into the lakeside town of Cate-maco. The ride through the southern mountains had been breathtaking. Though Meg had been tired, she stayed awake for the entire trip and tried to soak in every sight. Now, the town known for witches and dark magic loomed below them, and Meg felt a small shiver go down her spine. While many people made light of things such as witchcraft, she was convinced that evil existed in the world and the source of that evil was at work all around them.

The streets were crowded with what Meg assumed to be both residents and tourists as Jon drove toward the lakeside hotel where they had reservations. Night was still a couple of hours or so away, but everyone in the car agreed that their first order of business needed to be to find a place to eat. Jon and Jose hurried into the hotel to secure three rooms for their group and returned to the car in less than ten minutes.

Lacy got out of the car so Jose could crawl into the back next to Ann. Once he was settled, Jon started the car and looked at Jose. "Tell them about La Casita, Jose."

"The lady inside told us that there are several good restaurants around. She suggested we try out one called La Casita that's just down the street. They offer a variety of food, including seafood and steaks."

Meg's stomach growled as if on cue. "Obviously, I'm ready for dinner," she said as everyone laughed. "If we don't eat pretty soon, I'm going to start eating the leather on this seat. Anything sounds good to me."

Jon stopped in front of a yellow building that was several blocks away from the lake, and everyone hurried inside. The place smelled incredible. Jon ordered a seafood salad for everyone for starters. While Lacy and Ann both ordered grilled shrimp, Meg wanted to try Chicken mole. Chocolate and peanut sauce over chicken didn't sound good at all, but she had always heard that it was a wonderful Mexican dish. She ordered Coconut shrimp tacos for Carla. Judy decided to try the chicken mole as well, but the two men wanted the biggest steaks the place served.

After dinner, the whole group leaned back from the table quite satisfied with their meals. Over coffee, Meg guided the group in discussing all of the things they could do the following day. It was obvious that they would need to spend at least two nights in the exotic place. They planned to take the lake tour on a boat first thing in the morning and then follow it up with hiking some of the trails in the area. Judy was mostly interested in Monkey Island where Sean Connery filmed *Medicine Man*. Meg noticed that even Lacy perked up when Jon started talking about the ancient stone head carved by the Olmec people.

"Who are the Olmec people?" Lacy wanted to know.

Meg pulled out her phone and typed a few words into Google. "Wow. This says that they lived in this region around 1200 BC until about 100 BC. That's unbelievable. Do you realize that means that around the time Moses was leading the Israelites out of Egypt, the Olmec civilization was born? Well, maybe the Exodus happened a little earlier, but that's amazing to think about."

"That is interesting," Jon agreed. "You know King David died in 970. These people were definitely quite ancient. Rome didn't even exist."

"It says here," Meg continued, "that they are the oldest civilization in Mexico. The stone head is in Santiago Tuxtla, which isn't too far from Catemaco."

Jose looked up from his smart phone. "There's also several waterfalls around. It would be a shame not to get to see them."

"Okay," Jon said. "It's settled. We're staying here for two nights, and even that may not be enough time."

"What about all this witch stuff," Lacy mentioned. "Doesn't that make you feel a little creepy?"

"I'm sure there's a lot of fake stuff for the tourists," Meg said, "but I'm also sure some of it's real. It's creepy all right. Like any other time, we just need to always stay together. As long as we're together, we should be safe. We'll also need to try to get in touch with Andrea."

Chapter Thirty-nine

Hospital Hope

Kerrick pulled the diaper snug and taped it in place. Noticing the gaping hole around their son's legs, he wondered how in the world this diaper was going to hold anything. He just hoped that a newborn wouldn't need much diaper support.

"So, what are we going to name him, Kerrick?"

"I have no idea, Hannah. I'm still trying to get used to the idea of being a father."

Hannah pushed the button to raise the bed a little. "What are we going to do? I mean, we're going to have to leave here tomorrow. Are you going to live with us? I'd like that."

"Uh, I don't know, Hannah. I'll have to figure all of that out."

Kerrick turned at the sound of the door. He doubted it would be Hannah's family, and he hadn't even told his family anything about this crazy turn of events. His mother would be devastated.

A nurse whom Kerrick didn't recognize walked to the side of the bed. "How are you feeling, Hannah?"

"I feel okay, but I really need some sleep."

"I'm sure you do. Last night was probably a rough night for you. You may want to let the nursery keep the baby tonight, so you can rest."

"I've been thinking about that," Hannah agreed.

"I'm going to come back in a little bit with your Rhogam shot. I checked your records and saw where you had one at twenty-eight weeks. We weren't sure if you'd need another one, but your little boy insists on it."

Kerrick cocked his head as if trying to remember something. "Uh, can you remind me what the Rhogam shot is for?"

"Sure. In this case, it is to protect your…, I'm sorry, but I don't know your marital status."

"We're married," Hannah insisted.

Kerrick knew that they must think his last name was Thompson. He didn't know if it was right to go along with Hannah's deception or not.

"Well, Mr. Thompson. Your wife has an Rh incompatibility with your son. If we don't give her this mixture of antibodies in the Rhogam shot, she would develop antibodies that would harm your next baby, that is assuming you're going to have another child. If your son had been Rh negative, she wouldn't have needed the follow-up shot. It's perfectly safe."

Kerrick was stunned. He sat motionless repeating in his mind what he had just heard.

"Mr. Thompson? Did you have additional questions?"

Kerrick suddenly realized that the nurse had been talking to him. "No, ma'am. Thank you."

"Oh, I almost forgot," the nurse announced. "Hannah. We serve you and your husband a steak dinner as our way of congratulating you. Here's an order form that you'll need to complete so we'll know how you would like your meal prepared." The nurse laid a card on the small table. "I'll come back with the Rhogam in just a little bit, and I'll pick up your meal order then."

After the nurse walked out of the room, Hannah pulled a pen from her purse that was lying on the meal table and looked at Kerrick. "How would you like your steak?"

"Uh, well, I guess medium."

"Baked potato and salad good for you?"

"Sure."

"And what kind of salad dressing? You'd think since I just had your son that I should know your favorite salad dressing. I'm sorry."

"Ranch will be fine," Kerrick said with a smile.

When the nurse returned forty-five minutes later with the shot, she asked if they had chosen a name yet for the baby.

"No," Hannah confessed. "We need to figure that out still."

"Well, you'll have to decide before you go home. You could go home tonight, but since your baby was born later in the afternoon, you may prefer to wait until tomorrow to leave. I suggest you wait. The rest will do you good."

The nurse administered the shot and left them alone again. Kerrick and Hannah spent the afternoon talking in between naps. Kerrick wanted to figure out what Hannah had planned to do once she had the baby. It seems that she didn't have many options for a place to live, and it became clear that she was hoping Kerrick would figure all of that out for her. While he arrived at the hospital the day before with no plans on them living together, Hannah had already been working out the details for their little family.

When the attendants brought in the steak dinner, a nurse from the nursery appeared to take the baby away for the night. She informed Hannah that she would be bringing the baby back to nurse, but other than that, Hannah should be able to get a good night's sleep.

After they had finished their meal, Kerrick leaned back in his chair. It had been quite good.

"Kerrick, you know there's plenty of room in my bed for you. There's no need for you to sleep in the chair tonight. You can sleep with me. I'm sure you'd be more comfortable."

Kerrick didn't know what to say. For starters, the bed wasn't really big enough for two, and the floor nurse would have a stroke if she came in and found them both in the bed. When he didn't reply right away, Hannah got up and eased over in front of Kerrick. She sat carefully down on his lap, and Kerrick noticed that it must have been quite painful.

Hannah placed her hand on Kerrick's cheek. "Kerrick. I know this has all been kind of crazy, but the fact is that I've always liked you. I'm assuming that since we, well, you know, since what we did that night, I assume you like me."

Kerrick took Hannah's hands in his. He stared at their hands for a moment and then looked into Hannah's dark eyes. He thought of Lacy's brilliant blue eyes and longed to be with her. "Hannah. What did we do that night?"

"What do you mean? I assume it's obvious."

"No. It's not. The fact is that I'm not the father of your baby, and I think you've known that all along."

The color drained from Hannah's face. "I don't know what you mean, Kerrick. Of course, you're the father."

"Hannah. Listen. I'll help you as much as I can. I know that you are in a bit of a situation, but I also know beyond a shadow of a doubt that I'm not the father. Your baby is precious, and I'm so glad you chose to give your baby life. I'm also glad you didn't have to go through your child's birth alone."

Hannah lowered her head, and Kerrick saw tears beginning to run down her cheeks. She sobbed with her face in her hands. After a few minutes, she reached for a tissue and blew her nose. "You're right, Kerrick. You can't be the father because we never had sex."

Kerrick was stunned. Though he realized earlier that day that he was not the father, he had never imagined that they didn't have sex. He knew that they had been together in the bed that night, or at least it seemed that way. He distinctly remembered Hannah getting out of bed, getting dressed, and leaving the room.

"We slept together that night, Kerrick, and I wanted to have sex with you. You are the kindest person I know. All those other boys just used me, but as hard as I tried to get you to…well, you know, to want me, you just didn't. When I say we slept together, I mean just that. We slept. I'm so sorry, Kerrick. I just wanted a good father for my baby. I've been so wrong."

"Didn't you think I'd want a paternity test?"

Hannah sobbed again. "I guess I hoped you'd think we, well, you know, had sex. You've got to remember us being in bed together. I'm sorry I've done this to you, Kerrick. You deserve better."

Hannah got up, shuffled into the bathroom, and closed the door. Kerrick could hear her weeping. He wanted to go in and comfort her, but he knew that he didn't want to give her the wrong signals. Once she came out, he directed her to sit back down in the chair.

"Hannah, I'm going to call my mother. She'll let you come home to our house for a while, and she'll take care of you. She and my dad will help you figure out what to do next."

"Are you coming with me?"

"I can't, Hannah. I have something I need to do in Mexico right now."

"I don't blame you for hating me, Kerrick. What I did was terrible."

"I don't hate you, Hannah. You were desperate. It doesn't make it right, but I don't hate you. I think somewhere in your life, you have taken a wrong turn. It seems to me that the birth of your baby could be the thing that sort of jolts you onto the right path. I know that my parents will help you."

"They would do that for me?"

"I'm sure of it. I'll call them in a few minutes, and they'll probably be here in the morning to take you home. I'll stay with you until they come, and then I have some things I need to go clear up, someone I must see."

Hannah hung her head. "I've been very selfish, Kerrick. Please forgive me."

"Like I said, Hannah. You've been desperate. What you did was wrong, but I'm sure you were just trying to take care of your baby. Let's walk down the hall a few times and then try to get some sleep."

The following morning, Kerrick's parents arrived at the hospital and were so kind to Hannah. Kerrick witnessed the selfless compassion of his parents and was moved by their generosity. They agreed to take him back to the airport on their way home with Hannah and baby Josh.

When he got out of the car at ticketing, he turned back to Hannah's open window. "You're going to be fine, Hannah. I'll check back with you in a few days when I call home. You're in the best hands."

He waved goodbye and strolled into the terminal. He found himself whistling as he walked up to the ticket agent. Fortunately, Jon had graciously purchased him a return ticket to Veracruz and had promised not to tell Lacy anything about what had happened. Kerrick wanted to give her the surprise of her life.

****

Jon hung up his phone and smiled at Meg. They had left their hotel that morning and driven toward San Andres Tuxtla, but they planned to stop at Salto de Eyipantla falls on the way. The lady at the hotel told them earlier that morning the falls was one of the most popular waterfalls in that part of Mexico. Jon had stopped for gas and a snack, and Meg got out of the car when she heard his phone ring. She would have heard his conversation with Kerrick, but the gas station attendant seemed excited to practice her English with an American. When he slipped his phone back into his pocket, Meg walked over to him with a raised eyebrow.

Jon leaned toward her and whispered, "Let's just say I have an outstanding surprise."

"Like what kind of surprise?" Meg whispered back.

"If I told you, it wouldn't be a surprise anymore."

"I have a feeling I know, but I won't even try to guess."

"Let's just say that our arrival tonight will be quite memorable. Our surprise will be waiting on us at La Parroqia, and it's not Pastel de Tres Leches."

Meg smiled and hugged her husband. "I can't wait."

"I need to make one more phone call to a particular airline, and then we can get back on the road."

Chapter Forty

Pastel de Tres Leches

All Lacy wanted to do was go back to her room at the vacation home in Veracruz and go to sleep. Their plane didn't leave for home until Tuesday afternoon, and she couldn't wait to get out of this place. She felt empty, and nothing in her world mattered anymore. Coming here had been a bad idea. Now, she didn't know what to do. For the last two days, she had thought about her future and considered her options. The last thing she wanted to do was to go back to Griffin to live with her mother, so her best option was to stay with Jon and Meg for the next few months. They hadn't offered to let her do that, but she was confident they wouldn't mind. She could finish her online classes in the Bahamas and spend time with Jon, Meg, and her sweet little cousin.

Small, colorful concrete houses whizzed by as Jon sped toward the capital city. It seemed that Jon was determined to get them back to Veracruz before dinner time, but the thoughts of eating something made Lacy want to throw up. She hadn't weighed in a while, but she was sure that she had lost a pound or two over the last couple of days. It was kind of odd, though. Judy wanted to go back to the steak restaurant, which Lacy knew that Jon absolutely loved. He insisted, however, on going to La Parroqia. La Parroqia was fine, but it wasn't El Asador.

"Jon," Lacy said from the backseat, "I'm really not hungry. You can just take me back to the house. I think I just want to go to bed."

Jon didn't reply. He must not have heard her.

"Uncle Jon. I'm really not hungry…"

"I heard you, Lacy. I just don't feel comfortable taking you back to the house by yourself. It may not be safe."

"I bet there are girls at home alone all over Veracruz. How is that not safe? I'll be fine. I think I'm sick. I probably have a virus, so you don't want me eating dinner with you."

Meg turned toward the backseat. "Lacy, we love you too much to risk letting something happen to you. We almost lost you this summer, and we don't want to go through that again. You won't have to eat, if you don't want to. Just come along and sit with us."

Lacy realized that it would do no good to argue with her aunt and uncle about this issue. She slumped back in her seat and crossed her arms. She stared out the window at an old house that was deteriorating from age. She felt like that was her. She didn't want to live anymore. She couldn't imagine killing herself and knew that would be the dumbest thing to do in the world, but she didn't want to face anyone right now. She might just move to California or Seattle. She could go work for Andrea in the film business and live in northern Mexico. *Isn't that where the cartel lives? Maybe I don't want to live in northern Mexico. Maybe Xalapa wasn't exactly cartel country.*

Lacy thought back to her time with Andrea in Catemaco. She had really enjoyed being with her new friend and hoped to one day visit her in Xalapa. Maybe Andrea could use another camera person.

Jon slowed to go over another tope in a small town a little
south of Boca del Rio. A man stood beside the road offering to
sell some kind of fruit in a plastic bag. Lacy wondered about the
family who lived in the little concrete house just behind the man.
It was probably his home, and they were evidently quite poor.
While some of the houses in San Andres Tuxtla and Veracruz
seemed to be a little more affluent, other homes in the outlying
villages were very simple. This one even had a thatched roof. She
thought back to the roof on the seafood place and remembered
that it was also thatch. The waiter had explained that the
thatched roof was a lot cooler. Lacy decided that the family may
not be poor after all, but then again, why was the man selling
fruit on the side of the road? A lot of people in Mexico lived on
much less in a year than she would spend in a month. Even buying a cup of coffee at Starbucks seemed a little extravagant to
her now as she stared at the bag of fruit.

Veracruz seemed busy for a Sunday night, but Lacy decided
that this place was always busy. It was a tourist center, and there
had to be thousands of people, maybe millions, who lived
around here. Jon opted to drive toward the old part of town by
taking the road that ran along the side of the bay. They passed a
music group setting up for a big outdoor concert. When Jon
pulled up to a red light, Lacy noticed a couple in a passionate
embrace leaning against the seawall near the aquarium. She
turned her head as a tear escaped her eye and ran down her
cheek. She would never date again. She would never marry. Men
were just not worth it, and they couldn't be trusted.

Jon pulled into a parking place and turned off the SUV. "I
hope you guys are okay with going straight to dinner. I figure if
we don't go now, Carla's not going to make it."

"Fine with me," Jose called out from the back. "I'm famished."

Everyone hurried across the street into La Parroqia. The place was bustling with people, but the attendant pulled a few tables together to accommodate the group. A small band of musicians were setting up to provide live music for the diners, but Lacy just wanted to leave. She considered excusing herself to go to the bathroom and then slipping out to wander around the shops, but then her uncle would kill her for going out of the restaurant alone.

"What do you want, Lacy?" Meg asked cheerfully.

"I'm fine, Meg. I don't feel like eating."

"You can't mope around for the rest of your life and not eat. You've got to get something."

Lacy looked over at Jon, who was eying the Carne a la tampiqueña the waiter was serving to the next table. "Okay, okay. I'll just take a ham sandwich and fries."

Ann put her arm around Lacy's shoulders. "Good. Getting some food in your stomach will help you feel better."

"You know you need to save room for Pastel de Tres Leches," Jon said from over the top of his menu.

"I don't think so," Lacy answered. "I don't even want a ham sandwich."

Nearly thirty minutes later, the waiter returned with a large, round tray loaded with food. Lacy barely acknowledged the guy when he sat a plate in front of her. She ate a few bites of her sandwich and three or four french fries, but she wasn't interested in eating. She spent the whole meal moving food around her plate wishing she could be home. The only problem she had was that she didn't really have a home. She certainly wasn't at home with her mother, and she didn't think she could go back to live in Miami.

The rest of the group buzzed with conversation about the Meso-American people and El Tajin. Jon was convinced that the clue to the lost city was somehow tied up with the carving from the cave back on Coral Cay and some of the artifacts he had seen at El Tajin. Meg had called their friend in Spain to see if she had been able to read anything on the picture Jon had sent to her. Lacy had stared at the picture until she was cross-eyed, but she couldn't make out a thing. It turned out that Cindy couldn't see anything either. She wanted them to mail the scroll to her, so Jon had called back to Roker's Point to have Diego get the scroll and ship it off to Spain.

Diego Rodriquez was a fine man, and Lacy knew that Jon and Meg trusted him with their lives. He was more than just a maintenance guy. She was surprised they had not brought him along on the trip, but she figured someone had to watch over the compound.

Lacy picked up a cold french fry and took a bite. She'd eaten enough.

"We ordered some Tres Leches, Lacy." Jon nearly had to shout across the length of the table to be heard. "Surely you'll eat some of that?"

"No thanks. I don't really want…"

A waiter walked up with a huge pan of the moist cake and sat it down in front of Lacy. Why was he setting a whole pan of cake in front of her instead of just a plate? She didn't even want any. She was shaking her head and telling the guy that he could put it on the other end of the table when she noticed that something had been written on the top of the cake. It wasn't Spanish.

It was plain as day English. She felt the blood drain from her face, and her stomach felt like the home of a thousand butterflies. She stared at the top of the cake trying to figure out what was going on.

The message written on the cake was crystal clear: "I Love You Lacy!"

I Love you Lacy? Who loves me? The waiter?

Lacy looked up to ask what the cake meant, and the man standing beside her was no longer the waiter. He had returned to the kitchen. She nearly fainted. "Kerrick? What are you…"

Kerrick pulled Lacy to her feet and wrapped his strong arms around her body. Their lips met in an explosion of joy, and a couple of men nearby began to whistle.

Jon and Meg were on their feet. As soon as Kerrick pulled away a bit, Meg wrapped her arms around him, and Jon slapped him on the shoulder.

"We're so glad you made it back," Jon said with a big grin.

Lacy was dumbfounded. "What's going on?"

Kerrick held Lacy's chair for her to sit back down, and Ann moved to the other side of the table so Kerrick could have her seat. Everyone sat back down and looked at Kerrick expectantly.

Kerrick grinned at everyone. "Well, it's a long story."

"If it's a long story," Jon interrupted, "cut us a piece of cake first and let me order some coffee. Lacy, do you want a lechero?"

"Uh," Lacy stammered. "Sure. I guess so."

Jon waved for one of the waiters and ordered coffee and lecheros. "Okay, Kerrick. We've got all night."

"Like I said, it's a long story."

Jon's cell phone suddenly rang, and he put it to his ear. "Hey, Sarah. I haven't talked to you in a while. I'm sorry that I haven't checked in more often." Jon shrugged his shoulders and stood up. "Hold on a second, Sarah." He looked back at the group. "I'm sorry guys. It's my assistant. I should probably talk to her for a minute. Kerrick, you can fill me in later." Jon left the table and headed for the exit of the restaurant.

"Go ahead with your long story," Jose insisted. "We're all dying to hear it."

Chapter Forty-one

A Vacation to Remember

Miguel looked out the window toward the Davenports' vacation house for the hundredth time. He had no idea how long it was going to take, but he was confident they would be back soon. The girl's dirty clothes were in a pile in the corner, and she had clean clothes in the chest of drawers in the room. He had gone back over to the house after his nap and discovered suitcases in three of the rooms. It seemed that Lacy must have stayed in the room upstairs by herself, but he couldn't figure out where the boy was staying. He must have been in Lacy's room, but there wasn't any sign of his stuff. Miguel went throughout the house trying to get a good feel for the layout because he figured that he may be coming back in the dark. He also unlocked the window that was in a storage room thinking that he may need a different way into the house. Whatever happened, he was going to be ready. He returned to the old man's house and prepared a lookout spot at the side window.

The Davenports had been a problem for Miguel for a while now, and he had to end this thing once and for all. He felt as if he might explode just thinking about the trouble they had caused him. He sat in the chair by the window and considered his plan. He had created some definite steps, but there was no way to finalize everything. He planned to somehow get hold of Lacy, but he wasn't sure how he was going to do that. He could slip into her bedroom at night and take her. That was probably the simplest option. He could confront Davenport as soon as they pulled into the garage, but that option could be messy. If he took her from her bedroom, she'd have to be knocked out.

As he processed the possibilities, he decided that he needed two things. He needed a way to get Lacy out of the house without making a sound, and he needed a place where he could stash the girl until Davenport came through with the medallion. Miguel assumed that the girl wouldn't have brought the medallion with her, so Davenport would have to go back to the Bahamas and get it. Waiting with the girl that long was going to be risky, but then again, the wait could be fun. He would just need to find the perfect place to keep her. Of course, he could just keep her right here in the Veracruz morgue. Miguel smiled to himself. *I currently only have one stiff on hand. She'll have to stay alive for a little while, so I can at least get some payback for the pain she's been to me.*

He'd have to come up with some chloroform or something in a needle that could knock the girl out. He decided that he had no choice but to go out for a bit to see if he could find the right solution to his problem. Now, he had another problem. He didn't exactly know where to go to find his drug of choice. He remembered seeing a strip club across town, so he decided to start there. It shouldn't be too big of a deal to just ask around. He could find someone who knew someone. Miguel thought to himself that people were the same all over the world. If you needed a product, someone would always have it. You just had to settle on a price. He got up, went into the old man's bedroom, and rifled through the man's drawers. Jackpot! He discovered a drawer full of paper cash.

Miguel looked over at the old man's lifeless body. "So, you didn't trust banks? Lucky for me."

Grandpa was becoming a problem. The old man's dead body was growing a little too obvious. The neighbors might eventually notice the smell, and it was starting to make Miguel a little nauseous. He found a roll of plastic in a closet and wrapped up the old man. If he was going to share a house with a corpse, it couldn't be a stinking corpse. He did the best he could to seal the body up with the plastic and some duct tape that came from a drawer in the kitchen. Once that job was complete, he left the house through the back door and walked casually up the street to where he parked his rental car. When he returned, he would park in the garage of the old man's house. Before it was over with, he may have to dispose of the dead body. He would soon be sharing the house with his little princess, and she might not fancy the stench of death. He just needed to get back before the Davenports returned.

****

Kerrick looked at Lacy. "Turns out that it's not my baby. We didn't even…" Kerrick looked around at the close proximity of all the tables around them. "Let's just say it would have been an impossibility unless you were the mother of Jesus."

Lacy sat in shock. She couldn't believe what she was hearing.

"How did you figure that out?" Ann asked.

"Lacy, do you remember a few days ago when I was telling you how special I am?"

Jose choked. "You were telling Lacy how special you are? This ought to be good."

Kerrick laughed. "I was messing around with her and told her that I have O negative blood. Only 15% of Americans have Rh negative blood, so I was just playing around the other night. Okay, so that's a little embarrassing."

"I always knew you were special," Meg said with a grin. "You are just more special than I realized."

"Last year in biology, we started talking about Rh negative blood and how rare it is," Kerrick continued. "My teacher took off on a rabbit chase because his wife is Rh negative. He went on to explain the genetics related to Rh negative and the probability of two people getting married who both had a negative blood type. He said that if the mother and the father were both Rh negative, the baby would also be Rh negative."

"Let me guess," Ann interrupted. "The girl in Florida is Rh negative."

"You guessed it." Kerrick beamed.

"So, they did blood work and told you she was negative?" Lacy stammered.

"No. Not exactly. You see, a mother with Rh negative blood has to get a shot of Rhogam when she gets pregnant to protect the baby. If the baby happens to be Rh positive, the mother's body will create antibodies that can actually kill the child. The shot protects the baby. If the baby turns out to be Rh positive, the mother has to get another shot within 72 hours of the baby's birth so that if she ever gets pregnant again, the next baby will also be safe. When the nurse came in to give Hannah her Rhogam shot, I knew that the child wasn't mine."

"Because you're negative and Hannah is negative, the baby should have been negative," Meg concluded.

"Exactly," Kerrick said and then laughed. "I waited until later on that evening when the baby was in the nursery and confronted Hannah with what I knew to be a fact. She denied it at first, but then she finally broke down and confessed to me the whole story."

"Oh, my God," Lacy finally blurted out. "So, you went through the whole child birth thing thinking this girl was having your baby?"

Kerrick sat quiet for a moment. "Sort of."

"I could kill her," Lacy nearly growled.

Kerrick put his hand on Lacy's fist. "The truth is that I feel sorry for her."

"I don't," Lacy hissed as she imagined herself pulling out the girl's hair.

"She's messed up, for sure," Kerrick agreed, "but she doesn't have anyone. The fact is that girl has been a mess for most of her life."

Lacy thought back to her own story. She was a mess, too. While this girl did the unspeakable that really turned Lacy's world upside down, she just acted out of the dysfunction that had been created for her.

"The sad thing is," Kerrick continued, "that she doesn't really know who the father is. She confessed that her life was so messed up that she just slept with whoever would take her. She had kind of become the fraternity's toy. She's got some real issues and really needs some help."

"What's going to happen to her?" Meg asked.

"My parents took her to their house. My mom said that she would handle it and for me to get back to Lacy as quickly as possible."

Lacy laughed for the first time in a few days. "I like your mom, and I haven't even met her yet."

Kerrick squeezed Lacy's hand that was no longer a fist. "They're sure eager to meet you."

"I'm guessing that your parents will find a home for Hannah?" Meg asked. "I don't know what's available in Florida, but I know of a few in Georgia that are really awesome places."

"Yeah. My mom said for me not to worry about it. She's done some volunteer work at a crisis pregnancy center in Jacksonville, so she'll probably get some help from them."

Lacy's heart melted as she watched Kerrick. She could just sit there all night with her hand in his. He was so kind and tender, even toward a girl who tried to wreck his life. He had come back! She couldn't believe it. Maybe there was a God, and maybe He really did care about her. She marveled at how her circumstances had suddenly changed. She went from homeless to once again being at home, at home with Kerrick. Meg had been right. You really shouldn't try to live tomorrow today. Lacy thought back to her attitude over the last couple of days. She had not been much fun to be around. She had the thought that she should probably apologize to everyone.

Jon returned to the table with a serious look on his face.

"What's wrong, honey?" Meg asked.

"Randal's mother called the office," Jon began.

Lacy's hand shot to her mouth as she thought about Randal. He should be living comfortably in his new house that Jon had purchased somewhere south of D. C., but evidently something must have happened to him. Her heart sank as she considered the fact that he had survived the diving accident only to be...*To be what?*

"What happened to Randal, Jon?" Lacy interrupted.

"Randal's fine," Jon reassured the group, and Lacy heard more than one sigh of relief. "He's getting stronger every day and physical therapy has really helped him. They think he's going to have a full recovery. His mom told me that our summer program had changed his life, and they all loved their new home. It's Randal's brother that she called about. It seems that he got hooked up with a pretty bad crowd in Washington. After they moved out to Belmont, Randal's older brother went off the deep end. He left home and went back into the city."

"Oh, wow," Ann whispered. "I bet his mother was heartbroken."

"I wish that was the only problem," Jon added. "His mother went into D. C. to get him, and he wasn't there. He and his girlfriend had run off."

"Run off?" Kerrick said. "To where?"

"It seems that Freddy had gotten mixed up with a pretty dangerous drug group. One of his friends said Freddy was going to Mexico to hook up with Pedro Escobar. Escobar is evidently a leader of some part of the Mexican drug cartel."

Meg gasped. "What are we going to do?"

"I figure that we have to at least try to find him."

"Jon!" Meg's tone got very serious. "We can't go up against the cartel."

"I know, sweetheart, but we have to at least try to find Freddy and talk him into going back with us. We're all exhausted. Let's get back to the house and go to bed. We'll work out a plan in the morning. We won't be able to stay much longer because Kerrick has to be in class on Tuesday."

"I could be a day or two late if needed," Kerrick conceded.

"Meg." Jon took hold of her hand. "We won't do anything stupid. I know you're thinking about the bus station thing, but don't go there."

"Bus station thing?" Jose raised an eyebrow.

"I'll tell you later," Jon said quickly. "We won't be doing that again. Let's just go home and relax for tonight. After a good night's sleep, we'll be able to think more clearly. In the meantime, let's celebrate the fact that Kerrick is back."

Lacy's hand went to the back of Kerrick's head. He was back, and he was hers. Jon and Meg may be planning to go back to the house and go to sleep, but sleep was the last thing on Lacy's mind. She was first going to ring Kerrick's neck for nearly shocking her to death with his little cake stunt, and then they were going to have a long talk. This episode with Hannah made her realize even more how much Kerrick meant to her. She wanted to know where their relationship was heading. They'd have a heart-to-heart talk, a midnight swim, and maybe…who knew. She just didn't want this crazy night to end. She knew it would be a night she'd never forget.

From the Author

Thank you for reading my book, *Love Waits*. If you enjoyed it, will you please take a moment to leave a review on Amazon? If you have missed reading any of the previous books of the series, you'll find descriptions on the following pages. You can pick them up from Amazon or your favorite retailer.

In the opening pages of Book 1, I offered the prequel to the series as a free gift. If you would like a free pdf copy of a story about Jon and Meg as teenagers, visit my website and click on the "free gift" tab (judahknight.com).

If you would like to contact me for any reason, I'd love to hear from you. You can reach me through my publisher (greentreepublishers.com), through the contact page on my website (judahknight.com), or through one of the social media links listed below. I look forward to hearing from you soon.

Thanks again for taking the time to read my book, and I'll see you in the next adventure.

Judah Knight

Follow me on Twitter:
    http://www.twitter.com/judahknight
Check out my website:
    http://www.judahknight.com
Have a discussion with me on Goodreads.com:
    http://bit.ly/1m5heLe

The Davenport Series

Book 1: The Long Way Home

He had a boat. She needed a ride. A simple lift turned into the adventure of a lifetime. Jon Davenport and Meg Freeman had a chance encounter in Nassau that would change their lives and destinies.

Book 2: Hope for Tomorrow
Our tomorrows can be different than our yesterdays!

Jon Davenport invited Meg Freeman, along with her friend Ann, to join him in searching for sunken treasure in the Bahamas. Though Meg thought that she was simply searching for gold, the treasure she found was far more valuable.

Book 3: Finding My Way
Bitterness. Betrayal. Brokenness.
Can the search for ancient gold help her find lasting treasure?

Meet Jon and Meg's niece Lacy Henderson as she joins the adventure in the Bahamas, along with summer intern, Kerrick Daniels.

Book 4: Ready to Love Again
She had given up on love until…

Lacy Henderson went to the Bahamas to help her aunt and uncle in a boys program, but she seems to be the one who had the greatest summer of all.

Prequel: A Girl Can Always Hope

In *The Long Way Home*, we learn that the two main characters knew one another as teenagers, and Margaret Robertson (Meg Freeman in *The Long Way Home*) had a crush on her brother's best friend, Jon Davenport. Read the fun short story of one awkward middle schooler's attempt to capture the impossible catch. This book is available as a free gift on the author's website: judahknight.com.

9 781944 483180